Deceive Me

Southern Nights: Enigma 2

Ella Sheridan

Dear Lydia —
Enjoy the heat!
Ella Sheridan

Also by Ella Sheridan

Southern Nights
Teach Me
Trust Me
Take Me

Southern Nights: Enigma
Come for Me
Deceive Me
Destroy Me

If Only
Only for the Weekend
Only for the Night
Only for the Moment

Secrets
Unavailable
Undisclosed
Unshakable

∞

For news on Ella's new releases, free book opportunities, and more, sign up for her monthly newsletter at ellasheridanauthor.com.

Copyright

Southern Nights: Deceive Me
Copyright 2017 Ella Sheridan

Cover Art Design by Mayhem Cover Creation

Editing by Deborah Nemeth

Published in the United States.

Praise for *Deceive Me*

"Overwhelming emotion and heart-racing excitement. Deceive Me is something special. Ella Sheridan's best book yet!"
— *Blogging by Liza*

"The suspense is riveting, the love scenes sizzling."
— *TBQ Book Palace*

"An edge of your seat thriller!"
— *Romantic Fanatic Blog*

"Full of action and suspense. A well-written and exciting read."
— *The Reading Café*

Dedication

To Deacon and Elliot.

My heart hurt for you from the very beginning. Here's to your happy ending. Both of you deserve it so much.

Acknowledgments

Stephanie Boting, thank you for all your insight and patience in sharing your country and culture with me. Someday I'll write a South African who isn't a villain, I promise. I appreciate your enthusiasm and willingness to answer question after question after question. Any mistakes regarding Africa are totally mine.

Heather Knight, I'm so glad you sent me that first e-mail. My life would be very different if we'd never met. Thank you for reading those first rough chapters and being honest about what they needed. Insight like that is invaluable, and you've shared yours graciously. Thank you, my friend.

Nikki Snider, my fabulous beta reader. Your encouragement and excitement every time I send you something makes my heart happy. Thank you for being willing to read, for being a cheerleader when I sorely need one, and for reminding me, over and over, that I have a gift readers enjoy. I appreciate you so much.

Dani Wade—critique partner, sister, partner in crime. I love you. I couldn't have made this journey without your love and encouragement. You've stood beside me for

TEN books (okay, more, but ten published books…). But even more, you've stood beside me for decades of life. Thank you for helping me find my voice and my feet these last few difficult years. Here's to many more!

And finally, to my daughter, S. You're patient when you don't have to be, act interested when I'm rambling on about my characters, and celebrate with me when I accomplish my goals. I don't know what I did to deserve such a kind, compassionate, smart, beautiful woman for a daughter. I'm looking forward to my vanilla Dr. Pepper on release day, hon. I love you.

Prologue

Two Years Earlier

Location: Namibia, Africa
Global First Security Team: Foxtrot
Mission Objectives:
- Rescue Senator Jeremy Ewing, wife, and twin daughters.
- Detain Andre Diako for questioning.
- Release human cargo.
- Incapacitate Diako's ship.
Entry: 2100 hours local time

The dock in the middle of nowhere, Liberia, smelled of rotting fish, fetid water, and the open sewers lining the streets nearby. Deacon Walsh ignored the stench and cursed as he directed his NVGs at the deck of the freighter moored at the end of the dock. The ship wasn't large, not as cargo ships went; that was how Martin "Mansa" Diako kept his operations under the radar. Every inch of space belowdeck would be crammed with illegal goods and human slaves, though.

Their target was a little higher end. Too bad Mansa wasn't on board with the hostages instead of shipping the senator and his family with his son. Mansa believed in earning what you got, not having it handed to you. Andre Diako had moved up in his father's organization if he had the privilege of "escorting" such high-profile prisoners.

The soldiers pacing the deck confirmed the senator's location—regular cargo wouldn't require that amount of guards, not in this out-of-the-way port. In the dim lights thrown by the few unbroken lights peppering the nearby dock, Deacon counted easily twice as many fatigue-clad figures as their informant had claimed would be there. If not for the fact that the fucker was already dead, Deacon would snap his fucking neck. His team needed to get in and out with as little fuss as possible, and that wasn't happening with thirty well-trained pirates between them and Senator Jeremy Ewing's family.

"What's the story, Deac?"

Lowering his goggles, he turned to his second in command, Fionn "Irish" McCullough. His best friend's eyes shone especially white in his blackened face. If not for those eyes, even Deacon wouldn't have been able to locate him—Irish's specialty was infiltration.

As much as the command left a bitter taste in his mouth, Deacon knew what they had to do. "Abort."

Trapper caught the command through their mics. His curse echoed in all their ears. They all agreed with the sentiment too, but Deacon wouldn't risk his six-man team against that many soldiers with no backup. They'd call in Team Lima. Now they just had to pray Diako kept his father's "cargo" presentable for the next twenty-four hours.

Except as Deacon swept the boat one last time, the light blinked on in the bridge. Andre Diako walked through the hatch, a sick grin of anticipation on his lips. Deacon saw why when the senator's twin eighteen-year-old daughters stumbled in behind him, thick metal chains looped around their throats. Tears tracked down the girls' dirty faces.

They were naked.

Shit.

Deacon allowed himself no more than a brief closing of his eyes, but deep inside, rage billowed. He knew what happened to women the Diakos—Senior or Junior—got their hands on, but watching it and not doing anything? Interference without the assurance of completing their objectives contradicted every minute of training he'd been given since he joined the military right out of high school. It risked himself and his team and everything they could accomplish.

Another glimpse through the binoculars had bile rising in the back of his throat.

Fuck objectives. Just fuck 'em.

"Scratch that," he barked into the mic. "Diako, wheelhouse, twin hostages."

Muttered curses from his team echoed through his earpiece, but not one objection. They were going in, risk be damned. Besides, no one had said they had to bring Diako in easy. Deacon would make sure they didn't.

"Trapper, Inez, take point," Deacon murmured. He lowered the binoculars, needing to focus. The two team members moved seamlessly along the wharf, keeping to the shadows, their bodies in sync with the ease of long practice. Their team had only been together four years, but Trapper and Inez had gone through Hell Week together, served their two terms as special forces together. They read each other's minds, it seemed, just as Deacon and Irish did. Maybe their expertise would get them through tonight without getting dead, but if not, it was worth it to give those two girls a chance.

Li and Farley followed the pair into the dark. Irish trailed Farley toward midship, Deacon covering their six.

The slap of waves against the hull covered the whisper of cloth against cloth as the six men closed in on their destination. Despite nightfall, the heat had melded Deacon's body armor to his skin with sweat. The air was thick with salt, scraping against any unprotected skin. Instant facial. He didn't think it would go over well back home, though. He'd rather be in the jungle than on the coast, even with the heat, but he went where the prey was. That's why he'd left the military, after all—why most of his team had left the military. The freedom to hunt bastards like Diako and his warlord father. And the freedom to make sure those same bastards never surfaced again.

Two guards stood at the gangway, their focus more on their cigarettes than their guns and possible intruders. Trapper and Inez had the two down before they ever knew a threat existed. Farley and Li dragged the bodies down to the dock and stuffed them out of sight while Deacon and Irish kept watch. Trapper and Inez were halfway to the lower deck passage before the rest of them hit the deck. At least the bastard informant had coughed up a map of the ship before he earned his broken neck.

"Go to stern, gentlemen," Deacon murmured into the mic. The passageway at the rear of the boat intersected with Trapper and Inez's near the cells the senator and his wife were likely still inside, frantic for their daughters. "Confirm."

None of the urgency he felt filtered through his words. Urgency made you sloppy. They couldn't rescue the hostages if they were dead.

"Confirmed," Farley answered. He and his partner peeled off, headed aft. Irish and Deacon headed the opposite, toward the bridge access. Guard after guard felt the final shock of their life before a silent knife sliced their throat or strong hands jerked their heads in the wrong direction without warning. With the boat in a "friendly" port, the men were lax, preoccupied, off their guard. Team Foxtrot took full advantage.

An outside ladder near the bow would allow them to access the bridge. As they neared the area, Irish looked over his shoulder at Deacon, signaling *eyes, forward*. Trouble ahead. Deacon kept himself in line with his partner, trusting Irish to assess the threat while Deacon watched their flank.

"Moving in." Farley. Deacon squelched the mic as Irish inched forward. Both men froze when a sudden shout from Farley and Li's location brought the pounding of footsteps along the deck.

Melting into the shadows, Irish and Deac waited as a contingent of four guards swept past. A fifth, a massive ape of a man with dead eyes, came to an abrupt halt right in front of their position, his head swinging back and forth as he searched for whatever had piqued his instincts. They all had it, the ability to sense a threat, even one they couldn't see. This man knew danger was at hand, but he couldn't pinpoint it. Then he made the mistake of turning his back to stare out toward the gangway.

In a sudden blur of motion Irish shot forward, crouched low to avoid alerting the target. His knife caught the guard across the backs of both ankles, slicing through the Achilles' tendons. Deacon caught a glimpse of the guard's gaping mouth and wide eyes as he fell. He hit the deck on his back, legs useless, but turned just in time to catch Irish's follow-up attack. The man blocked the downswing of Irish's knife with a meaty arm but left his torso unprotected. Deacon's blade swept past his guard and found the man's right lung a second later.

A strangled scream gurgled from the dying soldier's mouth. At the same moment, a pain-filled feminine cry filtered down from the bridge. Deacon went cold at the sound. A quick jerk of his knife sliced through the guard's vocal cords, cutting off any further sound or air. Deacon flicked the blood from his blade as he met Irish's grim gaze.

Mouth tight, his partner nodded toward the ladder just past the bloody sprawl of the guard's body. As he turned and stepped over the soldier like so much garbage, Deacon's earpiece lit up with calls from the other members of their team.

"Two targets located."

"Bastard—Li!"

"Farley, report!" Trapper.

Then Inez. "Senator and wife mobile. Deac, report."

A second scream, this one ending in a horrible gurgling sound, came from inside the bridge.

Deacon squelched the mic again in lieu of a verbal report. The men knew what it meant. This close to the bridge, a word spoken at the wrong moment would alert Diako and anyone else he had with him. Deacon tried to ignore the chaos in his ear in favor of completing the mission.

The hatch at the top of the ladder was part glass, the large rectangle illuminated with bright light from within. Irish ducked beneath, taking the entry side. Deacon glanced in quickly as he joined his partner. What he saw seared his eyeballs long after he crouched next to Irish, breathing low but ragged.

One twin was chained to the far bulkhead. The girl's face was red, tear-ravaged as she yanked on the hook her tether was attached to, so high up that she stretched just to keep her tiptoes on the deck. Diako was forcing the second twin toward a wide table at the back of the room. The child's desperate eyes had faced the hatch Irish and Deacon were set to enter, searching for rescue, for escape. He heard a soft scream and the impact of skin on the tabletop.

Christ.

Deacon forced the blinding rage away. He needed a clear head to rescue both girls from the bastard. Mentally he assessed positions, assets, limitations, searching for the best way to accomplish their new objective.

He tapped Irish's shoulder. When his partner's gaze met his, he signaled silently, giving Irish the plan. With a nod, Irish grasped the hatch handle openhanded, his fingers closing on a silent countdown to entry.

The hatch opened with a slight squeak that was drowned out by Diako's filthy play-by-play of his actions. Irish crept forward, staying low. Deacon followed, disgust curdling in his stomach in a way he couldn't detach from as the bastard's voice became more and more breathless, rough. A countdown to his death, whether he knew it or not. The knowledge allowed Deacon to focus—he wouldn't fail these girls when they needed him most.

They'd made it halfway down the room when a hoarse shout left Diako's mouth. Irish surged around the counter that hid them from sight, ready to tackle the fucker to the deck.

The second twin moved faster. Dangling chain now clasped in her fists, she rushed across the room, ready to swing the heavy metal at her sister's attacker. Despite his preoccupation, Diako saw the threat coming.

Later Deacon tried to remember where the knife had been—not in the hand he could see, planted on the table next to the first twin's head. The bastard might've had it in a sheath on his opposite hip, in his hidden hand, lying on the table. Wherever it was, it was close enough that Diako had time to raise it before the girl reached him. Flying chain and striking knife passed each other in the air, one slapping harmlessly across Diako's back, the other digging deep into the girl's belly. Irish shouted from directly behind their target, the angle of his raised gun lining Diako and the girl up, preventing his shot. Deacon jerked to the side, his approach giving him a clear shot of Diako's sick brain. The silenced spit of the gunshot sounded soft in the chaos, but Diako's head exploded anyway. Monster and child fell like empty puppets to the deck, their bodies settling mere inches away from each other.

Chapter One

"I'm not a fucking nanny, Dain."

"Not with a mouth like that."

Elliot shot a deadly look Saint's way, but her team member shrugged it off. She seriously considered strangling the man with the crucifix he wore around his neck, but it wouldn't matter. Their boss would simply replace him with someone even more annoying just to get back at Elliot for the inconvenience. Instead she turned her back to the room and sought calm outside the floor-to-ceiling windows providing a perfect view of downtown Atlanta.

Okay, the calm came from avoiding the three amused sets of eyes behind her, but whatever.

The members of her team remained silent, though she could feel their stares burning into her back. Good men. She couldn't have asked for better. Dain Brannan, or Daddy as they sometimes called him, was the head of their particular team here at JCL Security, the one who took care of the rest of them. Saint, or Iggy—the six-two, massive warrior took personal exception to the use of his full name, Saint Ignatius Solorio—was the joker of the bunch, always saying what everyone was thinking but would never politely admit. He also had an encyclopedic knowledge of weapons that made him invaluable despite the constant temptation to kick his ass. And then there was King—Kingsley Moncrief. No one would guess from looking into the man's assessing eyes that he'd been raised with a silver spoon in his mouth. Acting as their client and media liaison was a natural role for him, but Elliot had never doubted how lethal King could be in the field.

All three men stayed quiet, waiting for her cool head to take over. Waiting for the pressure of their silence to push her into complying. They knew her as well as she knew them.

"I don't want to be shoved into a role because I have the requisite vagina," Elliot bit out.

When Dain chuckled, she whipped around to glare at him. He raised a hand to stop her in her tracks, a smile still on his lips. "Think about it, Otter. A four-year-old girl. Look at us." He gestured at the two men flanking him, both over six feet and muscular. Tough. Scary, if you weren't Elliot. "Do you really think a child is going to be particularly comfortable with us? Or that she'll trust us as fast as she needs to? This isn't some forty-year-old visiting dignitary's wife we can simply talk into complying; it's a kid."

Elliot refused to let Dain's use of her call sign influence her. "She would trust you. Everyone trusts you." And they did. Dain wasn't called Daddy only because he watched out for his team.

"Maybe. But with you, it's guaranteed."

Because she was tiny. The truth of the knowledge burned in her gut. She didn't like appearing weak, though she wasn't above using it to her advantage. She'd taken down many a fighter in the ring because they thought she was an easy target. They learned otherwise quickly, much to their detriment.

So yeah, she got it. That didn't mean she wanted to admit it.

Elliot sighed like a teenager being forced to wash dishes instead of a kick-ass security specialist being assigned a new client. "Do I really have a choice?"

No, of course not.

The side of Dain's mouth quirked up in a smirk she knew meant he thought he'd gotten his way. Again. Bastard. "Not really."

Another sigh. "Fine."

That earned an all-out laugh. "Fine. Can we meet the client now?"

Elliot grumbled under her breath as she followed Dain to the door of his office. King chuckled as he fell in line behind her. Saint, of course, simply had to add an, "And don't forget to watch your mouth, little Otter."

Elliot growled back at him before she stepped into the hall.

JCL Security was headed by Conlan James and Jack Quinn. Their reputation in the United States security community was unparalleled. Even Elliot had heard of them before Dain found her and convinced her to join his team two years ago. She respected her bosses, and Dain's influence on her life had been such that she'd do pretty much anything he asked, but he'd also never asked her to babysit children. She knew nothing about children. Even when she'd been a child, she hadn't been "normal," so how the hell—heck—was she supposed to understand how to handle a child? The mere thought had her wishing for a paper bag to hyperventilate into as their group came to the door of Jack Quinn's office.

Dain glanced over his shoulder, one last assessment of his "troops" before presenting them to his commanding officer. His gaze settled on Elliot, and the warmth she recognized there eased the panic in the pit of her stomach. When he nodded, she found herself squaring her shoulders and putting on her game face.

Dain gave a peremptory knock and opened the door.

Here we go.

Her gaze shot immediately to the head honcho's desk, but the sight of Jack was blocked by a set of wide shoulders wrapped in a tight black T-shirt. Wide, muscular shoulders. Elliot saw the same sight nearly every day—all of her team members were "built," so to speak; they all dressed in what she called military casual, fatigues and tight tees. None of them had ever made the breath catch in her throat like this man did.

Brown hair left shaggy at the top, cut close in a semimilitary style as it tapered to a cropped V at the base of his skull. Tanned skin along his neck and heavy arms. The man's back narrowed to a tight ass and legs that told her he was just as strong as Saint or King or Dain, so what did he need with them?

Oh, right. Kid.

Forcing herself to stop eating up his manly form with her eyes, Elliot fell into line next to Dain to one side of Jack's desk.

Their boss made the introductions, alpha to alpha. "Dain Brannan, this is Deacon Walsh."

Deacon? Actual name or military call sign? Their team all had call signs they went by while on mission, but clients typically didn't. There hadn't been time to brief them on more than the very basics of the assignment—number of clients, degree of threat. A call sign gave her a small hint as to why the guy looked like he'd be the last person asking for their help, though.

"Please, call me Dain." The two men shook hands, and that was where Elliot focused. On their clasped hands, not on the sudden uneasy squirm in her belly. She didn't understand what was wrong with her. She didn't question clients, and she sure as hell didn't have a…reaction…to them. But there was no doubt that everything feminine in her, all the parts she'd thought were good and dead, thank God, were doing weird dances in this man's presence. And she didn't like it. She didn't like it one fucking bit.

"Deacon, meet my team: Elliot Smith, Saint Solorio, King Moncrief. Elliot will be assigned to your daughter's personal protection, of course."

"No, she won't."

That jerked her head up. Her gaze clashed with grim brown eyes in a grim, hard face. Deacon Walsh stared down at her like she was a puppy who'd just pissed on his boot. "Excuse me?"

"I said, no you won't."

Dain shifted next to her. "Elliot is the best member of our team to—"

"You're not assigning your weakest guard to my daughter simply because she's a woman."

It had been Elliot's argument too, sort of, but instead of cheering, she gritted her teeth. Was this bastard saying she was too little to kick ass if she needed to?

She didn't even realize she'd tried to step forward until Dain's hand came out, blocking her advance. Elliot settled back on her heels and waited. Of course, she glared daggers into the man's stern eyes while she did it, but what were they gonna do, fire her?

The thought almost made her snort. She held back just in time.

"Mr. Walsh…"

Dain's words were cut off with an abrupt slash of Walsh's hand. "My daughter is top priority on this assignment. Nothing else matters but her. She needs more than one scrawny wom—"

"Did you just call me scrawny?"

Elliot felt more than saw her team members take a step back, Dain included. A warm rush of pride filled her at their acknowledgment that she could fight her own battles, but she didn't allow it to get in the way of her focus on Walsh. His gaze swept over her, and though she thought she detected a hint—a very vague hint—of embarrassment in their depths, mostly his eyes held frustration and anger. So did his response.

"I sure as hell did."

The final word was barely past his lips when Elliot struck. A fake palm heel to the big man's chin had him jerking back instinctively, giving her a mere second to connect a kick with his inner thigh. She did avoid the groin, though—no need to thoroughly piss off the client, after all. Her grin was probably a tad too exultant as the strike brought Walsh's head forward, right into her elbow.

"What the fuck!"

"Smith!"

Chuckles from her teammates mixed with Dain's and Jack's shouts as she grabbed Walsh's closest arm and turned, putting her back to his chest. When she dropped to one knee, Walsh flipped over her head.

Ah, the joys of leverage. He hit the floor back first. A quick arch and push brought him to his feet—just in time for Elliot's swift kick in the ass. Walsh stumbled forward.

Dain caught him, fighting hard to keep the grin on his face under control.

No more than fifteen seconds had passed, but Elliot was already briskly brushing her hands together like she'd finished taking out the trash. Or proving a point. Said point might get her fired, but what the hell. They were used to her lack of communication skills around here.

Jack sputtered behind his desk, his face a shade of red she'd never seen on him before. Not very flattering.

A loud laugh pulled Elliot's focus to the client. Walsh bent, his back to her, the long furrow of his spine drawing her attention right down to the best ass she'd ever laid eyes on—and in her line of business, she'd laid eyes on a few. A warm hum that had nothing to do with a good fight sparked deep inside her.

Dain shook his head, one hand coming up to rub tiredly at his eyes. Elliot shot him a sheepish look.

Jack cleared his throat. "Mr. Walsh, I apologize—"

Walsh's raised hand precluded any apology. "No need, Jack." He turned, and Elliot read the amusement in his expression with relief. So maybe she wouldn't be fired today. "I believe I'm the one who should be saying those words. Nice job, Smith."

Not *Miss Smith*, which was what most clients labeled her with. Just Smith. As if she was one of the guys. The final bit of resentment fizzled out. *Okay, I can work with that.*

That was when she noticed the heat in her cheeks. Looking anywhere but at their client, her gaze met Saint's. When she moved to stand next to him, he leaned in to whisper, "Don't bother being embarrassed now, Otter. Too late."

She punched him in the ribs. His groan was covered by Dain clearing his throat.

"Let me assure you, Mr. Walsh"—Dain threw her a "we'll definitely talk about this later" look—"that Elliot will be much more circumspect with your daughter than she has proven to be here, won't you, Otter?"

If she said no, she might get out of the whole nanny duty thing, but one glance at Dain said she'd pushed as far as he would allow her to. She cleared her throat of rebellion. "Of course."

Walsh's gaze skimmed her before returning to Dain. "I have no doubt." He turned to Jack. "Now that we have that clear, perhaps we should get to the point."

"Right." Jack gestured them over to a conference area, where he, Walsh, and Dain took seats. Elliot stood next to Saint and King, lined up like good little soldiers behind Dain's seat, looking on as Jack opened a thick file on the coffee table before him and pushed it toward their team lead.

Dain planted his elbows on his knees and leaned forward over the intel. "Objective?"

"Protection," Walsh said before Jack could speak. "My daughter is the primary objective. Despite my performance here today"—Walsh didn't look her way, though his tone was filled with chagrin—"I don't need protection from this bastard. But I can't be with Sydney 24-7. I need someone who can."

"What bastard?" Dain asked.

Jack answered this time. "Martin Diako."

Elliot froze, even her breath stilling at the name. *Martin Diako.* She stared at the back of Dain's head, pinning her composure on her lifeline to the man who'd taken her under his wing.

Martin Diako. Fuck.

Deacon and Sydney Walsh needed protection from Martin Diako. The man known as Mansa in most circles. *Ruler.* The monster in charge of the biggest modern-day African pirating organization operating today. The monster responsible for ruining an untold amount of lives in the last forty years, including Elliot's own.

The monster who was her father.

Chapter Two

"Two years ago my team was responsible for the rescue of Senator Jeremy Ewing and his family."

"Team?" Dain asked. "That rescue was the responsibility of Global First."

And high profile; the senator's arrival back in the US, battered and bruised and grieving the loss of one of his twin daughters, had been televised live. Though Deacon's team had been responsible for his rescue, they weren't present for the media circus for obvious reasons—reasons that were coming back to haunt him now. "Yes. I'm still employed with them, though I'm not currently in the field."

"Why not?"

He had no desire to explain, to relive even through a few words the pain and anger of the last year, but the more the team knew, the better they could protect Sydney. "My wife, Julia, died eighteen months ago. I left the field to be with my daughter, though I still run computer support, mostly from home. I go into the office a few days a week, no more than a few hours at a time. Sydney began a private preschool in August, so I typically use that time for the office."

Dain nodded, tapping his finger against his jaw. "That was the raid that took out Andre Diako, wasn't it?"

Deacon's mouth tightened as memories of that night surged in his mind. For a moment he swore he could actually smell the salt-heavy air—and the blood.

"It was. The senator, his wife, and one of their twin daughters were rescued. The second girl, Shannon Ewing, was murdered by Andre before we could get to her." She'd bled out, naked and so damn scared, in Deacon's arms. "Andre was also killed."

"And now it appears that Mansa wants revenge," Jack stated.

Dain's intent eyes searched his boss's face. "How so?"

"Six months ago," Deacon told him, "one of our team members, Farley, went missing. Since he was on assignment deep in a South American jungle, we assumed it was related to his work. A month later, a second member, Inez, showed up murdered. Tortured."

Dain flipped through the file. Images of Inez's body—or most of it—flashed into view. Deacon bit back bile and rage, forcing himself to continue.

"A few weeks later Farley's body was discovered, buried in a shallow grave near the Bolivian border. He had the same...damage as Inez. Not long after, Trapper was attacked while on assignment in Beirut. He managed to escape before the assassin completed his objective, but he learned enough to know that all of them had been targeted for one purpose."

"Revenge," Jack inserted. "Mansa is tracking down the men who killed his son."

Deacon nodded. "The fourth member of our team, Farley's partner, Li, was killed during the rescue. That leaves my partner, Fionn McCullough, and me."

Dain continued skimming the pages before him. "Any direct threats up to now?"

"No." Frustration sharpened the word to a point. "Trapper has been brought here to GFS's Georgia campus and put in protective custody. Fionn and I are both stationed here in Atlanta as well. We're prepared, but Sydney... I won't risk my daughter becoming a target." As much as Deacon would like to believe he was infallible, he wasn't. Soldiers died all the time, especially when they were trying to protect others. Sydney had lost enough when her mother died; he wouldn't leave her without both her parents, alone. His pride wasn't worth that.

If he had any pride left after the little woman standing across from him had put him on his ass.

The thought actually amused him despite the seriousness of the situation. He'd have to make sure Fionn didn't find out or he'd never let Deacon hear the end of it. The spitfire had caught him off guard, something that had never happened before. No doubt she'd succeeded where others had failed because he'd been too busy ogling the perfect breasts under her tight T-shirt. Her white-blonde hair had caught his eye first, then the hard awareness in her eyes, but those breasts...goddamn. Only their slight jiggle had warned him she was moving, allowing him to relax enough that the impact on the plush but not too cushiony carpet hadn't fazed him.

It was the kick in the pants that had totally charmed him, however. Spitfire indeed.

She's here to protect your daughter, not tweak your libido, jackass.

Right. He'd have to remember that when she was ensconced in his home.

"So what's the plan?" Dain asked, pulling Deacon's focus out of his pants.

"Under normal circumstances, we would go directly to the threat, but we don't know where Mansa is right now. And with Sydney in the crossfire, I can't go anywhere. I won't risk leaving her unprotected."

"Why not go into hiding?"

"Because terrifying a child almost guarantees they'll act in ways that aren't natural for them," Jack said. Deacon met the man's look as something in his gut relaxed. Fionn knew Jack fairly well; the two men had crossed paths in Afghanistan more than once, and Fionn had highly recommended him, but trusting his daughter's safety to strangers had not set well. Jack seemed to understand the situation, though.

"At home," Deacon added, "I can pretty much predict her behavior, her reactions. We have bugout procedures we've practiced before, so she doesn't see them as unusual, more like a game. She knows what to do and where to go. In an unfamiliar environment, with unfamiliar people, she won't know what to do. And being on home turf gives us some small advantage." They needed every one to go up against Mansa and win. "Besides, each of my team members was caught by surprise. Let Mansa come to us, fight on our ground instead of choosing his own."

The spitfire spoke up from behind Dain. "Mansa isn't known for doing his own handiwork."

Deacon narrowed his eyes on her. "You know him?"

She shrugged. "I know of him."

Something about the look she exchanged with Dain said it was a little more than that. Deacon eyed the team leader. "What aren't you telling me?"

Jack's "Dain?" held an inquiry but no suspicion.

Smith met Deacon's gaze head-on. "Just an old case. I researched an associate of his."

"Really?" He didn't bother hiding the bark in his tone. "Because if it's any more than that, you don't want me to find out later."

She stayed relaxed under his scrutiny, something most men, innocent and not, had trouble doing. Her fists didn't tighten, nor did the skin around her eyes or mouth. Her stare was intent, but that seemed to be normal for this woman. One eyebrow went up as if she was more amused than intimidated. "Really. That's it."

Dain cleared his throat. "You've been given our files, of course, Deacon. You might not have had time to read them, but rest assured Jack and Con do a thorough job on the background of every member of their staff."

"Absolutely," Jack agreed. Resentment didn't color the word either. They all seemed to understand his suspicions.

Deacon nodded his acceptance of the explanation despite a slight reservation. He would definitely be looking over the files tonight, not to mention running his own background checks. Sydney would be safe; he refused to take anything for granted.

But that was later; right now he needed a plan in place to protect his daughter. "The fact that Mansa usually sends assassins instead of coming himself is what has made this harder, up to now."

"Why not now?" Dain asked.

Jack reached for the file, flipping to the very back where a still taken from grainy security footage waited. Deacon stared down at the gray-and-white image of the tall white male as anger built in his chest, vying with a fear he hated to acknowledge but couldn't ignore, not if he wanted to protect Sydney. "Mansa entered the US on a false Visa yesterday. West Coast." He turned the page, displaying copies of the ticket and the terrorist's forged ID. "He walked out of Los Angeles International Airport and disappeared."

"He has an endgame in mind." Dain's voice was tight with the realization.

"He does. And I'm very afraid that endgame involves my daughter." What better revenge than an heir for an heir?

"Why you?" Elliot asked.

"Because I'm the one who pulled the trigger and killed his son."

Curses filtered from each team member's mouth.

"Where is your daughter now?" she asked.

"She's with Lori in reception," Jack answered.

"You're not scared, are you, Otter? It's just a little girl," the Latino, Saint, said. Deacon had already identified him as the joker of the bunch.

"So is Otter," the one called King said. The words sounded serious, but he wasn't too successful at hiding his grin.

A faint blush colored the woman's cheeks. "Shut the fuck up, you two."

"Language!" the men yelled in unison, then laughed.

Deacon recognized the joshing the two male team members gave Smith; they respected the woman, obviously. They also weren't above ribbing her any chance they got. He was the same with his team—or had been. There weren't many of them left. Trapper would never go back into the field. Though recovering from his injuries, he'd lost power and dexterity in both hands, where critical tendons had been damaged. Deacon would eventually return to active duty, but for now had sidelined himself to stay home with Sydney. That left only Fionn, who'd refused a new team assignment since Julia's death despite Deacon's protests.

Fucking Mansa and his revenge.

Dain was shaking his head at the others' antics. "Can we bring her in?"

"No!" Smith's eyes went saucer wide. "No, we can wait. Work up a plan. Get—"

Chicken noises came from Saint. Smith glared back at him, her look promising evil things the minute Deacon or their boss weren't present. Deacon hoped the man had a good lock on his locker, though even that might not help if Deacon was any judge of character. And he was. Spitfire was beginning to feel like a pretty mild description for this female firecracker.

"I think that's an excellent idea," Deacon couldn't resist saying. Elliot Smith obviously wasn't looking forward to her assignment, although he got the feeling it wasn't distaste so much as fear that was behind the attitude. If he had to guess, he'd say her experience with children was severely limited. The thought of seeing her out of her element had anticipation sparking inside him. "Jack, would you call for Sydney?"

Jack stood and crossed to his desk. Deacon heard him chuckle along the way.

Smith crossed her arms and fumed. His attention dropped immediately to the delectable mounds pushed high by the position. Heat tightened his cock behind his zipper, and Deacon let himself enjoy it for a moment. When had he last taken the time to savor desire, hunger? Long before Julia's death. He'd been deployed, and despite what others might find acceptable, he'd remained faithful while away from his wife. Then her illness—she'd lasted no more than a few weeks after his return, the cancer already well advanced by then. Since her death, he'd been focused on grieving and work and Sydney. Women hadn't been even a blip on his radar other than as quick fantasy fodder in the shower.

And this one definitely shouldn't be on his radar. They would be working together, not sleeping together. Still, knowing that part of him hadn't been buried with his wife was something of a relief.

The arrival of his daughter moments later helped smack down his libido, at least a little bit. Sydney was holding the executive assistant's hand when they entered the room. The minute she saw him, she broke away on a run. "Daddy! Guess what we did?"

Deacon scooped her up when she reached him. Settling her on his lap, he smoothed her dark hair back from her face with his free hand. "What did you do?"

"We played with a puppy." Sydney practically quivered with excitement.

Uh-oh. "Is that right?"

"Yes," she replied smartly. "His name was Tebasterand. No... Sed— Um." She glanced back to Lori. "What was his name again?"

"Sebastian." An indulgent smile curved Lori's mouth.

"Right." Sydney turned back to him. "Sebastiton."

Deacon chuckled at the butchered name. "Right."

"He was so soft, and he licked me, right here." She pointed at her cheek. "I love him, Daddy." Imploring green eyes caught his, so similar to her mother's that Deacon felt a catch in his chest. "Can we get a puppy?"

He barely held back a groan. "Now where would that leave Katie, huh?" He palmed the ragged stuffed-animal kitten Sydney carried everywhere. He had to sneak it from her bed after she fell asleep at night just to wash it. "She wouldn't want to share you, would she?"

Syd contemplated the kitten with a seriousness far beyond her years. "I guess not."

Movement nearby pulled his daughter's attention from her best friend to Elliot Smith. The woman approached as if Sydney were a wild animal she didn't quite know how to handle—one that might bite at any moment. Deacon did his best to hide his amusement, but from the lethal look she shot his way, he wasn't succeeding.

"Sydney, I'd like you to meet some people." He settled her on her feet next to him and turned her gently to face the room.

Sydney eyed the men intently as each was introduced, but when it came to Smith, her face lit up. She left his side immediately to approach the petite woman. "Your name is Smith? That's weird. Like Walsh. I'm Sydney Walsh. Is it like that?"

Smith crouched to bring herself eye level with Sydney. A quick glance over at Deacon for approval amused him even more. He gave her a nod that visibly relaxed her tense muscles.

"Well, Smith is my last name like Walsh is your last name. You can call me Elliot."

"That's a boy's name."

"It can be," Deacon gently corrected. "Not always."

"Like my name's a city?" Sydney asked.

"Yes."

Sydney looked at him, then at Elliot. "Cool!"

Elliot smiled. The curve of her lips caught Deacon's attention. He wanted her to lick that lower lip and let him see it wet.

"Daddy? Daddy?"

Reminding himself he wasn't alone, he clasped Sydney's tapping fingers and curled them in his. "What, Little Bit?"

"Can Elliot come over and have a tea party?"

Deacon ignored the choking sound coming from the still-crouching Elliot. "Sure. In fact, everyone will be coming over to help me with some stuff at the house."

"Work stuff?" Sydney asked.

"Work stuff." He gave Elliot a wicked glance. "But I'm sure we can find time for you and Elliot to have a tea party."

"Yay!" Sydney skipped her way back to Elliot. "What do you like to have at tea parties? The tea is pretended. Or milk; sometimes Daddy gives me milk to pour. And cookies. Do you like cookies? What kind?"

Elliot, seeming flustered, finally said, "I don't know. I've never had a tea party."

"Never?" Sydney's distress was plain as she squinted between Elliot and Deacon, a look that said she didn't understand how anyone could get to the age of four without a tea party, much less be a grownup like Elliot and not have this vital experience. "She's never had a tea party, Daddy."

He wasn't sure he understood it either, but… "Well, we'll have to remedy that, won't we?"

If Elliot's glare had been a weapon, he'd be bleeding out on the floor. He couldn't hold back a chuckle. "See, Sydney, Elliot definitely wants to have a tea party."

Sydney swung her head around to see a quickly smiling Elliot.

"Sounds fun," Elliot said. The *not* she undoubtedly added in her mind was clear, at least to him. It made him want to kiss that look off her face.

Why did her bristly attitude attract him? He didn't know, but he liked it. Maybe because she was the opposite of Julia, everything out in the open for everyone to see, socially acceptable or not. Julia had been a wonderful part of his life and he'd loved her, but she'd been nothing like Elliot.

Nothing.

Of all the things he'd expected walking into this office this morning, Elliot had not been one of them.

Chapter Three

"You fucking lied to a client."

The slam of Dain's locker door as he flung it open told Elliot even more about his mood than his words did. Guess she was lucky he'd waited till the rest of the team left for Deacon Walsh's house before confronting her.

She tossed the duffel she'd been filling onto the bench and turned to face her boss. "And you fucking let me, Dain."

Dain squared off too, body tense, arms tight over his chest. "Of course I did; I've got your back, always. I wasn't about to contradict you in front of everyone."

"So it was just about allowing me to save face; is that it?" She snorted, hiding her hurt behind the usual sarcasm. "I've never given a rat's ass what anyone thought about me and you know it."

"I know that's what you tell yourself." Abandoning his locker, he crossed to tower over her from the opposite side of the bench. "It's what you've always told yourself, and it's a damn lie, because if it were true, I wouldn't be the only one in this building who knows you're Martin Diako's daughter."

"That's not why."

"Then explain it to me, Elliot."

I can't handle anyone seeing who I really am, even you. Dain had gotten her drunk and gotten the facts, but even he couldn't release her emotions. Sometimes she wondered if they were well and truly dead, except if they were, she wouldn't be afraid of them.

She turned to rummage in her locker for a T-shirt. The silence behind her became heavy with Dain's disappointment the longer it stretched, and when she turned back to him, her gaze refused to lift off the floor. "Knowing who I am won't help this case. It sure as hell won't help us protect Sydney Walsh."

"That's not your decision to make," Dain argued. When Elliot leaned back against the lockers, arms crossed over her ribs, a growl erupted from his lips. "Would you look at me, damn it?"

You're not two; you're a grown woman with a right to decide who knows about your past.

She met Dain's gaze. Barely.

He ignored her defiance. "Deacon's daughter is at risk. He has a right to know anything and everything related to his case. Period."

"This is my personal history, Dain, not a fact of this case. Certainly not something that will hinder it. If anything, you're lucky to have me on the team. I'm the only expert on Mansa that exists, whether anyone else knows it or not. I've studied his every move, his personality, the people he surrounds himself with and the people he eliminates—and why. You need that. You need me. Because Sydney will never be safe until I take Mansa out."

"Until *we* take him out, Elliot."

"Not we!" she shouted, the words shaking as hard as her body. "Never we. You're the one who pulled me into this fucking family, Dain. You're the one who made me put down roots, made me care, damn it! And now you want me to risk you? Risk being able to protect you?" She stepped over the bench and into his space. "One person is far more agile and able to infiltrate than a team; you know that. And if you think I'll let that fucker take one more person that I love from me, you can go to hell."

Dain's big hands wrapped around her biceps—to comfort her or keep her from attacking, she wasn't sure. It worked either way. His warmth seeped into her, slowing the shaking, breaking down her anger until she could see the compassion in his expression without wanting to kick him. Or kill something with her bare hands.

Damn the man.

"We have to tell him," he finally said.

"I can't." And that was the truth. In the end, the argument didn't matter because she would never be able to get the words past her lips.

"Then I will."

Something far too close to fear fluttered in her belly. "No. Dain…please."

"I have to." His hands settled on her shoulders, their weight reinforcing his authority. Elliot fought the urge to shake him off. "I'm responsible—for your life and theirs. We operate together; that's the only way this works. We need all our information on the table. We don't keep secrets from each other, Elliot, not when lives are at stake."

"You already have the information, Dain. That won't change by keeping my…parentage…a secret. But it just might if Deacon and Jack find out who I am. I'd become a security risk. They'd yank me off this case so fast your head would spin."

"No, they wouldn't."

"Can you guarantee that?"

Dain's lips tightened into a thin line. Point taken.

Elliot pushed a little harder. "Too many people knowing about my relationship with Mansa means too many possibilities of a leak. It would put more people in danger and turn this into a full-blown FUBAR. We're safer—Sydney is safer—if no one knows." Her father had long ago given up searching for her, at least she thought so. As far as she knew, he thought she'd died with her mother, which was all the better.

Dain shook his head. "No one on our team would leak this information."

"Not intentionally."

The pain that washed over Dain's expression, the loss of his hands on her shoulders felt like a blow, almost as hard as the one she'd delivered. Dain believed she didn't trust them; he couldn't see the truth, that she could protect them better if *they* trusted *her*. That trust would disappear, intentionally or not, once they knew Mansa was her father.

But even if she walked away, he'd still tell them—she could see it in his eyes. What other options did she have?

This feeling started up in her chest, fluttery, almost…panicked. If she didn't know better, she'd say it was fear. "Give me time."

"Elliot." His sigh sounded as if it came from his toes. "I can't risk my integrity or the integrity of this team."

"Then tell me to go," she said quietly. "Tell me I'm done, that it's over." Because she didn't have the strength to walk away on her own.

The words shook them both; she felt it down deep where she hid all the things she didn't want to see, but even worse, she saw it in Dain's face. Had she felt this way as she watched her mother die? When her world had exploded in a rush of fire? It had been so long she couldn't remember. Dain and King and Saint were her whole world; could she live through their loss like she had her family's?

Dain was silent so long she wasn't sure what he would say. When his hand lifted to cup her cheek, she went rigid, waiting for the blow, the pain. She should've known better.

"Whether you leave or not has always been up to you, little Otter." The tenderness in her call sign was almost more than she could stand. "Stay, walk away— your choice. I hope you'll stay and fight with us, but I won't force you." The tension in his frame eased the slightest bit as his hand dropped back to his side. "We need you. You know we do."

He didn't argue further; he didn't have to. His searing focus argued for him: *Trust me. Believe in me. Live what I've taught you, not what the past beat into you. It will work out all right.* She was letting him down, being a coward, and she knew it. His narrowed eyes watched her like a hawk, reading every nuance of expression that she couldn't hide, right down to the burn of fucking tears at the backs of her eyes. What the hell was wrong with her? First her reaction to Deacon, and now this. It had to be her damn hormones; nothing else would ever make her cry.

She couldn't trust her voice not to wobble like a little girl's, so she nodded instead.

Dain didn't rub in the victory. "You might have a point about Jack removing you from the case. We can't chance that—we need the information you can give us about your father."

The hated title caused her breath to catch.

"But I do think we can compromise. What about you?"

"How?"

"I'll give you five days. That's all," he warned. "Five days to earn Deacon Walsh's trust. Five days to tell him on your own, or I'll do it for you. In the meantime, anything you see or have insight on that involves Mansa, you come to me immediately, got it?"

She hesitated. Nodded.

"I won't tolerate you holding out on me, Elliot. I care about you. We all care about you. But that won't keep us from doing the right thing."

"What happens if I trust these people and they don't keep my secret? What happens if the information leaks?" She'd have to leave then. Maybe she was merely delaying the inevitable.

"It's not gonna happen. I promise you, Elliot—and I keep my promises."

"I know." He did. If she knew one thing about him, it was that. And she knew she trusted him as far as she could trust anyone, so his promise would have to do. "I know you're trying to do the right thing, Dain." She was too, but he'd never see it that way. She wanted to protect the people she cared about. Why put everyone at risk when they could put only her at risk? But she knew from Dain's face that this was as far as he'd concede.

His body relaxed even more as he ran a rough hand through the Mohawk lining his head. "You drive me absolutely insane. You know that, right?"

The words shouldn't hurt; half the time that was her primary objective. But she didn't think either one of them was joking right now.

With a negligent shrug, she grabbed her duffel bag and headed for the locker room door.

"Elliot."

She didn't really look back, more like at the floor just over her shoulder. Dain was having none of that; he walked right up until she couldn't help but see him—from the chest down, at least.

"Look at me, little Otter."

That fucking tenderness again. Funny how she could name it now; when they'd first met, her a fighter on the underground circuit, him a respectable "soldier" who shouldn't want anything to do with her, tenderness had been as foreign as normal. And yet he'd still managed to convince her to join him, to work for him. To become something far closer to normal than she'd been her entire life. And bastard that he was, he wasn't above using it to his advantage.

And damn it, hurt or not, she didn't want to leave her team. They needed her.

She turned to meet Dain's dark stare without flinching.

"Don't wait," he said earnestly. "Don't put me in that position. I don't want to betray your confidence, but even more"—he reached out to trace the line of her jaw, the look he gave her softer than she'd ever seen on his hard face—"I want you to come to terms with your past and realize it no longer has power over you, Elliot, except the power you give it."

"My past doesn't have any power, Dain."

"Yes, it does. That's why you can't say aloud that Martin Diako is your bastard of a father, that he killed your mother because she escaped, that he tried to kill you, that he ruined your life. You've built a whole new you out of the ashes of the torture he inflicted;

41

don't let him steal that from you as well. You're strong. You can face this."

"Can I?"

"You have to. Because if you don't, it will eventually destroy you."

Chapter Four

Deacon knew he should be in the library with the team leader, Dain, going through logistics, discussing their plans, explaining the setup here at the house. King and Saint had arrived around lunchtime with a shit load of equipment they'd laid out in the library at the back of the house. Dain and Elliot had been delayed at the office but arrived a few minutes ago, and yet Elliot still lingered out by the team's van in the driveway.

And where was he? Lingering in his own foyer, for God's sake. Waiting for a certain spitfire to come inside. He should probably feel guilty for watching her through the front windows, for spying, but he didn't; he was curious, a trait that usually served him well. He wasn't sure where that curiosity would lead him with Elliot, but he refused to back down from it.

The door finally opened, and Deacon released the breath he'd been holding as Elliot walked into his home. What kind of name was that, anyway? Elliot Smith. The men called her Otter sometimes, but if anyone asked him, she bore zero resemblance to the playful creature they'd nicknamed her after.

The second the words popped into his head, he understood.

They'd named her after her opposite, of course. Just to piss her off, more than likely—something his team would do to one of their own too. He grinned

43

imagining all the havoc that must have wreaked with the prickly woman.

Elliot didn't seem prickly now as she walked through the front door and stopped to eye the open area before her. Those intense blue eyes assessed the new domain, but her expression remained blank. Buttoned-down. He had the sudden perverse need to provoke her, to push her past whatever was holding her back and free the attitude that had so fascinated him in the office. Pushing away from the wall, he walked toward her.

That sounded easier than it was, because the closer he came, the more the sexual attraction that had flared in Jack's office gripped his balls in a vise of need. He couldn't remember the last time he'd felt hunger this strong, and with no effort whatsoever by the object of his interest. Elliot didn't startle at his appearance, didn't do anything but stand there looking around, and yet the sunlight streaming through the glass surrounding his double front doors set her white-blonde hair gleaming, brought a rich glow to the light tan of her bared neck and the slope of slender muscles in her arms. Her shirtsleeves were rolled up, the buttons open at the collar, creating a beguiling vee that drew his gaze down to places that had distraction written all over their tempting curves.

Her body was small but perfect. Just the thought of how small she'd be if he managed to get inside her had sweat breaking out on his upper lip. He forced himself to look back to her face, to stop at the base of the stairs and lean an elbow on the banister instead of moving right up into her space and seeing if she'd have the same kind of reaction to his body that he had to hers. Would those blue eyes widen? Would her pale skin flush, her breath quicken?

A pinch in his groin warned him to avoid that path, so he opened his mouth instead. "I wondered when you'd get here. You aren't afraid of working with a four-year-old girl, are you?"

Aaand inserted his foot. Damn it.

Elliot's back went rigid so fast he heard a distinct pop from her spine. Not the reaction he'd intended, but she wasn't indifferent to him, at least. He worked to control his grin. Elliot was probably a typical female in many ways, but in this she was just like every other man he'd had under his command—being called a coward offended her. The look she shot him could've peeled paint off the walls. "Do I need to be?"

He released his grin. "Depends."

She didn't take the bait by asking him to explain. Instead she went back to studying the layout of the house.

"What do you think?"

Elliot stared at the sweeping staircase reminiscent of traditional Southern plantations. Deacon had added the feature after he'd bought the house, replacing a plain staircase that had hugged one wall and closed the space in too much for his liking. "I'm thinking we could use this to our advantage in the event of a security breach."

Hmm. Well trained. And focused. What would that focus be like when it was on him and not his house?

His eagerness to find out surprised him, though given the fact that his dick had yet to subside, *eagerness* might be too mild a word.

"There are small hidden closets—cubbies, really—behind the staircase on each side," he pointed out. "Easily accessible from the back of the house, for either observation or an ambush. The foyer and the upstairs landing area are both open for obvious reasons." No one should be able to sneak in the front door and find cover, if they even managed to get past the three-foot-wide windows along either side and atop the doors without Deacon observing them.

"All this glass…"

A spark of ego lit inside him. "The windows here and in the back are coated with a special reflective film. We can see out, but no one can see in. I won't give anyone leverage." He was surprised she hadn't noticed, but then he'd gotten the distinct impression from Dain that something pretty intense was going on between the two. The vibes coming off the team leader when he'd entered told Deacon he was unhappy for some reason. Were they involved?

No, Dain wore a wedding ring. Elliot didn't. And they were on the same team. No way would Deacon put a married couple together, and he'd bet Jack wouldn't either.

"I noticed," Elliot said wryly. "I meant, what kind of glass?"

Now it was his turn to be offended. "Bulletproof, of course." What else?

"You designed this house for attack?"

He moved closer, just close enough to catch the warm female scent of her. Not flowers, definitely not perfume, just fresh, clean skin. "More habit than anything else. I certainly wouldn't have brought danger home to my family if I could help it, but I'm not one to leave it to chance." That was one of the reasons he hadn't intended to have children until he left the field, but Julia had been impatient. Or maybe they really had been careless as she'd claimed. He'd always suspected that she became pregnant on purpose during that short vacation in Sydney between missions, but once his daughter had arrived, why she'd been conceived no longer mattered. Sydney was the center of his world. And now that Julia was gone...if they had waited much longer, there would've been no children for them at all.

Elliot's snort cut his mental trip down a rabbit hole short.

"What?"

"If your intention was to not bring danger home to your family, you really fucked up, didn't you? Mansa's about the worst danger you could imagine."

"Granted. But it wasn't a fuckup." He tried to keep the bite from his voice but didn't quite succeed.

Elliot didn't seem offended—or intimidated. "No?"

"No." He realized he was stalking toward her about the time her shadow reached his boots. "If it's a choice between bringing danger to my daughter and letting that bastard rape a second eighteen-year-old defenseless girl, I'll stick by my decision. One child destroyed on my watch was one too many."

With the sun behind her, Elliot's eyes were shadowed, hard to read, but he felt their intensity even if he couldn't see it. That same intensity echoed in her voice. "Mansa has always been death on women; Andre Diako was raised to it. Not that that's any excuse." Her mouth went tight, her tone deadly serious. "You don't want him getting his hands on Sydney, Deacon."

It was the first time she'd said his name. A shiver tingled down his spine. "No, I don't—and he won't. That's what you're here to help me prevent."

She opened her mouth to answer, pulling his gaze down to the full curve of her lower lip. The growl of an engine outside the front door cut her off, followed by the harsh ping of gravel being thrown beneath abruptly braking tires. Deacon groaned.

"Looks like the rest of our backup is here," he said before allowing himself a small retreat. If he stayed that close to Elliot, he wouldn't be able to breathe—and Fionn would razz him endlessly over it. No way his best friend wouldn't notice Deacon's crazy reaction to this woman.

"The rest of our backup?" Elliot asked.

The front door opened. Deacon squinted against the harsh glare that left him momentarily blinded as Fionn slammed the door shut. A sharp wolf whistle split the air.

"Deac, you've been holding out on me. Who is this pretty wan?"

Elliot's eyes widened, the first openly honest emotion he'd seen on her face since she'd walked in. Her shock shone plainly as she turned to take in Fionn's appraisal of her ass. Deacon glowered at his friend as much as at the sudden urge to protect said ass from Fionn's view. He should be focused on the situation, not jealousy or ego or, God forbid, lust. And yet he was helpless against all three, which only added an even harder edge to his words as he made introductions. "Fionn McCullough, meet Elliot Smith. Elliot, Fionn, my best friend and frequent embarrassment."

"Elliot?" Fionn had moved on to appraising the front of her now. "What kind of name is Elliot for a pretty little thing like you? Ellie, maybe...now that's a name for a woman." The smile that had gotten Fionn laid more times than Deacon could count crossed his face. A charming smile.

Elliot didn't seem to be reacting the way most females did.

Deacon wondered how long it would be before Elliot put Fionn on his ass. Maybe slightly longer than it had taken her to put *him* on his ass, but not by much if her expression was anything to go by.

The men of Team Foxtrot were making a hell of an impression today, weren't they?

Elliot surprised him by taking a totally different tack with his uncouth friend. "Fin?" She tilted her head slightly. "Like on a fish? And you think *my* name is weird?"

"Irish, you know." The lilting flavor of his friend's language deliberately deepened, emphasizing his nationality. "That be Fionn with an O."

Deacon had seen this conversation played out more than once during their friendship. When Fionn's mouth formed the O, something about it made women want to mimic the shape of his mouth with theirs. Some kind of sexual spell, according to Fionn. Personally Deacon had seen Sydney do the same thing when he was trying to teach her to eat solid food, not that he'd shared that vital bit of intel with Fionn.

Now he watched with interest as Elliot's lips softened, parted just barely, then pressed firmly together. When disappointment flashed across Fionn's face, her mouth twitched like she was forcing back a smile—of amusement or triumph, he wasn't sure. He was sure Elliot would take it as a personal victory to deprive his friend of the reaction he wanted. Would she be equally amused to know Deacon wanted to punch Fionn in the face for flirting with her when Deacon had seen her first?

And on that note…

He cleared the growl out of his throat. "Elliot, your team is setting up in the library." He nodded toward the right hallway beside the stairs. "Would you like to join them or spend some time with Sydney before we tour the house?"

"The layout of the house is likely more impor—"

"Elliot!"

His daughter appeared at the head of the stairs, her tiny body practically quivering with delight at the sight of her new friend. Just like she had a thousand times before, Sydney grasped the banister at the top of the stairs, threw a short leg over with the aid of a little hop, and whizzed down the slick wood. Deacon was chuckling when Elliot's slight weight knocked him out of her way.

Chapter Five

Elliot fought the scream that rose in her throat. Years of training had ingrained the need to remain silent in crisis, but the sight of Sydney balancing precariously on the banister as she whooshed toward them from twenty feet up scared the shit out of her. Instinct moved her forward when fear would've stuck her feet to the floor. All she knew was she had to get to the child before she fell; nothing else mattered.

And when Sydney's slight body came to rest in her hands? That's when the anger hit. "What the hel— Fu—"

The only words that popped into her head were all curses, none of which she could say with Sydney's wide eyes staring curiously up at her. Instead she plucked the girl from the banister and settled her safely on the nice unmoving floor of the foyer, then spun on Deacon.

His eyes bulged when they met hers, seeming to recognize both her terror and her anger. She wanted to hide it, wanted to hide herself—she didn't react this way. Ever. She was always under control. But seeing that baby in danger…

And then Deacon laughed, which only made it worse.

Before she could kick his ass—which was really fast—Deacon had scooped Sydney up to his hip and cuddled his daughter close to that broad, muscular chest. "I think you scared our Elliot a bit, Sydney."

"Oh." Sydney wiggled out of Deacon's arms in a shot and raced to her. Tiny arms wrapped around her thigh; a tiny face tilted up to reassure her. "Don't worry, Elliot. Daddy made sure the rail's real wide. That way I won't fall. He taught me how to slide good. It's okay; he won't let me get hurt." The child's utter belief in her father shone from her eyes, clear as day and as foreign to Elliot as baby dolls and tea parties.

And now everyone was staring. She couldn't blame them. Her cheeks burned. Of course Deacon would make sure his daughter was safe; the man had hired a specialized team to protect his house from a murderer just for her. So why was Elliot's heart still pounding? And where the fuck had all her vaunted professional cool gone? "That's…uh… That's good."

Sydney chattered away, seemingly oblivious to Elliot's breakdown. Elliot realized her hand was atop the little girl's head when her fingers stroked along the silky brown hair pulled back into a ponytail similar to the ones her mother had put her hair into as a child. Looking down into Sydney's eyes, caressing her hair, Elliot realized something: Sydney was only a year older than Elliot had been when her mother escaped Mansa's island. Nora had risked everything to protect her daughter, and now, two decades later, Deacon was trying to do the same thing.

It had to stop. No more little girls should be at risk because Mansa was an egomaniacal bastard. No more parents should feel like this, like their hearts would pound out of their chests, like they couldn't breathe because they were afraid for their child's safety. Children deserved to be protected, and Elliot knew, whether she had experience with kids or not,

Sydney was hers to protect, just as Mansa was hers to kill.

She carefully pulled her hand away, retreating into the space she knew, the familiar, safe space of her professional persona. Her words slipped into a slight pause when Sydney stopped to draw a breath. "I think it's time for that tour. I'll go get the others."

"No need." Footsteps accompanied the words, moving down the hall, and then Dain appeared, Saint and King flanking him in their usual positions.

"Speak of the devils." Deacon introduced Fionn around. Elliot noticed that, after shaking the men's hands and giving them each a hard stare, Fionn turned to Deacon and gave his friend the barest of nods, the gesture seeming to ease the tightness around Deacon's eyes. Had Deacon called Fionn in for a second opinion? She could see him wanting an outsider's perspective; he had a lot to lose if they weren't the right team to protect his daughter.

Sydney squealed. "Can I show Elliot my room, Daddy?"

Elliot hadn't known a sound that high could emanate from a creature that small unless said creature was a mouse. She plugged a finger into the ear closest to Sydney and shook it, trying to stop the ringing, but didn't miss the fact that Deacon's gaze was still locked on her. It was a fight not to react to him, but every time her interest tried to rise, so did the memory of Dain's ultimatum. She needed to be objective, in control, not...whatever this was.

And a great start you've made with that, Ell.

Telling herself to shut up, she followed her charge up the stairs. Not that she had much choice given that Sydney had claimed her hand. Those tiny fingers twined with hers felt foreign, strange. She wanted to shake them off and clutch them closer at the same time. Between that and the heat licking along her spine at the knowledge that Deacon was directly behind her, right on level to get a great view of her ass, she wondered if she was having some sort of mental break. She never had to fight to focus on work, never worried what a man thought of her as a woman—hell, she barely thought of herself as a woman. Maybe the shock of Diako's reappearance in her life was the cause.

All the more reason to kill the fucker as soon as possible.

The second floor of the house was bisected by a long hall that jigged to the right at the end. It didn't extend far enough for that to be the back of the house, though. Elliot knew Dain had a copy of the house's blueprints, but reviewing them herself had had to wait. She made a mental note to commit them to memory later.

"The back half of this story is a Jack-and-Jill suite intended for guests," Deacon explained behind them. "Since the master is downstairs, I've taken one of those rooms for now to be close to Sydney." He opened doors as they went along, showing them a large study and third guest bedroom at the front near the stairs. Elliot glanced into each. Somehow Deacon was always there, right where she couldn't help but brush against him. And every brush made her breath catch, damn it.

"Saint and King can stay in the guest room," Deacon said. "I'm assuming you'll be downstairs, Dain?"

They continued down the hall, passing two additional rooms that were currently empty, one on either side. "I'll stay in the library," Dain said. "The couch in there will do fine, and I want to be close to the equipment just in case." They'd agreed to keep all weapons not currently being worn in a locked chest in the library under constant surveillance. Sydney had been raised around guns, but she was still a child and no one wanted to risk her safety. "We'll take shifts on a rotating basis, of course, but I'd rather everyone get as much rest as possible until things begin to heat up."

There was no question of them not heating up; they all knew that. Diako didn't travel outside the realm he easily controlled, ever. It was how he'd stayed alive, stayed on the throne of the kingdom he'd created. Retaliation for his heir's death appeared to be an exception.

Deacon acknowledged Dain's plan with a nod as he led them down to the end of the hallway. "I'm in this bedroom here." He indicated the room at the hall's elbow. The position of the door meant he could see anyone coming from the stairs; no one could get to Sydney's room without passing his. Good plan. "The adjoining room can be Elliot's so she'll be directly across from Sydney."

Not a good plan.

"Isn't that great, Elliot?" Sydney bounced up and down, practically vibrating with excitement. "You'll be right next to me. Almost like a sleepover; would you like to stay in my room for a sleepover sometime, huh?"

"Um, maybe. Let's get settled first, okay? We'll have plenty of time for sleepovers." As if she knew all about them.

Right.

Sydney pouted up at her, and Elliot wondered how the hell Deacon ever resisted that face. The kid was cute, no doubt about it.

Deacon gestured to a door down the short corridor at a right angle to the original hallway. "That's yours, Elliot."

She did no more than glance in. The sight of the connecting door open to the bathroom made her chest feel funny. She turned to Sydney. "And where's your room?"

Sydney's grin went wide. Elliot carefully surrounded the fragile fingers that slipped once more into hers, ignoring the tension caused by Deacon's gaze as it followed them into a room with pale pink walls and stuffed animals piled on the bed. Sydney went straight over and picked up a ratty-looking cat that Elliot recognized from this morning.

"This is Katie Kitty."

A favorite, Elliot had no doubt. She listened to Sydney discussing Katie's wonderful qualities, then introducing the rest of her animals while Elliot scanned the room for security issues. Though the usual kid clutter existed, Deacon had a toy chest against one wall that Sydney seemed to make use of for everything but her animals. A bookshelf overflowing with books occupied another wall, next to a large double window curtained with light, flowing pink material, not see-through but allowing in the sun. Elliot walked over to look out.

A second later Sydney ducked beneath the material with her, Katie clutched to her thin chest. "It's pretty, isn't it? Not like our old house. I didn't have a window. Now I can see everywhere, and the people next door have horses that visit our fence sometimes, and Daddy lets me pet them when we're out. And roll down that hill in the grass. And…"

Elliot lost track of the conversation as her gaze settled on the hill across the road from Deacon's land. For a second she swore she caught a glint of light flashing off metal or glass. On instinct she shuffled Sydney behind her hip.

The move brought a pause in Sydney's chatter.

"Uh-huh," Elliot said.

The little girl continued, unaware of Elliot's focus centered outside.

"Syd, c'mere and be telling me about this new baby doll," Fionn called through the curtain. Sydney bumped Elliot's leg as she turned away from the window, but Elliot continued to stand. To watch. In the back of her mind she heard Fionn teasing Sydney, heard Dain and Saint's low-voiced conversation near the door. The buzz of activity fell away as she breathed deep, in and out, allowing her warrior mindset to click online. Whoever was out there posed a threat to her team, to her client, an innocent little girl who'd been standing in this very spot a few seconds before.

She couldn't allow that.

Another breath, waiting, waiting. Seek and destroy. This was who she was, who—

Another flash.

Got him.

She turned quickly, flinging aside the filmy curtain. Sydney sat on a rug across the room, showing Fionn a line of baby dolls. Safe.

Three strides brought Elliot to the door and Dain.

"Surveillance. Opposite hill from Sydney's window, twenty yards below the ridge." A sharp glance at King and Saint brought their attention to her. She'd just lifted her hand to gesture for them to follow when Deacon appeared in the door.

"What?"

Dain filled him in. Elliot signaled her team.

"Where the hell do you think you're going?" Deacon barked.

She frowned. "Where do you think?" She literally squirmed, set to go, her body flooded with adrenaline and ready for the hunt. This was the lead they needed, that she needed, her first step in finding Mansa. And Deacon was holding her back.

His hard face reminded her that he wasn't just a client or a dad, but also a warrior. And this warrior wasn't happy, apparently.

"We need to go," she insisted.

"No, they need to go. You stay with Sydney."

"But..." There were five soldiers that could stay. "That's my team. Let me do my job, Deacon." *Let me protect you all.*

He gripped her arm, his hand wrapping all the way around until she felt the pinch of digging fingers underneath. "Your job is here, with Sydney. Or did you forget that? Fionn!"

Hell no. She was not handing her authority over to Mr. Playboy. "I'm protecting your daughter by investigating a threat." She needed to be out there doing what she did best, seeing the evidence with her own eyes, finding the clues, uncovering the slightest lead that would take her to her father's doorstep. She was the one with the intel, the one who knew the target better than anyone else. Why were they stopping her?

Because you screwed yourself, remember? Deacon doesn't know how valuable you are.

"Elliot."

When she glanced at Dain, he shook his head. She glared back at him. When Fionn arrived, she kept her gaze on Dain as she repeated the information he needed.

"Sniper?" Fionn asked, his voice low enough that Sydney couldn't hear them across the room.

It was Deacon who answered. "I don't think so. She was right in the window and he didn't fire. Take King and Saint to check it out."

Fionn jerked his chin in acknowledgment and gave them a wide berth as he jogged toward the stairs. Instinctively Elliot pushed forward to follow him.

Deacon didn't let her go. Elliot clamped down on the urge to break his fucking fingers.

Deacon leaned in, his brown eyes darkened to near black the closer he came, his irises taking over her world, his gravel-filled voice vibrating deep inside her. "You are my daughter's last defense; if anyone gets through us, then they have to get through you. Keep that in mind, Elliot—it's the only position that matters on this op. So don't fight me again. You might not like the instinct it stirs up." His smile took on a feral edge. "Or maybe you will."

Shock sizzled down her spine. "What did you say to me?"

"You heard me."

Without another word, he turned to follow the team—her team. Elliot stood, frozen, until small fingers gripped her hand. Shaking fingers. "Elliot?"

Guilt surged in Elliot's chest. Yes, her first instinct had been to verify Sydney's protection, but it had also been to leave the child there.

She dropped to her knees instead. "I'm here."

Green pools of worry stared up at her. "What's going on?"

For a moment Elliot was lost in the far too innocent depths of Sydney's eyes, eyes that reminded her of her own distant past, when she'd had a mother who loved her enough to die for her, a mother she'd trusted to take care of her. *Just like Sydney trusts me.*

"Everything's okay, baby. I won't let anything happen to you." With a quick scoop she gathered the little girl into her arms and stood. "Come on."

The sound of boots on the stairs faded as the team left through the back of the house, but she refused to dwell on it any further. She had a job to do—she had to trust her team to do theirs.

She'd have to find some other way to get to Mansa before he got to them.

Chapter Six

Deacon had Fionn take point. He'd spent his life leading, and if there was one thing he understood about command, it was that the most important trait of any leader was knowing when to step back. He was, frankly, too damn pissed to be at his best, and his team deserved the best.

What he didn't understand was why the defiant little spitfire he'd left back at the house got under his collar the way she did.

He knew better than anyone how hard it was to send his team out on a mission without him. Elliot's role as Dain's second meant she would normally lead this op, but she'd made sure Sydney wasn't alone before trying to leave—so why had Deacon felt the need to challenge her? Because he truly wanted her with Sydney, or because arguing with her was slightly less disturbing than wanting her?

And yet, if the heaviness in his gut was any indication, arguing with her had merely heightened his secondary issue. Again.

His gut also told him that Elliot would guard Sydney till her last dying breath, not because she was a woman but because of the way she reacted to his daughter. The fear in her serious blue eyes when Sydney had slid down the bannister. The way she touched his daughter's hair, knelt to talk to her like Sydney was her equal instead of a nuisance. Elliot might not understand children or childhood—for what reasons, he didn't know—but she already felt some connection to Sydney; he'd seen it in her eyes. And he knew better than anyone what that connection would drive someone to do. It didn't matter who he had to kill or sacrifice, he would make his daughter safe. Elliot, warrior that she was, would do the same for anyone she cared about. He wanted her focused on his daughter now more than ever, if only to grow that instinct inside her. For Sydney's sake.

Right. Not your own.

Of course not.

He grinned at Fionn's back, his steady footsteps in perfect sync with his friend's as they traveled at a fast clip through the thick woods outside of the perimeter fence to the south of Deacon's property. At the road they chose the heaviest cover and crossed, then split up, Fionn and Deacon to the left, King and Saint to the right, spreading out to approach their target from both sides. Based on the position Elliot had indicated, the observer would not have been able to see them leave from the back of the house. Deacon hoped that meant he'd still be there when they arrived.

Only it couldn't be that easy. He'd learned in the past two years that, when you thought you had an advantage, that's when the universe tended to punch you right in the kidney. So he wasn't surprised when their stealthy approach brought them to an empty rock ledge jutting out from the slope.

Fionn's hissed "Feck it!" was heard more through the earbud Deacon had slid in before leaving the house than aloud. He silently agreed with his second's sentiment as he took in their surroundings for any clue that would tell them where their prey had scrambled off to. The rock was clear, no more than a couple of scrapes bearing evidence of its recent occupant, but there had to be something…

The sound of a crack and a low, rough curse echoed down from farther up the slope. "Got him," King commed, his voice heavy with the effort of racing up the hill. Deacon and Fionn ran, their path a parallel line to the other two, not bothering with stealth any more than their prey now was. They could hear the man scrambling through the brush, catch occasional glimpses, but whatever had caused him to break his silence was also slowing him down. The team converged on him before he managed to reach the crest of the hill.

Fionn's GLOCK was out and pointed at the man's head before he could turn to look at them. "Hands out!"

The man froze, all except for his hands, which moved slowly out from his sides. A heavy camouflage coat and pants might've led a civilian to mistake him for a hunter despite the lack of an orange vest, but the rifle in his hand was no hunting weapon. It was a sniper rifle.

The sight made Deacon's blood freeze in his veins. His daughter had been in that window. Elliot had been in that window—and were it not for her, they wouldn't have known a sniper was staring straight at it.

So why hadn't he taken the shot?

"On your knees," Fionn barked. When their target complied, Fionn jerked his chin at Saint. The other man approached their target from behind, then summarily stripped him of his weapon, the equipment strapped to his body, and finally the freedom to move. As the zip tie tightened around his wrists, the target gave a low growl of discomfort.

Good. "Get used to it," Deacon said, stepping around to face the bastard. Fighting the urge to punch him. "Cutting off your circulation is the least you can expect until I get some answers." Maybe not even then.

"Look"—the man didn't turn his head, didn't move except to talk—"I got no quarrel with you. This is just a job, okay? No harm done."

"Fecking bastard." Fionn's gaze burned with the promise of retribution Deacon was sure they all felt. "You had a sniper rifle pointed at a wee one, and you're telling us there's 'no harm done'?"

Deacon saw fear creep into the man's gaze. "No, no!" the man insisted, shaking his head frantically. "That's just for protection. I didn't point it at the girl, I promise. Just the camera. Only the camera, I promise!"

"And why should I believe you?" Deacon asked. From the corner of his eye he saw Saint stalking toward him, a wallet in his hand. He passed Deacon the man's driver's license.

Gary Lawrence.

"Well, Gary?" He transferred his gaze to the man on his knees. If Gary's face was any indication, Deacon's rising anger was coming through loud and clear despite the low, careful tone he used—or maybe because of it. "Tell me, why should I believe you?"

Gary cursed. "'Cause I ain't no baby killer."

"Your boss is," Fionn said, casually fingering the long knife attached to his belt. "If you're helping him, that makes you just as guilty."

"No, I'm not! I don't even know him. The job was just to get some pictures, that's all, not hurt anybody."

At the casual dismissal of a threat to his daughter, Deacon's temper got the better of him. He lunged, one hand already drawn back, a feral growl tearing from his lips to echo through the quiet woods. The crack of his fist against the man's hard cheekbone was even louder.

The punch tipped Gary off balance. Without the use of his hands, he fell heavily onto his side, a trickle of blood escaping where his skin had split open. No one moved to pull him upright.

Deacon rubbed his knuckles, pushing the pain into his bones, savoring every pulse as he stared down at the crumpled figure.

"Deacon."

Turning to King, he stalked over, leaving Fionn to pick up the asshole—or leave him where he was. Fine with him either way.

King knelt in the circle of Gary's equipment. One hand held a digital camera with a telephoto lens attached. The other held a cell phone he'd switched on. "Take a look," he said, passing the cell to Deacon.

The e-mail app was open on the screen to Sent Messages. Only one e-mail was on the list.

"Sent ten minutes ago," King confirmed. "Looks like a Dropbox location."

"Can you empty it before they access?"

"Checking now," Saint assured him, staring down at his own phone, tapping frantically.

Deacon held his breath. Saint was the techie in the group; if anyone could do anything about the images, it was him. But long minutes passed until finally Saint shook his head. "No go. Anything he uploaded has already been downloaded and deleted," he confirmed unnecessarily. Then, "Damn it." More tapping. "Now the account's gone."

From behind them, a gruff laugh sounded. It cut off abruptly when Deacon jerked around to stare down at their captive, now back on his knees.

"You think this is funny?" he asked.

"N-no." A heavy swallow, followed by a wince as the simple movement obviously sent pain rippling through his already swelling jaw. "They're smart, though."

"Who're 'they'?" Fionn asked with a slight kick to the man's shin. Or not so slight, given the grunt that escaped their captive.

"I'm not stupid enough to have the answer to that question," the man said. "You think I want to know? Shit, all I'm looking for is some quick money; nothing else. I don't know who it comes from, and I don't care."

"Well, at least you're smart about one thing," Deacon agreed. He nodded to Fionn. "Make sure he's not hiding anything else, Irish."

Fionn drew his knife like he'd been given permission to play with his favorite toy, grinning sadistically down at the man on the ground. The last ounce of arrogance melted into blubbering pleas for mercy and promises to spill his guts. Deacon left Fionn to it and turned back to King and Saint. Once Irish was finished with the guy, he'd be trailing piss as he ran so far, so fast, he wouldn't even remember the money he'd been paid until it was far too late to retrieve it.

"Whatcha got?"

Saint glanced up from the two phones he now held. "I can't get anywhere else with this without pulling the SIM card. I'll need the equipment I've got back at the house. I might be able to find a trace of the download then. I can start on Douchebag's bank information too. No doubt he's got an off-shore account where the money was wired. Won't take more than a few minutes to find out. It's tracing the deposit that will be difficult."

Deacon grunted his agreement. Mansa wasn't a pirate king for nothing—the man knew how to hide anything to do with money; otherwise he'd no longer have any. "Anything else, King?"

The other man didn't bother glancing up from the bag he rummaged through. "Other than the license info, no. He really is an idiot if he knows anything more and made it so easy to find his identity. But then there's also the fact that he had the sniper rifle, as well as this"—he pulled a handgun from the bag, ejected the cartridge, checked the chamber— "and never used either, so he's not all that experienced with being hunted. My bet is on him telling the truth, such as it is."

The cries of pain behind them, occasionally interrupted by Fionn's threatening voice, continued unabated. "We'll know soon enough."

Neither King nor Saint seemed to have a problem with that, a point in both their favors. And the rest of the team's. Deacon was used to working outside the law when he was in the field with GFS, mostly in third-world countries where the law was more about who could pay a bribe than who was in the right. On home soil, they rarely went to such lengths, but Mansa would have no such scruples.

They had to be as willing as their enemy to push the boundaries if they wanted to stay one step ahead. That Dain's men wouldn't fight him on that was a good sign.

When King had everything packed back up, Deacon sent the two men to find their new friend's vehicle. Maybe a clue would pop up there. In the meantime, he tapped his earbud twice and settled onto a nearby rock. He'd check in with Dain while Fionn finished up.

Chapter Seven

"What if—"

"Dain said no." King kept his gaze on Sydney as she played at a kitchen set toward the middle of the preschool classroom, but his words were enough to shut Elliot down.

Frustration kicked at the restraint she was trying to show. She had to watch more than her cussing in a roomful of three- and four-year-olds. Still, a hint of impatience leeched through. "To me taking the night shift?"

"To any changes you suggest," King told her. The closed expression on his face gave nothing away, not even a hint of curiosity about Dain's order. But they both knew it didn't really matter if he understood or agreed; he'd still follow Dain's command.

"But—"

"Anything. Period."

Damn it, why couldn't Dain understand?

Because he cares about you and isn't about to use you to bait a madman?

She'd had this argument with herself more times than she could count, and the one thing she kept coming back to was this: The longer they waited, the more advantage Mansa had. Her team would either become complacent or, more likely for them, hypervigilant, jumping at every shadow and gradually wearing themselves down. Getting Mansa to make a move before he was ready required one thing, giving him a chance at what he wanted. And since she refused to do anything to put Sydney in harm's way, the only thing Elliot could think of that he might want was inside information.

And the seemingly "weakest" member of the team would make perfect bait. There was just one problem. Bait needed to be alone to be taken. And the only time Elliot could be alone wasn't preschool duty.

Maybe an early morning run around the perimeter? Mansa would have surveillance somewhere. If he saw an opportunity to snatch her and took it, he'd be handing her the chance she needed.

"Stop thinking about it, Elliot."

Shaking the haze from her attention, she glanced at King's set face before returning to Sydney. "Stop what?"

"Whatever it is you're planning." Turning to lean a shoulder against the wall propping them both up, King scowled down from his considerable height. Elliot ignored a twinge of resentment. "Deacon is the client, which makes him the boss. But not only that, Dain is team lead. We've always respected his leadership, you especially, not because he demands it but because he's earned it. I don't know what's buzzed your ass, but whatever it is, forget it. Don't compromise this team for a personal agenda."

"Language," she murmured as a stocky little boy brushed past. It wasn't what she wanted to say, which was *hell yes, this is personal.* It was about keeping the only people in the whole fucking world that she truly cared about safe. She hadn't been able to do it for her mother, but she was older and stronger now. No matter what it took, she would not let Mansa hurt her family again.

Maybe King and Saint would get it if she told them the truth about her past. Dain didn't, though, so spilling her guts on an off chance seemed useless. Not that Dain was giving her a choice. She had four days left—if her boss waited that long. Over the past twenty-four hours, several opportunities had arisen to confess, but every time she kept silent, the vein in Dain's temple would begin to throb. He'd held his tongue, though, his burning gaze reminding her the whole time that she was disappointing him with every half-truth that left her mouth. But even Dain's disappointment couldn't seem to overcome her fear of what would happen when the words left her mouth.

She, Elliot Smith, was scared shitless—of how her team would react, and yes, how Deacon would react. There was something about the man that made her want his approval almost as much as she wanted it from Dain, Saint, and King.

It made no sense. None of this did.

You better start making sense of it somehow, Elliot, or you are a hundred percent fucked.

No shit.

Fortunately Sydney chose that moment to run over to their silent corner of the room.

"Elliot, would you color with me?"

She ignored King's amusement. "I don't think—"

"You think too much." King nudged her away from the wall. "Go color with the girl."

The way Sydney's face lit up at the prospect had Elliot swallowing her refusal. At least this she knew how to do. Her childhood hadn't been perfect, with tea parties and baby dolls and shit like that, but coloring had been a quiet way to occupy a frightened child on the run. And the supplies were cheap and fairly compact.

She bet she could color King's ass under the table.

Making a mental note to challenge him soon, she took Sydney's outstretched hand and wove the two of them through the obstacle course of playing children and discarded toys. At the coloring table Sydney dug through a stack of pages before pulling out an outlined image of a horse eating grass near an apple tree.

"This looks like Benny." She settled the paper in front of her and began her search again. Elliot waited, assuming the girl was finding an image for Elliot as well. "Here."

Elliot choked. The picture was Sleeping Beauty, her fair prince bending over her narrow bed, prepared to offer a kiss. "Isn't there another horse?"

"You don't like this one?" Sydney asked, eyeing the paper. "He looks like Daddy, doesn't he?"

Did he? She hadn't noticed.

Keep telling yourself that.

Elliot picked up a blue crayon and started in on Sleeping Beauty's dress.

"My mom had dark hair like Sleeping Beauty in the movie. Have you seen the movie, Elliot?"

Did she want to admit she hadn't? Settling for a noncommittal hum, she tried to decide if it would be sacrilege to give the renowned fairy-tale princess blonde hair.

Like yours? Do you really want to color yourself into the role of Deacon's lover?

She refused to answer that question. Instead she eyed Sydney's thick, dark hair. "You must look a lot like your mom."

That earned her a smile. "I even have her eyes." The smile slowly faded. "She's been gone a long time."

Something soft mixed with the remembered kick of pain and panic that rose whenever Elliot thought of her mother's death. She'd been thirteen when her mom and stepdad got into their car, turned the key, and ignited a bomb that killed them instantly. Sydney was far younger than thirteen, and though the little girl had her father, that didn't make up for all the moments in the future when Elliot knew the need for a woman would arise. She'd faced each of those moments alone. Would Sydney? Or would Deacon find a new wife to take Julia Walsh's place?

"What's your mom like?" Sydney asked, rubbing a brown crayon absently over the horse's legs.

Elliot drew up the memory of her mother. It had been so long she sometimes wondered if what she remembered was real or just an idealized version of the woman who'd birthed her, protected her for as long as she could. "She was always telling me stories and reading with me." Nora had wanted her to be able to escape their life on the run—the constant vigilance, the unending training. By the time she'd lost her mother, Elliot had been proficient with a knife. She probably wouldn't have arrived at General Ingram's compound otherwise. He'd been a friend of her stepdad's, if men like that had friends, and had agreed to take them in if an emergency arose. Instead he'd been saddled with a thirteen-year-old girl, orphaned, half-starved, desperate.

That trip cross-country had been the first time she'd used her skill with a knife to protect herself. She didn't think she'd share that aspect of her childhood with Sydney.

The four-year-old was focused on something else, though, her eyes wide and round. "Your mom died?"

"She did. I was a little older, but I know what it's like." She didn't know what it was like to share her grief either; by the time she'd talked about it openly, she'd been an adult, the grief a faint echo of the savage pain she'd first experienced. Searching for words, she finally settled on, "It's…hard. We never stop missing our mothers."

Sydney stopped coloring to stare up at Elliot solemnly. "Daddy's home now. He used to go away a lot. But I miss her." The child's green eyes welled with tears.

Elliot couldn't resist the urge to settle a hand gently on Sydney's head. The little girl's hair was soft beneath her fingers, warm. She knew from last night's bedtime routine that it smelled of baby shampoo, lightly floral, a scent she remembered from her own childhood, oddly enough. Another thing they had in common.

"She was sick for a long time," Sydney was saying. "Daddy took her to the doctor so many times, but the medicine didn't work. Not like when I had an earache."

"Cancer isn't like an earache or the flu," Elliot agreed. "We wish it was, but it's not."

"Did your mom get sick?"

"No." How did she explain to a child that a terrible man, one who might be after her now, had planted a bomb in her mother's car in hopes of killing her and Elliot? "She was in an accident."

Sydney finished with the brown crayon and set it back in the pile. Elliot picked it up absently and went to work on Prince Charming's hair.

"Elliot?"

She was beginning to see why Deacon was so far gone over his daughter. Every time those green eyes stared up at her, Elliot felt this melting inside. And yet she couldn't afford to lower her guard, not with Sydney as their primary target. She glanced back at King, arms crossed, gaze missing nothing as he swept the room—even her attempt to connect with him. All he gave her was a wink.

Big help he was.

A tug on her wrist pulled Elliot's focus back to Sydney.

"What?"

Sydney gave Elliot what could only be described as puppy-dog eyes. "Maybe you could read to me the way your mom read to you. Daddy does it sometimes. Or Fionn—he does really good voices. But…"

But Sydney wanted to connect with another female. It was only natural. Elliot couldn't bring herself to feel impatient in the face of those big eyes. She wasn't going to get night shift anyway; Dain had made certain of it.

Early morning run it is.

"I think we could arrange that," she told the little girl.

Sydney's grin prompted a tugging at Elliot's lips that she quickly squashed. "Great!" She looked down at Elliot's picture. "He really does look like Daddy, doesn't he?"

With the brown hair and black shirt Elliot had given him? Yeah, he did. Too much like Deacon for her taste.

"Five minutes, class! Please start cleaning up your station," the teacher called from the front of the room. Elliot helped Sydney scoop crayons back into the bin and stack coloring pages and books. As Sydney joined her classmates at their desks, Elliot folded the coloring page she'd been working on and slid it into her pocket. She'd throw it away later. Deacon might look like Prince Charming, but they didn't live in a fairy tale and she was no sleeping princess. She was more likely to break someone's nose if she woke to find them bending over her.

At least that's what she tried to tell herself as she went to join King at the back of the classroom once more.

Chapter Eight

Security waved Deacon and Fionn through after a quick swipe of their IDs and fingerprint scans. One thing about Global First—they never took security for granted. Deacon led the way through the entry and down the long hall toward the medical wing where Trapper was being treated.

"What did Sheppard say about surveillance?" he asked Fionn as they walked, nodding to staff members along the way.

"We'll be swinging by her office on our way out," Fionn said.

Deacon hid his grin. Fionn showing up in her Bat Cave, as they called it, should make Sheppard's day. How his friend could be oblivious to the girl's interest in him, Deacon didn't understand. Not that she was Fionn's type. Young, on the geeky side, with a keen mind for electronics and all things computer related but shy and nervous around people, especially the infamous ladies' man, Fionn McCullough. Sheppard's tongue tripped over itself whenever Fionn was near, adding to the impression of a socially awkward nerd. Personally Deacon thought she was adorable. Too many women fawned all over his friend, a situation Fionn took full advantage of. Their resident geek didn't wear makeup or sophisticated clothes—more like glasses and her hair up in a messy ponytail. She was just her normal shy self, whether she had a thing for Fionn or not. Take her or leave her, she was who she was. Deacon admired that, even if it didn't earn her the notice of his man-whore friend.

All thoughts of Fionn's tangled love life fled as they approached the swinging double doors leading to the medical suite. GFS kept a mini hospital on the grounds, both for their personnel and for any clients that required medical attention during their contract. Regular hospitals were a security nightmare. Besides, GFS's clients were more than willing to shell out the cost for personal, secure care at a guarded facility. Trapper had been flown here after his initial treatment, and GFS had brought in every specialist they could to help heal the damage done by Mansa's hit man. Unfortunately some things couldn't be fixed; when a man lost the ability to do his job, more than his body ended up broken. When he lost his long-time partner and best friend, like Trapper had Inez, *broken* wasn't really the word for what it did to a man.

Necessity had Deacon behind a desk for now, but eventually he would be able to go back to active duty; Trapper would not.

Coming to a stop outside Trapper's door, Deacon glanced at Fionn, sharing a long look as they braced themselves for what waited on the other side. Soaking up strength. After a deep breath, Deacon rapped his knuckles on the door.

"Come in."

Trapper's voice had always been rough, but the damage his attacker had inflicted on his vocal cords made it even rougher. Today it was downright guttural. When they entered, Deacon saw why. The company physical therapist, Edward Cho, stood over Trapper, placing stim pads along their friend's scarred and mangled upper body. "You gentlemen arrived just in time. We've finished our daily torture session, and our friend here is ready for a relaxing electrical massage."

"Would be better if we had a masseuse," Trapper muttered.

"Certainly easier on the eyes," Fionn agreed with a grin.

One side of Trapper's mouth lifted slightly. "The parts of me that still work would appreciate it."

Progress. Until the last month, their visits had found Trapper close to monosyllabic, uninterested in the world around him, often lost in a haze of pain. Though the pain was still there, a faint shadow in his dark gray eyes, any effort at interaction was a step in the right direction. When Deacon met Cho's gaze and received a small nod, the tightness that had constricted his breathing since he'd entered the building eased the slightest bit.

"I'll see what I can do," Cho was telling his patient as he laid several weighted heating pads over Trapper's skin. As the electrostim began and the warmth seeped into what must be tired muscles, Deacon watched the whiteness around Trapper's mouth ease. From personal experience with PT, he knew what a relief the post-session ritual could be. Cho wasn't sadistic, but he'd never been easy on any of the men. Extending the range of Trapper's damaged muscles was more important than comfort, Deacon knew.

When Cho had his patient settled, he set a timer on his watch. "Since you've got company, I'll be back in ten to free you," he told Trapper with a grin.

"Don't forget me this time."

The words, half teasing and half something dark and fearful, twisted Deacon's gut. Cho's eyes narrowed the slightest bit, but his answer was playful. "I'll try not to." With a wave to Deacon and Fionn, he was out the door, leaving the men alone.

"You look better," Deacon said after the door had clicked closed. He wasn't lying either.

Trapper grunted. "Hard not to when you started out looking as fucked up as I did."

"And now you're only half fecked up." Fionn chuckled as he lowered his big body into the chair beside Trapper's bed. "By the time you're down to a quarter, we'll be considering you back to normal."

"Speak for yourself, pecker face."

Deacon laughed along with them, watching carefully to be certain no more than a grimace of pain flashed over Trapper's face.

Silence settled for a moment, but it wasn't strained. They'd spent more time together silent than they had talking over the years, the state natural for them. If anything it was the weight of their missing team members that pushed them to fill the emptiness in the room. Trapper spoke first.

"You get in touch with JCL?"

"I did." Deacon brought his teammate up to speed. "Sydney is under careful watch. Quinn's employees know what they're doing, Trap. They'll help us keep her safe."

"It helps that they've got a woman on their team," Fionn added slyly. Deacon resisted the urge to roll his eyes.

"A woman? You're letting a woman guard our girl?"

As much as his team's concern for Sydney warmed his heart, Deacon had no illusions. Trapper was tough, old-school; women were smaller, weaker, less capable. A woman wasn't good enough for Sydney in his eyes.

But Fionn was already laughing. "Sure as shit we are. This woman isn't feckin' around either."

Ignoring the glowering look Deacon leveled on him, Fionn embarked on the tale of Elliot's surprise attack at their first meeting. The bastard didn't leave out a single detail.

"She kicked his arse—literally, at the end. I'm telling you, there's nothing like seeing a tiny woman plant her boot in Deac's backside and shove him across the room."

"You didn't see it either," Deacon reminded his friend.

"I'm imagining it, though—Saint described the scene in detail."

Great.

Trapper's skeptical gaze landed on Deacon, who shrugged. What could he say? He certainly wasn't going to tell them why Elliot had gotten the jump on him.

"She surprised you?" Trapper asked.

Well… "Yeah."

Fionn snorted. "More like he was surprised by what the little spitfire's tight jumper sho—"

"Fionn."

At Deacon's growled warning, his friend subsided into a chuckle. Even Trap gave a faint, rusty laugh. "Well, that explains it."

Deacon shifted against the wall, trying to ignore the effect that memory had on his cock. Thank fuck his fatigues weren't snug, though if he didn't get himself under control soon…

"It's not all one-sided, though. That tough little wan isn't striking me as one who gets flustered very often, but around Deac? She can barely talk—unless she's defying him, that is."

Funny that Fionn could see Elliot's interest so clearly but was completely oblivious to Sheppard's attraction to him. If Deacon wasn't such a gentleman, he'd point that out, if only to push the topic away from his own…curiosity…where Elliot was concerned. Instead he clamped his mouth shut and let his closed expression speak for him.

Trapper eyed Deacon speculatively across the room. "Is that so?"

"Course it is." Fionn seemed to take offense at anyone questioning his intuition when it came to the opposite sex. "Not that she's flaunting it. Elliot Smith's a professional through and through, despite her tendency to defy Deac."

"There's only one way to deal with defiance," Trapper said. "Bring it to heel ASAP."

"Amen." Fionn crossed his arms over his chest as he tilted his chair back on two legs. "Be using the best tools you got. Sex is my top choice."

"And the fastest choice," Trap added.

"I'm not going to seduce a team member just so I can keep her under my thumb." Although the idea did have merit. Kill two birds with one stone.

No, he couldn't—

Trapper grunted. "Believe me, Deac,"—he lifted one wrapped arm about six inches off the bed before grimacing and lowering it back to the sheet—"these men have no qualms using women, men, children, anything they can, and they won't hold back or show common decency when they do. You've got to be on your toes, and you've got to have a team you can trust a hundred percent to follow your orders without question. Without hesitation."

Deacon tightened his lips against his agreement. Just because their enemy acted a certain way didn't change his own ethics.

Except, if he was honest, he needed something to counter the willfulness that seemed to rise in Elliot whenever he was around. He'd already acknowledged it; he simply hadn't come up with a plan. Could his conscience accept using sex to get a member of what was essentially his own team, however temporary, to obey?

There was only one way to get Fionn off the subject of sex, and when Cho entered the room, Deacon took it. "We need to have a chat with Sheppard real quick. Why don't we let you get settled and come back in a few?"

Sheppard's office was in the next building over. When they arrived in the Bat Cave, it was to find her staring intently at one of five screens, her eyes tracking code faster than Deacon could read *The Cat in the Hat* to Sydney. "Hey."

Sheppard spun around, jerking the cord for her headset from its plug. Pounding hard rock flooded the office. Sheppard's blush hit about the time her gaze landed on Fionn standing at Deacon's back. "Oh, hi." She cleared her throat.

The words were drowned out by the music. Sheppard wavered, her hands doing this funny little dance as if she couldn't decide whether to usher the two of them into her office or turn down the god-awful noise. Finally she reached for the mouse on her desk. With a couple of clicks, the sledgehammer beat cut off.

"What's the story, Bat Girl?" Fionn asked in the same teasing tone he used with every woman he'd ever encountered. The memory of that tone being used on Elliot had Deacon gritting his teeth.

The pleasure in Sheppard's eyes dimmed. "Not much, Fionn." She turned back to the screen, closed the program she was working on, then faced them again. "I suppose you want to talk about Trapper."

"We do." Trapper was a loose end, and if Mansa decided to clip him, they needed to be ready. Few would have the balls to bring the fight to GFS's compound, but Mansa was definitely one of the few.

The girl nodded toward a screen on her left. "Here's what we have set up."

For the next few minutes they talked security. GFS owned a three-hundred acre complex situated between Atlanta and the northwest corner of the state. They were guarded both by woods and hills shrouding the location, and the best in security and personnel. Sheppard walked them through the details of the extra security they'd implemented, answering questions and showing them reports. Deacon didn't miss that the sidelong glances she threw Fionn's way went completely unnoticed.

When he was satisfied with the setup, he asked about the surveillance on his home. He had his own security system, but everything from door sensors to camera feeds were being monitored by GFS as well. They couldn't have too much backup when it came to Sydney's safety.

"Everything's in place, sir." Sheppard switched monitors and clicked through the items like she had a checklist in her head, which he wouldn't doubt. She might be young, but he'd known her several years, and she never missed anything. The girl's mind was a steel trap.

"Anything further on Mansa's movements here in the US?" he asked.

"Nothing." The tightness in her voice said she didn't like the answer any more than Deacon did. "He's totally off grid. Believe me; if there was anything to find, I would've found it. Mansa knows how to stay hidden."

"Maybe because the man barely left his tropical island for twenty past years," Fionn bitched.

"That we know of, anyway." Straightening up to stretch his cramped back muscles, he sighed. "So we're basically still at square one."

"You're at the most defensible square," Sheppard reminded him, her soft voice determined, no longer hesitant. "He has to come to you; that was the plan, and it's still the best one."

She wasn't telling them anything they didn't already know. "I need you to do some digging on a local named Gary Lawrence."

Sheppard flipped a switch on a speaker near her keyboard, then said, "Tell me what all you need."

As he spoke, the device Sheppard had activated dictated his words onto the nearest computer screen. Fionn whistled. "That's nifty."

"I do like my toys," Sheppard said absently, clicking the mouse. And then her words seemed to register in her mind, because a dark red stain worked its way up her neck to her cheeks. Fionn grinned.

"Uh…o-okay." Another click. "I'll get this to you in a couple of hours, sir."

"Deacon, Sheppard. His name is Deacon." But Fionn was the one insisting; Deacon and Sheppard ignored him. Deacon had given up trying to get the girl to call him by his name a couple of years ago. Come to think of it, he had no idea what her first name was; he'd never heard her referred to as anything but Sheppard.

He gave the desk a light rap and turned to go. "Let me know what you find. And thanks."

"Anytime." She was answering him, but Deacon had no doubt the girl's eyes were on Fionn's broad back as they walked out of her office.

"When are you going to put her out of her misery, Irish?" Deacon asked as they walked toward the elevator at the end of the hall.

"Who?"

"Duh! Sheppard, maybe? She's only been drooling over you since you met three years ago."

Fionn reached for the Down button, a grimace twisting his lips. "I don't do teenagers."

That shocked a laugh out of Deacon. "She's twenty-four, not fourteen." He remembered because he'd walked into her office a few months ago and found the girl reading one of those musical greeting cards. He'd caught the theme music from *Star Wars* before she'd slammed the card closed and hidden it, but he'd managed to wrangle the fact that it was her birthday out of her.

Still, he couldn't deny that no matter how old she was, he'd always thought of her as *girl*. Maybe Fionn had a point.

"I don't think I'm the one to be worrying about a wan right now, do you?" Fionn asked.

The elevator doors slid shut. "What are you talking about?"

"Go on outta that," he said before Deacon could get the words out of his mouth. "Elliot Smith—and don't bother denying it. I'm seeing the way you two eye each other; everyone is. The anticipation is so thick no one could miss it, bro."

"We're on an op, Fionn."

His friend leaned against the wall. "Let me be telling you something, Deac—that woman is a distraction. You want that distraction gone? Fuck her. Then your brain won' be fogged by wondering what the sex would be like. Get it out of the way, and everything will go easier."

"Is that the only way you see sex?" He'd been married to Jules since high school. The whole "sex for sex's sake" hadn't been a part of his experience. Now...

Could he do it? His cock screamed yes every time he thought about the petite fighter, but when his brain wasn't fogged with lust, it sounded a firm no. And then there was Elliot's team—not one of those men would be okay with sex on an op. Dain might just rip his head off.

Fionn had no such qualms, obviously. "That is how I'm seeing it! Everything else is too much fecking drama."

Fionn would know; some of the women who'd chased him after a one-night stand had certainly caused drama. Deacon suspected Elliot was exactly the opposite. The expression on her face when he'd confronted her over the surveillance...

Yes, she'd run, and the part of him that was pure predator wanted the chase. He would never admit it to Fionn, but he was beginning to wonder if the man was right. She wouldn't go down easy, though. And her team…

He needed a plan, and he needed one fast.

Chapter Nine

Deacon was elbow-deep in suds and dishes when Fionn came into the kitchen that night. "Time for you to tuck the wee one in."

He glanced up at the clock, then made a hasty grab for a towel.

"There's no fire; stop making a mess. Sydney's enjoying a story with her new friend. A few minutes won't be mattering."

Now it was Deacon's turn to grunt. He let his friend take his place as he dried his hands. Fionn called his name, stopping him at the door. "Yeah?"

"Say good night to Elliot for me. And don' be doing anything I wouldn't do, right?"

Considering there was very little Fionn wouldn't do, that was unlikely. "Enjoy your cold evening patrol, dickhead."

Fionn shot him a bird as he left the room.

Even knowing Fionn and Dain and probably Saint, who had inside patrol duty tonight, would check the house, Deacon followed his normal routine, starting at the back to check windows and doors. Only the front door would be used during overnight patrols, and the fingerprint pad on the lock assured them there would be no unauthorized entries. He passed the library, nodding to Dain, who was talking on the phone—for a good-night call of his own, if the tone of his voice was anything to go by—and made his way to the front stairs.

The guest-room door was closed, the faint sound of snoring filtering through. King had midnight-to-five shift with Dain, which meant he was the source of the snoring. Around the corner, the soft glow of the bedside lamp in Sydney's room illuminated the space between her open door and Elliot's. Deacon deliberately avoided glancing into the darkness of Elliot's room as he walked down the hall. Even empty, it stirred far too many temptations.

The object of those temptations sat in a chair close to Sydney's bed, *The Cat in the Hat* in her hands. He'd paused in the door to listen to the soft cadence of her voice reading the lilting words when Sydney spotted him. "Hey, Daddy."

Elliot whipped around, the thin book flying from her grip to hit the floor with a thump. He hid a knowing smile. No man wanted to make a complete fool of himself; every time she reacted to him in a way that didn't include punching and kicking, pleasure lit inside him. Of course at the thought of a possible sparring match with the petite firecracker, things he'd like very much to remain quiet while in his daughter's presence started kicking up a fuss as well. He shut that line of thought down quick.

"Hey, sweetie. Good book?"

Elliot had retrieved the inadvertent missile and closed it. She stood before Syd could respond. "I'll leave you two to say good night."

"You'll be right across the hall, right?" Sydney asked.

"Right across the hall, just like last night. I've even got that monitor, the one I showed you, remember? I can see and hear everything. Don't you worry." She moved the chair back against the wall, then sent Sydney a mischievous glance he immediately coveted for his own. "You know, I swear I heard snoring last night."

His daughter's eyes went wide. "You did?"

"I did."

Deacon noticed how the lines around her mouth tightened as she tried to suppress a grin.

Sydney glanced between the two adults. "I don't... Do I snore, Daddy?"

"I don't think so," he said. Her obvious relief made him smile.

"Well, that's good," Elliot said. "It must've been King. He sounds like a chainsaw when he sleeps. I bet the monitor picked up all that noise." She even winked at Sydney before cautiously approaching the doorway he was currently blocking.

He told himself team members slept in the same room all the time. Hell, even he knew King snored—he'd walked past the man's door a few moments ago. But the jealousy rising in his gut wouldn't accept a reasonable explanation. He wanted to question how close she was with King, Saint. He wanted to tell her she didn't have to leave on his account. He wanted her in the room, in his presence for just a moment longer—but he didn't do any of those things. Instead he moved farther into the room, making sure his arm brushed hers as he passed. "Thanks for reading to her, Elliot."

He savored her name on his tongue.

"No problem." She looked like she wanted to elaborate, but she didn't, simply walked out the door without a backward glance. He knew because he watched for it. So did Sydney.

His daughter and he were both infatuated, it seemed.

Approaching the bed, he eyed the mound of pillows and stuffed animals Sydney had buried herself in. Elliot knew they needed to be removed—they'd gone over the rules the first night—but he'd noticed the woman never forced the issue. And obviously Sydney wouldn't do it without being told.

"Did you forget something?" he asked his daughter.

Sydney pouted but began throwing the clutter to the floor on the far side of her bed. Normally Deacon let her get away with that if she picked it up in the morning. Now, aware of the need to keep the area clear just in case something happened, he gathered the discarded toys and pillows and stacked them near the toy box. By the time he finished, Sydney eyelids were drifting open and closed in long sweeps.

Deacon leaned over for a quick good-night kiss. Sydney clutched his hand. "Would you rub my face, Daddy?"

Deacon's heart clenched. It was a ritual they'd begun after Jules died, one Syd hadn't asked for in a while. Obviously the turmoil around the house had affected her more than she let on. He sat close, leaning over to plant a hand on the opposite side of her body. Something about caging her in, about being the strong Daddy who could protect and comfort her, felt more powerful than a gun in his grip. And when he brought his free hand to her cheek and she snuggled her tiny face into his big palm…Jesus.

"Close your eyes."

She did. He ran his fingertips lightly over the lines of her cheeks, her forehead, down her nose, which wrinkled in response. It wasn't more than a minute, though, before her breathing went deep and she fell into sleep. Deacon stayed awhile, tracing her little-girl face and marveling at the beauty created by the mix of his and Julia's features.

When he drew away, Syd stirred, rolling onto her side. "Daddy?"

"Hmm?"

"Tuck Elliot in too."

Out of the mouths of babes.

Sydney drifted back to sleep, unaware of the conflict her words had incited. He turned her bedside lamp off, leaving the room illuminated by a small night-light, and returned to the hall.

Elliot's open door called to him. He found himself walking toward the darkened room, unable to resist any longer.

A bright white line shown around the closed bathroom door, a direct contrast to the ghostly greenish glow illuminating the area near the empty bed. The glow emanated from a small four-by-four screen on the nightstand showing a video feed from the camera in Sydney's room. The screen reminded him of the baby monitor Jules had insisted on until their daughter was one, the kind with a camera that showed the baby's crib. She'd worried constantly that Sydney would stop breathing during the night, that an intruder would get inside the house and enter the nursery—so many fears that never came true. And yet the one thing she should've feared, illness, had taken her away from the daughter she'd loved. Deacon could never remember those last few weeks after he'd taken a leave of absence from work without anger. Jules had worked so hard to be the perfect mother, and she'd neglected her health in the process. Now he and their daughter were both alone.

The bathroom light blinked out. When the door opened, he didn't so much hear it as sense it, the change in the air of the room, in the pace of his heartbeat. He wanted to see her, feel her. How could a woman he'd only met yesterday affect him like this? It was ridiculous—and as real as his need for his next breath.

He should leave. His body was silhouetted in her doorway. She couldn't miss seeing him. Being a creeper wasn't going to impress her any more than his hard-ass attitude at their first meeting.

He didn't move.

Elliot's voice reached through the darkness toward him. "Saint has inside patrol tonight."

"I know."

"What are you doing?"

"Tucking Sydney in. Parents do that."

"I'm not Sydney."

No, but you are a mystery, and I can't seem to stop myself from trying to figure you out.

He still didn't move.

The sound of cloth brushing against skin tightened his cock. Elliot stepped into the gloom midroom, her legs bare, the hem of her jogging shorts cupping her upper thighs, her flat belly and rounded breasts lovingly outlined by a cotton tank top. The curse that rang in his mind almost escaped his mouth.

The confusion in her expression held it back.

"Did you need something, Deacon?"

At least she hadn't called him Mr. Walsh. "No."

Her brows drew tighter together. "Then what do you want?"

He glanced around, searching for an excuse to be here. His gaze landed on the monitor. "Just making sure you have everything you need."

She crossed her arms over her rib cage. Did she realize how that position plumped her breasts up in mouthwatering display? How it made his fingers itch to touch her?

He couldn't, not yet. If he moved too fast, Elliot would kick his ass. And yet, despite the tension spiking the air between them, she didn't look like she wanted to kick his ass—she looked...shy. And aroused, if the nipples he could plainly see outlined by the soft cotton of her top were anything to go by.

His mouth watered at the sight.

"What do you really want?" Elliot asked, suspicion obvious.

He couldn't resist a grin, nor the retort that rose. "I'm getting what I want right now, thanks."

His feet moved him forward before he was fully aware of the urge. Elliot didn't back away, not this woman. Fearless. Defiant. And hungry. Drawing close, he let his gaze trace where he wanted his fingers, down the material next to the swell of her breasts, her naked collarbone. She could just as easily have been going running in this outfit, but here, in her bedroom, in the dark, there was nothing sexier than that slim strip of cloth over her shoulder. "Is this your nighttime uniform?"

She couldn't miss the husky tone of his voice, but though she tensed, it wasn't fear he read in her face. Not even close. Her shrug wasn't as casual as she probably intended. "Whatever works. Fatigues don't make for easy sleeping."

"No, they don't." He'd slept in uniform more times than he could count.

"What are you doing, Deacon?"

The words were rough. His groin tightened even more. "Getting to know you."

Elliot snorted.

Deacon grinned at the sound. It turned to a frown when the sound of footsteps approaching in the hall registered.

Patrol. Saint.

Elliot startled.

Deacon's foot didn't want to move, but he forced it back anyway. "So…you have everything you need, right?"

"Right."

Saint appeared behind him in the doorway, light flashing off the silver crucifix lying against his black tank. A frown formed a vee between his eyebrows. "Everything okay?"

"Perfect," Deacon assured him. "Just checking in." He turned to leave, throwing back over his shoulder. "Good night, Elliot."

Her quiet "good night" kept him up far longer than it should have.

Chapter Ten

Elliot was awake, staring at the dark, blank ceiling, when her alarm gave a single low beep. A push of the button on her watch shut the sound off as she dragged heavy limbs over the side of the bed and rubbed her tired eyes. Fucking conscience. Between its constant demand to spill her guts—in a voice remarkably like her boss's—and the remembered feel of Deacon's silent gaze on her every second they were together, sleep was getting hard to come by.

But she had a job to do.

Shaking off her fatigue, she dragged on running clothes in the predawn darkness of her room. A trip to the bathroom was accomplished without sound, and then she was walking into the hallway, her shoes clutched in her fingers instead of on her feet. No way in hell did she want Deacon finding out about her little morning forays outside. It was bad enough Saint would know about them, but there was no getting past her teammate if she wanted a little freedom. At least that's what he thought she wanted.

He wasn't completely wrong. Elliot carried tension every moment that she was on a job; they all knew that, knew she occasionally needed to blow off steam. But this job? The tension was even higher because Deacon was watching her. She knew surveillance when she saw it, felt it. And she did with Deacon, but there was also something else, something more that she couldn't quite put her finger on. Something that made her...restless. She itched for a break in the pressure, a fight, anything to distract her from the electricity running under her skin anytime he came into the room.

Mansa was the perfect distraction, but the bastard hadn't even hinted at a move. He was taking his fucking time. And Elliot was scrambling for ways to avoid telling Deacon the truth. The urge hadn't left the tip of her tongue all evening, and when he'd come into her room and stood there, staring at her, studying her? She'd wanted to confess then, in the dark where it was safe, but nothing she did made the words come out, and it wasn't because his eyes on her made her tongue-tied. They just wouldn't pass the huge lump in her throat.

Maybe she was a coward like General Ingram had always claimed. Every hesitation, every question had been beaten out of her, literally and figuratively, during the five years she'd spent in his compound. By the time she'd turned eighteen, fighting was all she knew. Traveling the underground fighting circuit, feeding the thirst for blood, for pain, had been a natural choice until the night Dain came to one of her fights. The night he'd convinced her to come work for him.

Dain had taught her about free will. He was still teaching her, so why couldn't she man up?

As she walked into the foyer, the faint night-light down the hall struck a gleam on the crucifix lying on the outside of Saint's T-shirt. The silver chain might be a sexy piece of jewelry for most men, but not for him; he took that shit seriously. The necklace never came off her teammate's neck unless they were fighting, and only then because he didn't want it broken. A gift from his grandmother, he'd told Elliot once. She had no idea what it was like to even know your grandmother, much less carry a piece of their spirit with you, a tie to the religion they'd handed down through generations. She was the only generation of her family left that she knew of.

Well, not the only one. But she was trying to make up for that with these early morning runs.

Saint nodded at her from his position to one side of the staircase, his dark eyes narrowed. "Fionn just started his morning patrol," he said quietly. "I'll let him know you're wandering."

"I need the exercise."

His eyes narrowed farther. Damn it. There was no need to be defensive if her motives were innocent, but she couldn't help the edge accompanying her words. What Fionn knew, Deacon knew. She could do without that.

Any doubts Saint had went unexpressed. A jerk of his chin urged her out the door. "Then go run the ants out of your pants, little Otter."

She flipped him a bird as she opened the front door. His faint chuckle followed her until she closed it behind her.

Little? She'd show Saint Dickhead little the next time they were on the mat.

Her irritation fueled a quick startup as she headed down the long drive. Deacon's home lay on the outskirts of the city metropolis, well off any main thoroughfare, surrounded by twenty-five acres of hills and woods that probably still cost a small fortune despite being a long way from Atlanta proper. The man liked his privacy—if the location didn't prove that, the security fence enclosing the property did. Elliot took the gently winding lane toward the large wrought-iron gate, warming up in the winter cold, then turned to follow the fence around.

Cross-country in the dark gave her enough of a challenge that her mind finally settled into the thudding rhythm of her feet and heartbeat as she circled the perimeter, eyes and ears open for the faintest hint of a threat. Her first circuit passed quietly, no lights or movement that she could detect aside from the occasional flushed bird. As she topped the back hill a second time and broke out of the woods, a dark shape loomed up in front of her. Inside the fence. A split-second assessment assured her the figure wasn't a threat, at least not in the way she'd hoped. Her heart did skip a beat, though—because it was Deacon.

Fuck Fionn anyway.

A silent growl rumbled behind her breastbone, accompanying the crunch of lightly frosted grass and fallen leaves as she approached the one man she definitely didn't want to see at five thirty in the morning. "You're up early," she tossed out, running by.

Deacon matched her pace with ease, the bastard. "So are you."

How could his mere presence make her warmer? It was like having a heater running next to her, which made no sense because he wasn't touching her. Apparently he didn't need to.

He was more dangerous than she'd thought. Either that or she was losing her mind.

"Trouble sleeping?" he asked.

With your room right next to mine? "No."

Liar.

"Hmm."

What did that mean?

Their footsteps punctuated a few long minutes. Elliot couldn't help but notice that, despite his heavy muscles, Deacon wasn't breathing any harder than she was. She resisted the urge to speed up, to push him. The faint glow on the horizon wasn't enough to light their way, and she wouldn't risk either one of them getting a careless injury—despite her perverse need to provoke him. Despite how the silence stretched her nerves to the breaking point.

She didn't have nerves, not like this.

Deacon's voice broke through the thoughts chasing their tails in her head. "Tell me about yourself."

Elliot stumbled—imperceptibly to some, but she knew Deacon would notice. He seemed to notice everything where she was concerned. Why did that make her gut tighten?

"You've read my file."

Deacon's sigh, like she was a particularly contrary child, rubbed her the wrong way. "Reading a file isn't the same as getting to know you, Elliot. And just so there's no doubt, I do intend to know you. As well as possible."

That jerked her to a stop.

"Why?"

The first hints of sunrise cast a faint shadow between his brows as they drew into a V. "Why do I want to know you?"

"Yeah."

Deacon moved ahead, walking this time instead of running. Dread dug in phantom claws—walking meant more time to talk, and she didn't want to talk. She didn't want to get to know him. She didn't want anything with him but a professional relationship.

Liar.

Damn conscience. *Shut the hell up!*

Deacon came to a stop, his hand on her arm forcing her to join him, and she knew with that single touch, his strong, rough fingers sliding along her skin to wrap completely around the smaller expanse of her wrist, that she wasn't going to be able to ignore this. Deacon wouldn't let her, and neither would her body. It came alive whenever he was near; there was no other way to describe it.

And now that she'd admitted it, her heart thumped harder for a whole different reason.

"Here's the deal, Elliot." When she refused to look at him, staring instead at his broad, muscular chest—so yeah, not a bad view—Deacon tipped her chin up until his equally sexy face filled her vision. "We got off on the wrong foot; I know it and you know it. I don't think it would've gone quite that sideways were it not for this...attraction between us. And I don't know about you, but resisting this feels pretty futile to me."

"No." The word was more whisper than speech. Elliot wasn't even certain what she was saying no to.

And Deacon wasn't taking no for an answer, it seemed. His fingers tightened the slightest bit. When he moved to cup her face with the other hand, Elliot jerked back, but his hold wouldn't allow her to go far. She watched with breathless anticipation, her stomach clenching and, lower, wet heat pooling as his rough palm pressed against her jaw. Long fingers reached to just below her ear, where he stroked the sensitive skin to painful life.

Elliot fought the need to tip her head, push herself harder against his touch like a cat.

Deacon's searching gaze took it all in, stripping her bare. "I'm definitely interested in you, Elliot, and I believe you're interested in me. Why fight it?"

"Why give in?"

"Because I'd like to think about something other than getting you beneath me," he said, "and that's only going to be possible one way."

Her breath choked off in her throat. Her eyes feeling like saucers, she finally managed, "So...what? We fuck and get it out of the way?"

She cringed as her own words registered in her ears, but Deacon merely laughed. The rich sound seemed to settle in her nipples, which budded up tight against her sports bra.

"I wouldn't have put it quite that way. Look..." His hands dropped. Relief and disappointment warred inside her. When he began to walk again, she instinctively moved with him. "I'm not the kind of man that jumps from bed to bed, especially not with someone I work with. But I'm no idiot, either." He glanced her way, his firm lips curving in a smile. "I want to get to know you; that's all." He paused again. "For now."

Fuckin' A.

She wanted him. He wanted her. But in less than three days, she would tell him something that might make him very, very angry.

Everything inside her screamed to give in, but was it worth it?

And then the analytical part of her brain spoke up. Maybe blurting out the truth about her father wasn't the best strategy. Maybe this was the in she needed, a way to soften the blow—for both of them. If she could reveal herself gradually, maybe the final bomb would be easier to drop. Cause less devastation.

Maybe.

Except when she opened her mouth, nothing came out. For some reason saying *we should fuck* was a lot easier than saying *I'm interested in you.*

"Deacon, I—" What? She found herself staring hard at the woods beyond the fence, away from him, away from that searching gaze and the awkwardness it sparked inside her. Or maybe that was heat.

Of course it is, idiot. If her tongue would just untangle—

A sudden blaring filled her earpiece, jumpstarting her heartbeat. She whirled toward Deacon. The white cast to his face said he was receiving the same alert. "What is it?"

Deacon tapped his earpiece without answering. "Dain?"

Her boss's voice came through the team line. "Perimeter alert, north corner."

"Visual?" Deacon gripped her forearm tight and dragged her along as he jogged in the direction Dain had indicated.

"Nothing on visual."

"Fionn?"

Deacon's second responded immediately, his heavy breathing indicating he was already on the move. "Coming in hot to your west."

Deacon nodded as if Fionn could see him. "Dain, send Saint."

Elliot wondered for a moment why they needed the extra man. Then Deacon threw over his shoulder, "Did you see any issues with the fence earlier?"

"No." She'd inspected the entire perimeter looking for her target. There'd been no sign of a disturbance until the alarm.

Deacon topped the rise closest to the north corner and stopped in the shadow of a thick pine, taking in the scene as instinctually as she did around his shoulder. No more than a second passed, but she knew he saw the same thing she did: nothing unusual.

"Get back to the house," he barked. Elliot's gaze shot to his, surprised, but the moment their eyes met, she knew exactly what he was thinking: *Sydney*.

"I've got her," she assured him. Surprisingly, the need to put his fears to rest was nearly as strong as her own to have the little girl in her sights, in her arms. Without waiting for a response, she hurried toward the house, wondering the entire journey how this little family had managed to squirm its way into her loner psyche so fast and so thoroughly.

Chapter Eleven

The woman's hair tangled around his rough fingers, but her mouth slid, silky and warm, over his cock as she deep throated him again and again. Tears leaked from her eyes onto his pants legs, wetting the material. Martin "Mansa" Diako hummed in pleasure, equally derived from the blowjob, the tears, and the frantic movements of the tiny figures on the screen in front of him. Those granular images in a hazy black-and-white palette told him the game had begun in earnest—his enemy had been dealt the first blow, and though not lethal, it was nonetheless effective. After all, nothing caused more chaos than the unknown, the unexplainable.

He had his ghost to thank for that.

A strangled moan from his lap pulled his attention downward. The woman was a mess, just as he liked them. He stroked a heated cheek with his free hand. "You are doing well, cherry. More now," he murmured and held her still for an even deeper invasion. A choked gag escaped her throat, sending a fierce tingle down to his balls.

Not yet. He clenched his jaw, forcing the urge of completion away, wanting to draw out the lazy thrusts into her throat awhile longer. He wanted her sobbing from the pain in her jaw before he finally let himself go.

She was not far from that edge when the door to the study opened and Kivuli entered. Most men who walked into Mansa's presence automatically dropped their eyes to the floor, either out of respect or, more often, fear. Walking into a room where another man was receiving a blowjob? Look away.

Not Kivuli. His black, dead gaze landed on the woman kneeling between Mansa's knees, her head bobbing over his lap, and…nothing. No reaction, no emotion. Not even the hint of embarrassment at seeing another man's erect penis. Nothing. Often Mansa wondered if his enforcer was a eunuch, unable to feel the surge of lust Mansa so often enjoyed. A curl of disgust settled in his gut, just above the woman's competent mouth, but he shrugged it away. Whatever Kivuli was, it made him a cold, efficient killer. A shadow, undetectable to the enemy, to Andre's murderers—the perfect weapon.

The tall, lean warrior approached the deep leather armchair where Mansa waited, silent as always, the scent of herbs and incense moving with him. From his belt hung a small pouch, one Mansa knew held the black *muthi* of the ghost, the herbal mixture obtained from a *sangoma* to make him invisible. Witch doctors. Mansa did not believe in such things; he believed in his own power, his own might. His ancestors were dead by his hand, their strength surrendered to his knife long ago. He pulled at the woman's tangled hair with rough fingers, savoring the evidence of the empire he had built. Everything he needed was at his fingertips.

Everything except his heir.

Remembering why he was here, in an unfamiliar house and not in his compound on Dhambi Isle where safety was ensured and everything he could want waited at the snap of his fingertips, tensed his body in a way that had nothing to do with the pleasure surrounding his cock. Andre had been groomed from the second of his birth to inherit Mansa's kingdom—not for many, many years, of course, but Mansa would have controlled that just as he controlled all around him. No son of his would do to him what he'd done to his own father. That memory sent a frisson of pleasure down the length of his cock to the tip, buried in wet heat. His father's blood spilling through his fingers had been equally wet, hot. His sisters, brother. All of them… Magnificent. Only his ma had been spared his determination to take over his father's domain, build something more than the small pirating operation Kam Diako had been satisfied with. The name Mansa had taken for himself now held true—he ruled the largest fleet of pirate ships in the seas surrounding the African coasts; he owned an entire island stronghold in the middle of paradise. He controlled it all.

Andre would not—because of Deacon Walsh and his team. Plans Mansa had put in place twenty years ago had been shattered with a single gunshot. And now they would pay; they would all pay. Mansa would see to it personally. He would ensure his reign and reinforce his power until the new heir was chosen from the crop he'd bred in secret. In the meantime…

"Your mission was a success, *ja?*" He waved a hand toward the screen where the drone's feed still ran. The UAV hovered at a high enough altitude to be unheard by those on the ground, low enough to give them viable surveillance. "Already Walsh and his compatriots scramble like rats on a sinking ship, and with a mere warning shot over the bow. Excellent."

Without a word Kivuli handed over a slender manila folder.

"And what is this?" Mansa asked. Why the urge to force Kivuli to speak always rose, he didn't know. Perhaps it was the alpha in him recognizing the alpha in another. Kivuli followed his own path, which was one reason Mansa had come to trust him. A man like him would never want the burden of an empire. He was too much of a lone wolf.

Still, he waited for a response. Kivuli gave one, but not the one Mansa wanted: a nod, not a word. Mansa grunted and opened the folder. As the intel spilled into his hand, the woman at his crotch paused in her movements. He used the photos he clutched to slap her lightly across the face. "Keep going, cherry."

She squeaked, cringed. The barest edge of her teeth scraped the sensitive column of his erection.

"*Jy fokken moer!*" He slapped her hard on the opposite cheek. The crack of his knuckles against her cheekbone calmed the rise of his anger.

"Watch the teeth, cunt. Remember what you've been taught."

A careful glide of the slave's tongue along the vein lining the underside of his cock allowed his attention to return to his lap and the images waiting there.

Deacon Walsh. A black-and-white photo of the man walking down the front steps of his home had hatred swelling in Mansa's throat. This was the man who had killed his heir. Mansa intended to guarantee that Deacon Walsh lost everything and everyone he loved before he died a slow, painfully inventive death.

Kivuli cleared his throat, more to prepare his voice for infrequent use than to show deference,

Mansa was certain. "The house and grounds match the satellite surveillance we obtained. Security is top-notch, as expected. In addition to the teammate, Fionn McCullough, we've managed to ID the other men our informant captured on film. Walsh has hired a prominent firm in Atlanta to provide backup security at his home." He reached for the photos, hand brushing the top of the slave's head as he flipped to one halfway through the stack. His expression remained blank. "I obtained detailed information on each of them."

Of course. Kivuli expected results; his team would've had answers before he returned to report to Mansa. One more reason to ignore the man's idiosyncrasies—nothing inspired subordinates faster than sheer terror, and Kivuli excelled at sheer terror without even trying.

Resisting the urge to shift under the weight of that dead stare, Mansa glanced back to the folder. "What firm?" he asked, rifling through the images.

"JCL Security, headed by Jack Quinn and Conlan James. They specialize in personal safety situations."

Mansa grunted. Smart man. Not that the extra manpower would keep Walsh or his child safe. The entire private army employed by GFS could not keep Mansa from his objectives in this godforsaken country.

His attention turned to the next surveillance photo. Slurping sounds rose from his lap, the only break in the quiet as he read the accompanying information.

Each photo showed a fit male in his prime, trained in all the latest hand-to-hand techniques, no doubt, given the intel on JCL Security. Most weaponry was concealed, though Mansa knew it existed. These men with their warrior backgrounds would not go into a fight unarmed. They were—

His breath caught as he flipped to an image near the bottom of the stack, every muscle tensing at what it revealed. *Blerrie hell.* This team member was no fit male, but a woman—a small, beautiful, and, as he looked closer, intriguing female. The image was grainy, much like the drone feed, but he could see that she was clothed in the same pseudo-military gear her teammates wore, only her arms and neck bared. The fatigues couldn't hide her feminine build, however. And that short, starkly blonde hair resting in shaggy hanks along her neck...there was something about it, so light as to be almost white in the dark photograph...

He knew that hair, he was certain of it, but the woman wasn't one he'd had the pleasure of meeting. He would remember. He never forgot a face or a grudge; his enemies knew that fact even better than he did.

He never forgot a grudge...even after the payback. And only one woman, a woman with white-blonde hair flowing down her back, had ever made him work for payback. He'd possessed Nora with the same steel hold that he possessed his island and his fleet and his other slaves.

He'd possessed her until she escaped him, and then he'd killed her. But not her daughter.

He drew the photograph closer. Kivuli must've been right out of her sight; the close-up contained more detail than some of the others, as if he was standing next to her, seeing the tension in her body as she pointed to the fence in front of her, the intelligence and challenge in her seemingly fragile face. The chin, the cheekbones, the eyes—all confirmed his suspicions. There was no mistaking that face. He'd watched it for too many years crying beneath him to not be certain.

"Who is this?" he demanded without lifting his eyes.

Kivuli stepped forward. "Elliot Smith. Second in command of the team JCL assigned."

Elliot Smith? Mansa doubted that was the name she'd been born with. What had his rebellious cherry called the babe she'd clung to for the three years before she escaped? He'd only tracked its growth as a commodity; she'd been number fifty-seven, not a name.

"She's not Elliot Smith." He gave his enforcer a smile that made most men soil their pants. "Find out everything there is to know about her. She comes first. Everything, Ghost. Do you understand me?"

Kivuli nodded sharply. Without permission he turned to exit the room.

"Kivuli."

The man stopped, turned, gaze still unreadable.

"What of our other plans?"

"On schedule."

Mansa dismissed him with a jerk of his chin. Long moments passed after the door closed, filled with the faint ticking of the clock and Mansa's breaths as he stared at the close-up of the blonde he held in his fist, memories of years past spilling from the vault of his mind.

His Nora.

His property. And now Elliot Smith was also his property.

The slave stirring between his legs brought him back to reality. Grip tightening on the picture, he pushed his free hand into her tangled hair and shoved down, forcing himself deeper and deeper.

Smith looked so like her mother.

He remembered the first time he'd shoved himself inside the tiny woman, claiming her virgin cunt for himself. His hips surged of their own accord, mimicking the act he pictured so vividly, and just like that the need to release made itself known. He pulled forward on the woman's head as he forced his way in, spilling hard to the chorus of her gagging shrieks and the memory of a long-ago slave's screams filling his ears.

Chapter Twelve

When Deacon entered the library, it was warm, a small fire crackling in the grate to push away the afternoon chill—a haven of peace in the frustration that had filled the day. Dain sat, his big frame sprawled on the couch closest to the fireplace, a phone to his ear.

"No, you're not going by the office. They don't need you that bad. You're going straight home." A pause, then Dain growled low in his throat, obviously not pleased with whatever response he was getting. "Carla can damn well wait!"

Deacon turned to the chair across from Dain, taking his time settling in, hiding the smirk he knew would piss the man off. Some things about marriage you never forgot, and one of those was exactly how well barking orders at your wife worked. He wasn't surprised when the sound of an equally loud yet feminine tone came through the phone. The working of Dain's jaw proved Livie wasn't the lie-down-and-obey type.

"No. You are going home and taking care of our baby—and no conference calls either, you hear me? Rest. That's it."

After a pause, Dain leaned forward, elbows on knees, and rubbed at his forehead. "Livie, wife…" He heaved a heavy sigh. "Please go home. I know everything's behind with so many people out sick, but work will still be there tomorrow. Take my wife and baby home."

Man, he's good.

"I'll have Lori drop by tonight with some of that chicken soup from that hole-in-the-wall you like. Yes, there. Now get some rest. Okay. Love you too." Dain clicked the call off and zeroed in on Deacon's smirk. "What the hell are you grinning at?"

"Your masterful play."

Dain had the grace to look chagrined. "Hey, when your wife is sick, you do whatever it takes to get her well, even if you can't be with her."

Yes, you did. Deacon knew that all too well. "Nothing serious, I hope?"

"The flu, but she's pregnant, and…"

And Dain had almost lost her recently. Deacon remembered that from a conversation with King their first day here. No wonder the man was beating his chest like King Kong. *Me, boss. You, go home.* Deacon certainly remembered that feeling. "How far along is she?"

Chagrin turned to masculine pride. "Five and a half months."

"Know what the baby is yet?"

"No, damn it. Livie says she needs something in her pocket to control me for the next few months."

"She's probably right. Men like us can drive a woman crazy when she's pregnant." Jules had complained loud and long about his overprotective bullshit—not that she called it that. He couldn't help grinning about it now.

"Damn straight," Dain agreed. "Not that it's gonna change. We've been married almost eleven years—you'd think she'd be used to it by now."

They shared a look full of mutual understanding. Deacon and Julia had dated in high school, married straight after, and stayed together till her death. Their marriage had lasted almost a decade and a half. Their eighteen-year-old mindsets had grown, matured, but some things didn't change. The protective nature of an alpha male was definitely one of them.

When Jules had died...fuck, the pain. Knowing he couldn't protect her, could do nothing but hold her as the cancer slowly stripped her away from him. He'd spent days, *weeks* shaking with the need to fight an enemy that couldn't be touched. And then, so fast, she was gone. Her father, a general who'd rarely been home, had arrived drunk and ranted over her casket about Deacon's inability to keep his daughter safe. For a while Deacon had thought the old man might be right.

That only made him more determined to protect Sydney from any and all threats—including this latest one. But to protect her, he had to discuss it, and he and Dain both were in avoidance mode. Probably because they both felt helpless.

"Any developments from the intel?"

Dain turned serious immediately. "No. The trigger of the alarm seems random, no patterns, accompanied by nothing on camera, no indication of what set the system off, nothing on diagnostics. Nothing on radar. Just...nothing."

"How do we know it's not a malfunction?"

"I can't assure you of that. We simply have to wait and see if it happens again. All we do know is that all readings are normal."

That was impossible.

"What about hacking?"

Dain's mouth twisted in a grimace. "My thought as well, but your friend over at GFS assures me the software is intact, no sign of intrusion."

And Sheppard knew her stuff. So no cyberattacks, and seemingly no physical attacks. They were missing something big-time.

"So let's go with the worst-case scenario and say this was an attempt to penetrate, even if we can't explain how he or she did it. Who's behind this?" They both knew it wasn't Mansa—the man wanted Deacon's head on a spit, but he wouldn't dirty his hands with anything but the final kill. Deacon wasn't aware of anyone locally who could do the job this seamlessly.

"Whoever this was didn't just get inside our guard," Dain said, pushing rough fingers through the strip of dark hair over his head. "He bypassed cameras, security, even Fionn's and Elliot's presence along the perimeter. And yet he didn't come inside."

"Taunting us." Psychological warfare—with his daughter as the target. The knowledge that next time might not be a mere taunt wound him up in knots. "Someone connected to Mansa. The question is, how?"

"Could be as simple as an anonymous bank account, but I don't think so." Dain reached to a side table to pick up a file folder. He flipped it open to scan a page. "I shared this with the others just a little bit ago. Mansa's secretive to the extreme about his inner circle. We do know he keeps a team of bodyguards, but they're rotated regularly, probably to avoid any one of them being susceptible to bribes." He handed Deacon the open file. "But since his son's death, there's been some chatter about Mansa acquiring a new right-hand man."

Deacon narrowed his eyes before glancing down at the report.

"He's known only as Kivuli." Dain jerked his chin at the file Deacon held. "The name means 'shadow' or 'ghost.' Not much is known about him, but we managed to track down a little information. People say he's able to get in and out of anywhere without being tracked, without showing up on surveillance. And once he's in…" Dain cleared his throat. "He's meticulous, efficient, and when Mansa requires it, deadly. Mansa's own personal assassin."

Deacon went back to the beginning of the report and started reading in earnest. The details made his gut churn. This man might be coming after his four-year-old daughter? God. "Dain…"

The team lead's voice dropped a notch, going quiet. "The thing to remember, Deacon, is that Mansa is on a personal mission. He wants his hands on you, not Kivuli's. He'll be sending his assassin after us, not you."

"That's not exactly good news." Despite the fact that Sydney was priority, he didn't want to lose any members of Dain's team. The decimation of his own had been almost more than he could handle.

The knowledge that Elliot would be in that line of fire? He had a hard time breathing as the weight of it settled on his chest.

"So we can't see him, can't track him, can't stop him—presumably." He glared at Dain, knowing it wasn't the man's fault but unable to stop. "What do we do?"

Dain remained calm despite the edge in Deacon's voice. "Nothing right now. Until Sheppard can give us more or we find something on our own, we check every alarm that sounds, we stay ready, and we stick to the plan."

"Will security be weakened by constant triggers?" Because if there was one, he had no doubt there would be more.

"No, thankfully. And no doubt Kivuli knows it. The goal of a series of alarms would be to wear down our ability to stay alert, push us off guard. He won't succeed."

Deacon handed the file back with a heavy sigh. "Global First hasn't heard anything about this man or I'd know. So how did you discover him?"

When Dain stood and walked toward the table to put the report down, Deacon knew he wasn't going to like the man's answer.

"Elliot knew."

Not what he'd expected. "How?"

Dain leaned back against the table, arms crossed over his chest, his stare boring into Deacon for so long he wondered if the man was planning on lying. "What she told you in the office is true: she had a case involving him. I don't know too many details, but I do know it was early in her…career. The death of a couple in the Midwest. Car bomb." Dain's words were heavy, revealing how much the case had impacted Elliot—and Dain. Deacon tried to ignore the niggle of jealousy that rose at the thought. "The bombing was tracked back to Mansa, though they were never able to get enough conclusive proof for a formal indictment or request for extradition. But Elliot… That case was hard on her. She hasn't forgotten them, or him." He shrugged, the action stiff. "She's tracked Mansa ever since."

So she wasn't just familiar with Mansa; he was her obsession. That explained so many things. He'd thought her drive was normal, was how she operated, always pushing to the front, always needing to be in charge, not submitting to anyone but Dain. Not on this case, apparently.

Deacon ran a rough hand through his hair. "Why didn't she just tell me this upfront, when I asked?"

"Elliot is…complicated."

Deacon snorted. That was the biggest fucking understatement ever.

Dain grinned, his tense posture finally relaxing as he moved back to the couch. "Look, Deacon…" A heavy sigh left him as he sat. "Elliot has a lot of things she doesn't talk about, but it's not because she's subverting you. It's just…her life hasn't been easy. Anything personal that she shares with you is up to her, not me, but if it has to do with your daughter, with this case? If I feel like she knows something we need to know? I'll *make* her tell you."

Deacon rolled the man's words around in his brain, looking for loopholes, looking for double meanings that could lead him to the truth. More and more, though, he wanted the trail to Elliot's bed more than he wanted the trail to anything else. Her secrets were just a part of that.

The library door opened and Elliot walked through.

"Speak of the devil."

Elliot glanced behind her. "Me?"

Dain stood, grinning. "You." He walked toward the door, pausing next to Elliot. "Everything quiet?"

Elliot's gaze shifted between Dain and Deacon warily. "Yes."

"Good." With a pat on Elliot's back that was hard enough to bump her forward, he continued toward the door. "I'll go check the kitchen for a dinner menu."

The silence after Dain deliberately shut the door behind him felt thick and uncomfortable. Elliot didn't continue into the room, and Deacon didn't know what to say. But then Elliot crossed her arms over her ribs, plumping the soft mounds of her breasts up to the low vee of the paper-thin white T-shirt she wore, and his brain said *fuck it* and pushed him to his feet.

"Where's Sydney?" he asked, stalking toward her. The glide of her tongue along her full bottom lip caused his blood to pool in his groin.

"She's having a short nap; all the excitement, I think. King is outside her bedroom door."

"Good."

Elliot took a step back.

Never give ground to a predator.

She seemed to realize her mistake, jerking herself to a stop despite his advance. "Good?"

"Yes, good. We have loose ends from this morning that need to be tied up."

She waved toward the closed door. "I thought that's what you and Dain were doing."

"Not loose ends with Dain. Loose ends with you."

"Oh."

The crease between her brows said she didn't understand why he'd want to tie up anything with her, which was almost cute, if Elliot could be called cute. But the word didn't really fit. Warrior. Powerful.

Strong. Those fit. The idea of having all that strength under him, around him…

Fuck.

"I never did get an answer this morning," he reminded her.

Her grip on her ribs tightened. As he stopped, so close that breathing might actually bring their skin together, Deacon couldn't help but look. The height difference gave him even more than a glimpse of her creamy skin, and *damn.* Elliot had a knockout pair of breasts. Were her nipples dark or rosy? From her coloring, he was betting on pink—and not just on her nipples.

"Deacon…"

He met her eyes. "What?"

"You can't… This isn't…" She shrugged, frowned. "I guess I thought you weren't really…serious. About—"

"Why would I not be serious?"

She shrugged again. But she didn't back away.

"Elliot." Taking a chance, he tipped her chin up with a finger, both so he could look into her eyes and because he simply had to touch her or die trying. "Why would you think I wasn't serious? You're a beautiful, strong woman. This can't be the first time someone has been interested in you on an op." Not that he wanted to be lumped in with every other man she'd been attracted to, but still…

"No." The word was breathless. His finger and thumb clenched on her chin.

But the uncertainty was still there. It looked foreign on this woman's face.

Something definitely wasn't adding up here.

He stilled, watching her, calculating the input, drawing conclusions. What his brain came up with surprised him: she might've been propositioned before, but she definitely wasn't used to being interested.

His chest puffed up, like he was some stupid buck preening at winning the healthiest doe. Now he just had to gentle her.

"I am definitely serious. I'm also not pressuring you." *Much.* "No is no, okay?" She couldn't very well bow out of staying here if she was uncomfortable, and he wouldn't make her feel she had to. "I'm interested, yes. If it's not mutual, just say so. I'll back off. But I don't want to—and I don't think you want me to either, do you?"

Her lips pursed like she wanted to answer, but nothing came out. But her face softened, her body relaxed. When he stroked his fingers along her jaw to cup her head, her tongue sneaked out again to wet her full bottom lip.

Every drop of spit in his mouth went dry. "Can I kiss you?"

Funny, he was the toughest ass out there when it came to work, but women? Even the toughest ass hated rejection. And he'd never wanted to hear a yes so bad in his life.

"Yes."

A long breath escaped him—relief. He leaned down nice and slow.

Elliot's hand settled on his chest. His heart slammed against it.

"Wait," she whispered.

Her fingers clenched in his T-shirt. When his breath hit her mouth, she parted her lips.

Deacon didn't close his eyes; he wanted to see, wanted to feel. He didn't want to miss a thing, especially not the flutter of Elliot's eyelashes on her cheeks, the flush of pink in her skin, the soft glide of her lips across his as he brushed lightly, back and forth, back and forth, along them. And then he couldn't wait any longer.

His tongue breached her mouth. The taste of mint and something distinctly Elliot, something that made him growl with delight, met him. He couldn't help the way his fingers tightened on her nape, forcing her closer, harder, forcing his tongue deeper.

Elliot moaned around him, her own fingers tightening to draw him against her.

The sound of male laughter drifted in from the hall, registering a vague warning in his roaring ears.

Dain didn't lock that door, damn it.

He didn't want to move, but he forced his head back anyway. There was no resisting the awed look in her eyes when they opened, though.

Another small kiss, two.

Footsteps in the hall, drawing closer.

He took a step back. His hand tensed in her hair before dropping to his side.

Elliot was still breathing heavy when Saint opened the door. "Ready to eat?"

You have no idea. "Sure," Deacon answered for them.

"Good, you can help cook." Saint threw him an unapologetic grin, but his gaze was far more serious as it brushed Elliot's back.

She felt it; he knew by the way her shoulders stiffened, her chin lifting just a notch. And then she was turning toward her teammate. "KP duty it is."

She didn't look back. Deacon closed his fist around the feel of her fragile neck in his palm and followed her out the door.

Chapter Thirteen

The punch connected before Elliot could slip it, the burst of pain in her cheekbone going farther to wake her up than the black coffee she'd had half an hour ago. Good. Restless night or not, she should be awake enough to avoid Dain's strike. She'd trained her team from the beginning not to pull their punches with her—she could take anything they dished out, often allowing a hit if it meant getting inside her opponent's guard—and the swelling on her face would remind her to keep her head in the ring and on her opponent.

Normally a reminder wasn't needed. She fought more fiercely than any of the men. This morning, though…

"Where's your head, Otter?" Saint growled from the sidelines.

Thanks for pointing out my mistake, dickhead.

"Right here." Before the last word was finished, she swept her foot toward Dain's front leg. He shifted around, avoiding her sweep but not the elbow to his ribs—or the back fist to his face, right on his prominent cheekbone.

Dain cursed around the mouthguard protecting his teeth.

"Payback is such a bitch, isn't it?" she asked, shifting on the balls of her feet as she waited for Dain's retaliation. The man knew his stuff too—he didn't bother replying with words. A flurry of punches and kicks flew at her. Dain's size meant he could overpower her if she let him drive her back to the edge of the ring, but she held her ground, blocking his fists and going low to grab a leg as it came up for a kick.

Dain landed on his ass.

"Nice one."

Deacon's voice jerked her attention to the side just in time for Dain to grab her ankle. Next thing she knew, she was in the air. Instinct made her drop to her ass as best she could and curl her back, minimizing the impact and keeping her head from slamming into the mat.

Dain was laughing, splayed out on his back. He knew what had happened—she'd let herself get distracted. By a fucking man. Embarrassment added heat to her cheeks and spark to her fighting instinct. Scissoring her legs, she flipped to her side and grabbed Dain's head between her knees. When she squeezed down, he choked on his laughter.

"Gotta pay attention, right, Boss?"

The rich sound of Deacon's laughter behind her mixed with Saint's and sent an unfamiliar flutter through her belly. She released Dain's head in favor of facing this new opponent on her feet.

Why she thought of her attraction to Deacon as an enemy, she didn't know, but it was.

She turned to exit the makeshift boxing ring Deacon had set up in his home gym. The place was bigger than some official gyms she'd been in, taking up the whole top floor of the three-car garage attached to the back of the house. In addition to the ring, there was an area covered in mats for wrestling or jujitsu, a treadmill and elliptical machine, weights, and a rowing machine Deacon was currently walking toward. She told herself not to stare at the man's ass in his slick jogging shorts, but damn… Staring wasn't optional when a man's backside looked like that. Her fingers curled as if gripping the firm slopes of each cheek, startling her. She'd never thought of herself as particularly sexual or having the same kind of cravings as other women; she was around sexy men every day and night, and she'd never fantasized about fucking them. They were more like brothers, comrades, friends. Deacon was…an aberration, apparently, one she seriously needed to get a handle on.

She grabbed her water bottle from the bench against the wall, trying to look like she wasn't eyeing Deacon's bulging muscles as he rowed. And failing miserably, if the side eye she was getting from both Saint and Dain was any indication.

Fuck. Fuck fuck fuck.

As images of just that rose behind her clenched eyelids, she realized she needed to find a new favorite word, damn it.

She snatched her towel from the bench. "I'm gonna grab a shower."

"Library, one hour," Dain called after her as she stalked toward the stairs. She raised a hand in acknowledgment without looking back. That would be a disaster, because she felt Deacon's hot stare on her back, and seeing it, knowing what she felt was, in fact, happening would only drag out this stupid infatuation even farther.

If infatuation was even the right word. Strong attraction, maybe. Very strong. *And stupid, don't forget stupid.* She'd known the man all of four days, for fuck's sake.

But that kiss…

Don't think about kissing, Ell. Just don't. A cold shower—that's what she should focus on.

The shower helped…some. She spent a good bit of the time pushing away thoughts of Deacon coming through the connecting door while she was naked. Running the towel across her wet skin, she realized how sensitized it was, how her nipples stood out—and not from the cold. Her lower belly felt warm, heavy. Empty. When she pressed her palm against it, the muscles clenched, grasping on nothing and yet making her far too aware of what it would feel like to clench on something.

No, this was not good at all.

A shudder went through her, part unbearable arousal, part revulsion. The only time she'd allowed herself to pursue a man, to give in to desire, it had been a pale shadow of this hunger. She'd been a teen, barely sixteen. Dating had been forbidden in the general's compound, but teens being teens, there'd been plenty of sneaking around. Elliot had done it only once, with a boy a year older than her. Josh. A clumsy fumbling encounter in a closet had divested her of her virginity, though not of her ignorance when it came to the opposite sex. When General Ingram discovered them, he'd locked her in solitary for a week. She'd emerged, embarrassed and still angry, only to find Josh was no longer in the compound.

She'd never heard what happened to him. And she'd never allowed herself to think about another man the way her teenage self had thought about Josh. No illusions, no fantasizing, and definitely no sex.

Her attraction to Deacon didn't seem like it would comply with the rules she'd laid out for herself.

It had to stop. And if her body wouldn't listen to her, she knew just who it would listen to. The only man she'd ever willingly followed orders from.

Dain was alone in the library when she arrived, fifteen minutes ahead of the daily briefing. He glanced up at her entry, his hair still wet from his own shower. Elliot watched the greeting on his lips die as she locked the library door behind herself.

"What's wrong?"

She crossed the room to the table where he sat, holding her breath the whole way. All it did was make her light-headed; no answers appeared in the ten seconds her steps took. "Dain…"

Those dark brown eyes had seemed menacing when she hadn't known him. Added to the thick Mohawk that striped his head, the light brown skin, and the hawkish features, Dain was an intimidating man, but he'd never intimidated her. This was the man who'd found her when she was lost and given her a place to belong. She opened her mouth, not completely sure what would come out.

"I have a problem."

"No, you don't."

"I don't?" Dain knew her better than anyone. If he said she didn't have a problem, maybe she was hiding it better than she'd thought.

"No. You don't have problems, do you, Otter?"

I never have before.

"This is definitely a problem," she argued.

"With Deacon?"

How did he know that? "Fuck."

Dain laughed.

She punched him in the arm, cutting off his laughter but not his amusement. "Don't make fun of me, asshole."

He raised his hands in defense. "I'm not making fun, I promise." He grinned. "I'm just relieved."

"Relieved?" What was there to be relieved about? And why wasn't he helping her? She needed help, not encouragement—that was the road to hell, one she wouldn't allow herself to take.

"Relieved." Dain's stare felt like a microscope searching out her innermost secrets. Or maybe a spotlight. He was revealing things she really didn't want revealed, even to herself.

Seeming oblivious to her turmoil, Dain slid back in his seat—just out of punching range, she noticed—and continued. "I was beginning to wonder if you even had a libido. Figured it was all channeled into extreme aggression." He shrugged. "I'm a bit relieved to realize you're normal."

"I'm..." She sputtered for a moment, not sure how to react, then settled on a growl. Dain rolled back in his chair, clutching his belly as laughter spilled out.

"Only you would take being normal as an insult, little Otter."

The truth slapped her hard. "I— No, it's not an insult." Was it? Maybe she'd taken a bit more pride in being different than she'd realized. Her identity had been tied up in being a kick-ass female for so long. "I didn't— I—"

Dain stood then, moving toward her. She felt the hug coming, felt the instinct to shrink back, but she clamped down on her muscles, refusing the urge. Dain's arms came around her shoulders, and when he tugged her out of her seat, she let her hands settle on his chest. No zing, nothing sexual, just warm comfort. It was at once odd and familiar—confusing—but she let it happen anyway.

Dain held her for no more than a moment before stepping back to pin her with the intensity of his stare. "Yes, you're normal. You always have been. Normal doesn't mean all the same. You may feel even more out of the loop because of your background, but that doesn't negate your normalcy; you're human."

She nodded, at a loss for words.

Dain plowed right on like he hadn't just thrown a bomb in her mental playground. He sat, gesturing her back into her own. "So…Deacon."

"Deacon." Her closed throat strangled the name.

"That's not a problem, Elliot. That's natural."

"Not for me, it isn't."

"Apparently you're wrong."

His grin made her want to punch him again, hug or not. That frustration mixed with the emotions already churning in her chest, forming a compound she was pretty sure would cause a big fucking mess when it exploded in her face. "You're not supposed to make this okay, Dain. You're supposed to tell me I'm wrong, shut that shit down, fix whatever's wrong with me before I make a mistake on the job and put everyone in harm's way because I can't keep my hormones under control!" The words were hard and ragged, but she couldn't hold them back.

And yet Dain was shaking his head like she was a not too bright child. "There's nothing wrong with you other than the fact that you are completely clueless— about this, anyway." He reached over to grip her forearm tight. "If there was any question in my mind that you of all people would ever actually lose control and put your team or your charge in danger, you wouldn't be working with me."

She dropped her gaze to his grip, the only thing keeping her from breaking apart. "So I can, what? Flirt? Make goo-goo eyes at the client when I should be keeping my focus on Sydney?" She couldn't keep her irritation hidden. Dain's amusement made her want to kick him. But that grip—she didn't want him to let go.

"Have you been doing that?" he asked. "Because from where I'm sitting, you've done fine despite the obviously mutual attraction between you."

"'Obviously mutual'?"

Dain quirked an eyebrow at her. "I'm male. I can see his reaction to you, Elliot. Yours took a little longer, but it's definitely there."

Great. Having this conversation was bad enough. She really didn't need to know Dain could tell what she felt. Really. It was a bit like being stripped naked; she preferred her naked privately.

Dain's smirking didn't help. Her cheeks went supernova hot. "Damn man."

"Elliot…" His smile faded, became tinged with worry as he stared at her. That look made her wish she really was normal like he'd said. "Stop being so hard on yourself. And stop worrying. I don't. As long as you're not fucking on duty—which I'd never doubt—you aren't doing anything wrong."

That wasn't going to happen. Nothing was going to happen; she wouldn't allow it to.

So why did that not make her feel any better?

"Stop. Worrying, little Otter." Dain's hand came up. She knew from the trajectory that the bastard was going to pat her head. The block was instinctive, as was the lunge out of her chair. She hated having her head patted, and he knew it, damn him.

Dain laughed when she growled at him. "Go unlock the door." He waited until she was halfway across the room to add, "And Elliot? Don't do anything I wouldn't do."

"That covers pretty much everything," she muttered, reaching for the doorknob.

"Yep, pretty much."

She was still shaking her head when she opened the door.

Chapter Fourteen

Deacon stood in the door of his daughter's bedroom and stared in bemusement at the tea party taking place inside. Sydney sat on the rug, princess crown atop her head, the tea set that had been Julia's as a child laid out before her. Chocolate cookies and cheese crackers graced their small plates. Elliot poured thin brown liquid into the china cups carefully, following Syd's instructions to the letter. He noticed she used the same care with the china as she had earlier today when he'd caught her cleaning her gun in the library—meticulous to a fault, and thorough.

Would she be as thorough in bed? The remembered feel of her lips, her mouth, her tongue against his said it didn't matter. If he got her in bed, he'd be too involved to keep score.

"And now a little milk," Sydney said. Elliot set the teapot to one side, then took up the small creamer dish.

"I don't know if I like hot tea." Elliot's tone was careful, as if she was trying not to offend.

Apparently this wasn't the first time Elliot had mentioned her uncertainty about the tea, because Sydney's sigh was long-suffering. "You have to have tea at a tea party, Elliot."

The strained patience in his daughter's expression made him want to laugh, but he choked the sound down. Elliot had said in Jack's office that she'd never had a tea party. He wasn't about to ruin her first time—or Sydney's, for that matter. She'd never played tea with any woman but her mother, and even then she'd barely been two. Did she truly remember those rare, precious moments with Jules, or was she imagining the stories Deacon had told her since?

The question cramped his heart.

Elliot was stirring spoonfuls of sugar into each cup. Deacon watched both girl and woman pick up their tea, bring it to their mouths, blow gently. A small sip, right at the same moment. Swallows. Sydney's expectant gaze stayed glued to Elliot, whose clear blue eyes turned thoughtful.

"Not too bad," she said.

Sydney grinned. "Told ya."

Elliot stuck her tongue out at her companion. They both laughed before getting down to the nitty-gritty of enjoying their tea party.

He gave them a few more minutes—and gave himself a few to enjoy watching them—before interrupting. Elliot's head jerked up as soon as he entered, a bright pink blush staining her cheeks. "Deacon."

It took him a moment to work through the reaction to her eyes on him, that kick to the solar plexus that hadn't changed since that first moment in Jack's office, and remember why he was here. They were supposed to work with Sydney this afternoon. Deacon played "the game" with her at least once a month, reminding her of safety procedures without seeming to. Given the alarm yesterday, he'd wanted Elliot to see the plan, not just read about it in a file.

"Elliot." He came to a stop, staring down at her. "You have crumbs on your lips."

"Oh!"

Sydney giggled as Elliot grabbed a napkin to wipe her mouth. Elliot gave her a look. "I'm not the only one with crumbs," she said pointedly.

Sydney grinned and popped a cookie in her mouth.

Deacon chuckled. "We have a date," he reminded his daughter.

"Right!" Sydney jumped up, mouth still full of chocolate cookie. "Ha' to cwean up."

Deacon helped them stack china and move everything aside, promising to cart the dishes down to the kitchen in a little bit. First, "Are you ready to show Elliot our game?"

With a squeal that had both he and Elliot shaking a finger in their ear—there was nothing wrong with his daughter's lungs, obviously—Sydney made a wild dash for the bed. Deacon took the opportunity to reach for Elliot where she still knelt on the ground next to the tea set. She hesitated, eyeing his hand as if it were a snake she wasn't sure she could wrangle, and then her smaller fingers wrapped in his and he was pulling her onto her feet.

Her body heat warmed him across the foot of air that separated them, but she didn't meet his eyes.

"Elliot."

Her name was low and gravelly, containing all the command he could infuse into it. Elliot's gaze snapped to his. He let himself enjoy the faint pink blush that reappeared, sweeping across her cheeks, down her neck. Did it reach her breasts? Could he provoke that same reaction the first time he had her in bed, see exactly how far it spread without the barrier of clothes hiding her from him?

"Daddy?"

Shit. He could not keep doing this. He shook away the lust clouding his brain and turned to Sydney. "Ready?"

Her nod was excited, happy. The contrast between her childish innocence and the purpose behind this exercise made him ache. But just as she always did with these little "games," Sydney seemed to see them as fun, picking up Katie Kitty and dancing her along the comforter as she waited for Deacon's signal.

He motioned Elliot over to the corner and leaned against the wall.

"What are we doing?" Elliot whispered.

"Waiting."

"Why?"

Her face drew him, even when concern for his daughter felt like it would tear apart his lungs. Staring down, he saw the same concern reflected in Elliot's beautiful blue eyes. God, the color was stunning, almost a shock each time he saw them, especially in contrast to the white-blonde shade of her hair.

He slid his hand into the hip pocket of his fatigues. "To catch her off guard," he answered and pressed the button on the remote he carried.

A loud beep sounded from the small speaker mounted above their heads, similar to the one that sounded on the team members' comms when there was a breach, but aloud instead of only in their earbuds. Deacon knew the same tone was being repeated in every room in the house. No matter where Sydney was, no matter where he was, he wanted her warned as early as possible.

His daughter knew exactly what to do. Clutching Katie Kitty to her chest, she hopped off the bed and went directly to her closet. Just inside, she grabbed her small purple backpack and pulled it on as she ran for the door. So little, so eager.

Elliot took a step to follow.

"Wait."

She turned her head, probably to argue, but he laid a finger against her lips. "I know. I hate it too, but she knows where to go. Every damn time I have to force myself to stay put, wait it out, not help her—because if I have to sound that alarm, I won't be here to help her. She has to do it on her own."

A vee formed between Elliot's brows, but she clamped her lips shut against any protest. The drag of her skin along his fingers made his breath catch. He allowed himself a single soft tap, a small show of his gratitude, and then he dropped his hand.

"What's in her bag?" Elliot asked.

Was the hushed quality of her voice a reaction to his touch? "Cereal bars, water, juice boxes. A flashlight and a burner phone so she can call for help once she's secure. I replenish the perishables regularly, and each hiding spot is stocked with additional supplies, a couple of toys, and a blanket."

"A four-year-old shouldn't have a go bag."

"No, she shouldn't." Deacon shifted against the wall, remembering the arguments he'd had with himself, the uncertainty of how best to take care of Sydney on his own. In the end the conclusion had been simple: his daughter had to be prepared, and not just for criminals. "Families have similar procedures for severe weather, tornados, earthquakes out west. Fire. It's not comfortable to think about your child being scared and alone, but at least I have some small peace of mind knowing she has a chance."

Elliot nodded, but she wasn't looking at him; she was looking at the door to the hall, her eyes haunted. By what? And what would it take to get her to share it with him?

He glanced at his watch: five minutes. "Let's go."

There were four hiding spots in the house: one in the back of Sydney's closet, one in the kitchen, one under the stairs, and a final one in the gym above the garage. As part of the game, Sydney chose one of the cubbies that was not in the same room as Deacon, and he came to find her. Whichever cubby was locked closed, Sydney was inside. And once he discovered her, they started the game all over again. Deadly hide-and-seek—or practical parenting; it was all in how you chose to look at it.

The hiding spot at the back of the closet in the front room opened readily. Not there. He tried to check the locations in a random pattern, but today, with Elliot along, he went in order. The kitchen was empty except for King, who glanced up from a stack of reports spread out on the table at their entrance. Deacon closed the door silently, a finger against his lips to keep the man from speaking. He led Elliot toward the pantry, which extended approximately four feet on either side of its door before terminating in cabinets that lined the rest of that wall. Most of the space behind the wall contained the actual walk-in pantry, but on the left side a hollow had been built between the pantry and the outer wall. Deacon knelt to run his fingers along the baseboard, found the shallow dip barely noticeable to the naked eye, and pressed.

The cubby didn't open.

He sent Elliot a ragged grin. Using his knuckles, he rapped three times on the drywall, paused, then three more.

A two-foot-wide panel opened in front of him. Inside, Sydney sat on a fleece blanket, grinning up at him. "Surprise!"

Deacon held his arms out. When Sydney slammed into him, he wrapped them tight around her. "Surprise, Little Bit. You did good."

She leaned back to look at Elliot. "See?"

"I see." Elliot's smile strained across her face. Deacon recognized the emotion behind it, but she didn't dwell on it any more than he allowed himself to. "Ready to go again?"

And the game was back on. For half an hour he and Elliot tracked Sydney through the house, laughing and joking while inside they fought the sick juxtaposition their playing represented. Deacon had finally called a halt to get his daughter some lunch when an alarm sounded in his ear.

Damn it!

Elliot didn't hesitate; she scooped Sydney up as they walked through the kitchen door, ignoring the palpable tension to cross the room toward the fridge. "What are we having for lunch, Syd?"

"Ice cream!"

"I don't think so," Deacon called after them, gratitude filling his chest as he watched Elliot secure his daughter, care for her. That left him to confront King and Fionn, now leaning over King's laptop.

"What is it?" he asked quietly.

Fionn straightened, frustration and anger a mask sharpening his playboy looks. With a flick of his wrist, he twisted the laptop around until Deacon could see the screen. "You won't be liking it, Deac."

Chapter Fifteen

Elliot could hear Deacon's raised voice through the thick oak of the closed library door. Not that she blamed him. It had been a long afternoon of frustration and anger, not to mention hiding it all behind a pleasant mask so as not to upset Sydney. None of them wanted to worry the little girl, although Elliot had a sneaking suspicion her charge understood more of what was going on around her than the other adults realized. She certainly sensed Deacon's moods. Kids were like that, or at least Elliot had been. And she'd learned well to hold it all inside so as not to add to the burden her mother and stepdad carried. She'd never really had a chance to be a child, carefree and naive. Knowing Sydney was being forced along a similar path made Elliot itch to find Mansa and stop him as soon as possible—permanently.

Right now, though, it sounded like Deacon was the one who needed her, odd as that seemed. When had they gotten so close that she knew he'd turn to her and not Fionn? Or maybe it was just wishful thinking and aberrant hormones—that had to be it. She sucked in a deep breath, filling her lungs to the bursting point, grasped the doorknob, and walked inside. Her silent exhale was lost beneath the quiet whoosh as she closed the door behind her.

No one paid attention to her entry; like Elliot, the team was focused on their client. Deacon glared down at a large computer screen centered on the library table, the image of a young, geeky-looking woman trembling before him, face a blotchy red swath. Elliot felt a moment's sympathy for her, though from the volcanic anger raging across Deacon's face and the near-to-breaking tension in his body, the woman should be grateful she wasn't in the same room with him and call it even.

Elliot moved to the empty spot next to Dain.

"Sir, I can't find something that isn't there."

"Bullshit!"

Yeah, Deacon's attention wasn't going anywhere anytime soon.

"It has to be there, Sheppard. It's impossible for nothing to be setting off the alarms. Either something physical is causing this, or something electronic. Now which is it?"

"I don't know, damn it!" She waved a hand at the desk littered with more computer screens than Elliot had ever seen in one place, a dozen stacks of reports, and an astonishing number of coffee cups, coming close to knocking over one or two. "Every square inch of the grounds has camera coverage. You have manual surveillance. We have the satellite for only a limited time per day, but we do have it. There aren't any gaps that I can pinpoint from here. It has to be something on your end."

Deacon leaned harder into the fists he'd planted on the edge of the table, getting nose to nose with the screen. "Are you saying my team isn't doing its job?"

Sheppard's eyes went suspiciously bright. "I'm saying your team—and I—are doing the best we can." She blinked behind her glasses. A single tear escaped. A hasty swipe removed the evidence quickly.

"Why do you think he's not coming inside? Because I made damn sure he can't, not without being seen."

Deacon slammed one fist into the oak table. "It's not enough."

Elliot watched over Deacon's shoulder as Sheppard threw a shaking hand up. "It's all I can do, sir. Diagnostics are clear. Camera records show no interference—and believe me, my team has gone over it with a fine-tooth comb. Every feed is perfect. I've searched every line of code in the programs, every hidden niche, every back door. There's nothing wrong with your security."

"Sheppard, goddamn it!"

Elliot had her hand on his shoulder before she even realized she'd approached. "Deacon..."

He spun on his heel, his big body knocking into her, but the moment he saw her stumbling back, the worst of his aggression seemed to fizzle out. He grabbed her midfall and settled her on her feet, dark eyes burning with apology as the entire room seemed to hold its breath. Deacon ignored them all, however; for the longest moment it was as if no one but the two of them existed in the universe.

And then Fionn was easing himself between Deacon and the screen, leaving Elliot off balance and more than a little wary, though not of Deacon's aggression. She managed threats much easier than she did emotions, and that look had been a physical caress, a stroke of pleasure that sent a hard shiver through her.

When everyone's attention returned to the screen, Elliot took the opportunity to slip back beside Dain, giving herself some breathing space.

"Sheppard," Fionn asked, "can we be pinpointing the exact location on the triggers? We know about where they came from, but do the diagnostics give you specifics? Is he targeting points in the blind spots of the cameras? Is that it?"

"Even if he was," Dain pointed out, "we should pick up some hint on visual inspection. The north side is wooded, so minimal exposure. But this last alarm was on the opposite side, nothing but pasture and grass—nowhere to hide, no cover. How did he know patrols wouldn't walk right up on him, out in the open like that?"

"Maybe he didn't," King suggested. "Maybe he's a brazen bastard and took a chance."

Elliot could see Deacon absorbing the rush of information before he blinked hard and pivoted to face the room.

"It has to be some kind of hacking bullshit," Fionn argued.

"That doesn't sound like Kivuli's MO," Dain said, rubbing at the stubble on his chin. "How does the ghost know when he can be a ghost? Some kind of surveillance?"

The question shot through Elliot like a bullet finding its mark. She glanced toward the screen, her gaze meeting Sheppard's, recognizing the flash of awareness in the young woman's red-rimmed eyes. "A drone," they said at the same moment.

Hissed curses filtered through the room.

"Wouldn't the satellite pick it up?" King asked.

Sheppard's frown was their answer. "To be detectable, the drone would have to be flying during the same window as the satellite's orbit brings it over the area. If it's big enough, the machine can hover too high for human ears to hear the engines, which eliminates manual detection. For twenty-three hours a day it could be in the air with us completely blind to it."

"What about antidrone technology? Some kind of jamming?" Elliot asked.

Fionn frowned. "You're talking a feck-ton of money for anything like that. GFS has the technology on the compound, so we're somewhat familiar. The system they use can jam a drone's transmissions from two miles out, even interrupt the connection between machine and operator. But eliminating drone surveillance on private property is no' monetarily feasible."

Which meant they now had to adjust their security in response to a new threat.

"But the minute Kivuli or anyone else associated with Mansa steps directly onto Deacon's land, they'll be caught in the surveillance net, right?" King's elegant brows were crinkled together. "So what are we worried about? Let them wear themselves out trying to keep us on our toes."

"It's not the false alarms we have to focus on, per se," Dain agreed. "The question is, if Mansa is willing to spend six figures on a high-tech drone, how much more will he spend? Enough for serious long-range firepower? Enough to bomb us off the grounds, forcing us into a vulnerable position? Enough to—"

"Dain."

The barked command startled her, but one look at Deacon's white face, the stark fear in his eyes, and she got it. Without thinking she reached a hand out to grip his thick forearm.

Deacon turned blindly toward her, his back to the others. "I can't lose her, Elliot," he whispered, low enough that the rest of the room wouldn't hear.

"You aren't losing her. I won't let anything happen to her, and neither will they."

He nodded at her words, but she couldn't tell if they'd actually registered. Rubbing a hard hand over his head, he pivoted back to the screen and Sheppard. "You have anything else?"

Sheppard's trembling was no longer visible. She blinked at him from behind her glasses. "Not yet, sir. I'll let you know when I do, I promise."

Her final words were drowned out as a harsh beeping sounded in Elliot's earpiece. She closed her eyes against rising frustration, listening to the team scramble to face a threat they couldn't find.

Yet.

"Dain."

Elliot opened her eyes in time to see her boss lift an eyebrow in Deacon's direction.

"You and Sheppard work on real-time data." The security tech was already scrambling from computer to computer on the screen, hopefully tracking the threat better now than after the fact. "I want reports as soon as they become available. Fionn and King, do a visual sweep of the entire perimeter, not just the affected quadrant. Full-alert, weapons hot—don't miss anything, and if there's a threat out there, make sure they miss you. Elliot—"

A pause. Deacon's fists were opening and closing, his jaw clenching. Her heart twisted.

"I want you online," he finally said. "See what chatter you can track down. Anything new from anywhere you can get it." Without another word, he turned for the door. "I'll relieve Saint."

Tough-guy code for *I need to be with my daughter.* Her heart wrenched that much harder at the realization.

She got to work, but her search yielded no fresh intel. The rest of the team likewise came up empty. By the time she began filling a tray of food for Deacon and Sydney, they were all exhausted and frustrated, and she was more than happy to escape. Upstairs, Sydney's bedroom door stood open. The little girl lay sprawled on her rug, a board game set up between her and Deacon, who mimicked his daughter's position.

"Dinnertime."

Sydney jumped to her feet. Elliot quickly lifted the tray to safety before it got knocked from her hands. "I take it you're hungry."

"Yeah!" Sydney tugged Elliot toward the game. "What is it?"

"Nachos."

"With cheese dip?" Sydney asked.

Elliot gave the girl an incredulous look. "You do know we have Saint on the team, right? He's not letting anyone have nachos without the appropriate queso." And homemade salsa. And guacamole. The man was a slave driver when it came to his favorite foods, but at least his whip cracking had given them all a break from the futility of their individual searches. Sometimes you needed to work together as a team to meld once more, even if that was over a pot of cheese dip and chips.

"I hope Saint is also planning to clean up," Deacon said, the faintest hint of teasing in his tone.

He set a plate in front of his daughter's place on the rug before accepting one of his own.

"I think he said it was Sydney's night to do dishes."

"What?" Sydney paused with a chip halfway to her mouth, both eyebrows practically up in her bangs.

Elliot couldn't hold back a chuckle or the automatic way her hand moved to ruffle Sydney's hair. "Don't worry. I paid him five bucks to do it for you."

Sydney's shoulders visibly relaxed. "Oh." The chip went in her mouth.

Deacon shook his head. "Such a literalist."

"What's a litalerist?" Sydney asked, looking at Elliot.

"Your dad can explain."

Deacon speared her with dark eyes. "You're not staying?"

"I already ate," she said. "Think I'll take a shower before this munchkin uses all the hot water for her bath."

Sydney smiled a cheese-and-salsa smile, not the least ashamed of the accusation.

"Not with your mouth full, Syd," Deacon warned.

Elliot slipped out while the two took their next bites.

The shower was a godsend, the super-heated water pummeling her tense muscles, driving out the aches and easing the pain in her head. She took her time, conditioning her hair, shaving her legs. Imagining Deacon walking in.

No, she definitely wasn't imagining that. He was worried about his daughter. Sex was probably the last thing on his mind—and hers.

The heavy feeling below her belly button called her a liar, but whatever.

Saint wasn't doing the dishes, Fionn and King were, but that didn't mean she was duty-less. Before the hot water ran hot, she turned it off, dried, and smoothed lotion on, then dressed in her usual pajamas. When her hair was mostly dry and the bathroom was neater than when she'd come inside, she opened the door to her room and stepped out.

Into darkness.

The ghostly green light of the monitor barely illuminated its own corner, much less the room, the closed door to the hall guaranteeing no further light would assist. After a few moments to adjust to the dark, she noticed the faintest gleam of something pale near the window.

Skin.

"Deacon?"

He turned. The greenish glow caressed a few dips and hills—his shoulder, his bare chest. She'd seen dozens of male bodies in her line of work, but not his, and definitely not when she was alone in a private space with the body in question. Still she couldn't stop looking; she needed to trace every last inch with her gaze. Her fingers.

Her tongue.

She cleared her suddenly constricted throat. "Where's Sydney?"

Deacon faced the window again, staring out into the night. "Asleep."

The word was more growl than speech, rumbling with frustration and tension and an anger she understood all too well. She'd lived futility, waded in it—ultimately drowned in it. She'd choked on the dregs until she wondered why she bothered fighting to take another breath. And in the end she'd decided it was because the only other alternative was to let the fucker who'd killed her mother win, and no way in hell would she do that. So she breathed. And fought her way forward.

And now she had her chance. And so would Deacon, if he could keep his head on straight.

A glance at the screen showed Sydney curled beneath her fluffy pink comforter, Katie Kitty tucked into the crook of her elbow, eyes closed.

"I… Uh, I have the monitor on. You can take a shower if you want," she told him.

"No."

He didn't turn, didn't explain. A hint of uncertainty flickered in her belly. "Okay." A tilt of her head toward her bed, as if he could see it. "I'll just turn in then."

Nothing.

Okay.

She crossed toward him, eyes narrowed on his powerful shoulders silhouetted against the night. At five feet away she began to feel his heat, his tension. At three, she could see the rock-hard state of his muscles. At two, she could hear the heavy tone of his breathing, echoing with anger. He'd never sleep like this. He was a soldier; he knew better—

And sometimes all the head knowledge in the world wouldn't make the emotions go away.

She sighed, watching his skin pebble with goose bumps as her breath caressed it. "You need to relax, Deacon. You know it, I know it—"

"Of course I know, damn it. I've been on more ops than you'll probably see in your lifetime. That doesn't mean I can snap my fingers and feel better about this. My daughter's life is at stake."

I know it is. And he knew she knew, so pointing it out would only make him angrier. Still, "You can't help her if you're dead."

The roar that left his lips shook the floor beneath her feet, the curtains hanging in front of him. Even the little monitor, when she glanced at it, shook with tremors, but the child in the greenish-gray picture didn't stir. Elliot didn't want her to stir. She didn't want Deacon raging either, but when she opened her mouth, nothing came out. And then she found herself lifting her arm, placing her palm on his rigid back—stilling when he went still. Motionless, like he'd stopped breathing. Was he afraid of scaring her off? Because she was doing a damn good job of that without his help, thank you very much.

Deacon swung around without warning, bringing them chest to chest, so close a shallow breath rubbed her nipples along his ribs. Could he feel how hard they were? Did it disgust him or excite him?

For that matter, what did it do to her?

He stepped closer. The friction sent a shaft of tingles from her breasts to someplace low and heavy and hot in her pelvis. Elliot tried to stifle the moan that rose in her throat—because God, how embarrassing—but the tiniest bit escaped anyway.

It didn't stop Deacon; he slanted his chest across hers, chafing her nipples a second time. Confirming their hardness. "Is this what you're offering me, Elliot? Your body for my anger? Sex to calm me down?"

She couldn't answer. She didn't know for certain what words would come out of her mouth. For the second time in a week, her courage was lacking—and not because she was afraid of offering herself.

No, she was terrified he'd refuse her.

Deacon didn't bother waiting for a response. "Because you know what I'm gonna say, right?" One hand came up to cup the full weight of her breast.

Her shoulders went back automatically—a soldier under inspection, and yes, a woman desperate for one more touch. But it was the woman who spoke. "You want…?"

She couldn't read his eyes, but she could feel his stare. It was focused on her barely covered breasts, the hard tips begging for his attention. "I want whatever the hell you'll give me. Every time. All the time." A thumb tapped one sensitive point, pulling a gasp from her. "Could I resist you? I don't know. I don't want to know. I just want you."

Elliot let her eyelids slide closed, protecting her from the intensity of the moment, of his gaze. With a single deep breath, she let go. "Then take me, Deacon. Now." *Before I do something I'll really regret, like come to my senses.*

Chapter Sixteen

Elliot was good at hiding her emotions. There was no fear in her eyes as he advanced, his body and the hand still holding her breast forcing her backward. No uncertainty. The woman's secrets even extended into the bedroom, it seemed.

The knowledge only made him want to push her harder, strip her bare—and not just her body. He wanted everything.

Her spine met the wall. Deacon didn't stop until he was pressed flat against her, until there was nowhere else to go, not another inch to put between them. The sweetly supple mounds of her breasts yielded to the rigid plain of his rib cage. Diamond-hard nipples resisted the pressure, just like his cock did, pressed ruthlessly into the softness of her belly. When his fingers closed on her nape, she moaned, her head tipping back in surrender as his mouth came down on hers.

Nothing had ever tasted this good.

Sweet fire and melting need—that was the only way to describe her. Deacon pushed deep, his tongue sliding along hers, wrestling, circling, stroking. He tugged her tongue into his mouth and suckled it like he wanted to suck her nipples, her clit. Showing her how it would be. Elliot's nails dug into his biceps.

Hold on, baby. Hold on.

Her rounded ass filled his big hands perfectly. He lifted until her core met his hard abdomen, her knees coming up to grip his hips just tight enough that she could drag herself up his swollen erection. When she slid back down, he grunted at the hard surge of semen begging to be released. "Elliot, God."

"I…I need…"

She lifted again, dropped down. Again and again. Opening his eyes, he caught the desperation on her face, a tinge of something like fear. He didn't want fear; he wanted her so lost in him, in them, that all she could feel was hunger.

With a single step back, he allowed enough space between Elliot and the wall that he could tip her against it, splaying her in his arms like a goddess waiting to be devoured. He intended to do just that. "Pull your top down for me, Elliot. Let me see you."

Her hands shook as she reached for the neck of the tank she wore. Slowly, inch by inch, she eased the material over her firm mounds, over hard pink nipples, finally tucking it underneath. The shirt acted almost like a bra, lifting her to his needy mouth. Still holding her stretched out, ass in his hands, shoulders against the wall, he bent and took a tight tip between his lips.

Heaven.

At the first lick of his tongue straight over the top, Elliot bowed herself upward. Her earthy cry climbed a couple of notches when he sucked, lightly at first and then harder, pulling with all the hunger and desperation that had been roiling in his gut since the first moment he saw her. A palm between her shoulder blades held her writhing body steady as he feasted—there was no other way to describe it. He was ravenous, and she was the only thing that could satisfy his hunger.

Something pushing between their bodies finally distracted him, but only long enough for him to realize it was Elliot undoing the zipper of his fatigues. His cockhead pushed up as if begging for her touch, begging her to grip him and give him some relief. Maybe if he hadn't chosen that moment to bite down on the nipple in his mouth, giving her the slightest edge of pain, she might've. As it was, the slide of her rough shorts over him caused a preliminary surge that came very close to ending this all too soon.

He needed control, and the only way to get it was to slow down. He didn't think Elliot had the same goal in mind.

Time to take matters into his own hands.

He grinned against the valley between her breasts before turning his head to deliver light, sucking kisses around the inner curve of each. At the same time he wrestled his big hand down between them, into the loose waistband of Elliot's shorts.

No panties, just heat, wet heat. He couldn't hold back a groan. A frantic suck on her kiss-swollen nipple had Elliot rising into his touch, into the pleasure he showered her in.

His fingers found her lower lips and tucked between them. A slight shift of his hold on her ass and one slid inside.

Barely. She was so tight he wondered for a moment if she was, in fact, a virgin. But surely... Elliot was sexy as hell, a fighter. It had just been a long time for her, maybe as long as it had been for him—she was too tight for anything else to be true. But he had to be sure.

Releasing her breast, he demanded, "Tell me you've done this before." Because God, he didn't know how slow he could go.

Elliot opened drowsy eyes to stare up at him. "I've done this before."

Relief filtered through him even as he shook with the need to line himself up and drive inside until she gloved him from tip to root, but he clamped down ruthlessly on the instinct to take. Elliot needed him to give first. He could do that. No matter what, he would take care of her. She wouldn't break, but he might if he didn't give her the tenderness she deserved.

Her arousal slicked the way as he withdrew, then tunneled back inside. He set up a rhythm, reaching deeper each time, brushing the swollen pad of her G-spot on every pass. Elliot strained to open her legs, open herself to his invasion, and he adjusted his hold so she could do just that. She surrendered her weight completely, allowing it to force her down on his fingers, to grind herself on his hand until she was mindless to everything but the pleasure he was giving her—exactly as he wanted her to be. When his rough palm abraded her sensitive clit at just the right angle, she detonated with a loud cry.

Motherfucker, she was beautiful when she came. And when she melted against him after? He couldn't think of a single word worthy enough to describe the perfection of the moment.

When the clenching of her channel finally eased, he pulled out and gathered her body tight against him to walk across the room to the bed. Only laying her out on the cushioned surface brought a response, a protest.

"Shh. I'm coming, love." He stripped them both, then lay down alongside her, one arm pulling her close.

Her eyes opened. "Deacon?"

"Yeah?" Could his voice get any gruffer? But it didn't seem to bother Elliot. Her hand came up to trace along his stubbled cheek, the tightness in his jaw as he fought for control. When her fingers reached his mouth, he sucked them in, laving them over and over as he watched arousal blossom in her eyes once again.

"Are—" Elliot's lips tightened, then relaxed. "Are you sure?"

"I've never been more fucking sure of anything in my whole life than I am about having you."

A smile replaced the worry in her gaze. "You say the sweetest things."

"Like 'fucking'?"

"Yes."

"Good." Leaning down, he nuzzled her neck right behind her ear. "Fucking, fucking, fucking, fucking." A lick, a deep, deep breath until the only thing in his awareness was the scent of her, the feel of her breasts rubbing his arm as she chuckled. "Fuckin' A, Ell." He settled his body completely over hers, enjoying the feel of her tiny form overwhelmed by his much larger one. "Let me please you again. All the way. Let me have you. Now."

"Yes."

His heart stuttered at that single whispered word. Propped on his forearms, he dragged his chest over hers, the rough hair abrading her nipples until they stood up for him once more. Until her breath was a quick, rhythmic gust against his skin. Until she squirmed restlessly beneath him, trying to get closer, trying to escape, but his arms pinning her shoulders and his legs between hers kept her caged.

"Deacon, please. Kiss me. Touch me."

He did. Her lips were swollen, a soft cushion beneath his, but they moved against him, at once tender and hungry. Her mouth opened, and he breathed into her his own need. The thrusting of his tongue, the wet slide of her around it, echoed like an electric shock throughout his body. A ricochet of pleasure and the pain of waiting chased it.

Settling his pelvis against Elliot's core felt more right than anything in his memory...except the wet slide of her open labia along his erection. The way her knees lifted and tilted outward to make room for him. The heat of her hands as she began to stroke his stomach, his sides, his back. It was all exactly right. And when he shifted back, centered his cock at her vagina, and pushed slowly inside—that was the ultimate perfection.

His groan mingled with Elliot's. The tight clasp of her strangled him, shot pleasure through every cell in his body, even as the fit of him inside made him sweat. Elliot—she lifted to meet his entry, but there was also a grimace of pain twisting her full mouth. Deacon kept going, keep pushing, but lowered his lips to nuzzle at the sensitive skin of her neck. At his kiss, Elliot contracted around him.

"Fuck."

"My thoughts exactly." Elliot's voice was nearly as strangled as his dick.

He tried a little side-to-side shifting. "Open up for me, Elliot. Let me in."

Her back arched, the curve of her neck so beautiful in the faint light from the nearby monitor. "I'm trying."

Deacon retreated, advanced. It took three thrusts to push in to the hilt. When Elliot squeaked at the brush of his cock against her cervix, he held still. Not Elliot—she writhed on him like a worm stuck on a hook.

It had definitely been a long damn time for her.

"Shh. Shh." He nipped her throat, the join of neck and shoulder. Down to one full breast. "It's all right. Take your time." He traced the plump mound with his tongue, his breath. "It's all right."

"Why did you have to be so goddamn big?"

He chuckled. "Thanks for the compliment."

"It wasn't a compliment," she complained. Wiggled some more. "I'm lodging a protest."

"Really?" Planting his knees, he pulled back until only the tip remained inside her. On the return he angled to glide along her G-spot.

Elliot choked.

"Still protesting?"

Her knees canted higher, along his ribs; her pelvis tilted, allowing him deeper. "I don't think so."

He didn't like the touch of doubt in her words, so he tried again. And again. A slow and easy rhythm set to drive her mad before he pushed her to orgasm. From the way she clenched around him and the gush of wet heat on his erection, he figured he must be doing something right.

And then he sucked a turgid nipple into his mouth.

Elliot exploded like he'd lit a bomb in her core. Maybe he had.

"Again, spitfire," he growled. Switching sides, he locked the second nipple to the roof of his mouth and nursed hard.

"Ahhh!"

Elliot bucked, seeming unsure whether she wanted his sucking or his thrusts more. Deacon gave her both, harder and harder and harder until he was pounding against her clit and Elliot was clawing at his back. A tingle started at the base of his spine, shooting down to his balls, and he knew he was out of time. Releasing her breast, he licked his thumb and sought out her most sensitive spot. The hard nub strained from beneath its hood, seeming to eagerly await his touch. He gave it with a rough circling of the pad of his thumb.

"Deacon!"

"Come for me again, Elliot," he demanded. "Come on." A few more circles, a few more thrusts, neither on rhythm as pleasure broke him down, and the tension burst in Elliot's body. Deacon let himself go, a quick flurry of thrusts drawing out Elliot's climax until he joined her in free fall.

When sanity finally returned and he opened his eyes, he realized he'd gone limp over Elliot's body. *Too heavy.* Shoving his hands under her hips, he quickly rolled them over until she was splayed atop him.

Elliot moaned but didn't seem inclined to move, not until he softened enough that his retreat released a gush of fluid between them. Then she startled. "What... Oh God."

He rubbed his palm down her spine. "Hmm?"

"We didn't use a condom."

The words were like a brick upside the head. Shit, of course they hadn't. *He* hadn't. He glanced around frantically as if he could find a way to fix his mistake, but it was far too late and he forced himself to relax.

"God, Elliot, I'm sorry." He rubbed his chin along the top of her head, his thumb against the hollow at the base of her spine, needing to soothe her as much as himself. "My only excuse is that it's not something I've had to worry about for a long time. Years. I— Really—"

Elliot raised a hand to cover his mouth. "You know, sometimes you chatter like a girl."

He bit her fingers lightly. When she jerked them back, he tried again. "I'm sorry."

"It's okay, Deacon. I'm on birth control. No little soldiers running around down there will find a permanent home."

That was one way of seeing it. And though she didn't ask, he knew he was clean—Julia had been his only lover. "It doesn't matter. I should've taken care of you."

"I'm a big girl. I take care of myself."

You shouldn't have to. He didn't say the words aloud, though. Elliot was liable to kick him in parts he had no way of protecting right now.

"So…" How to phrase this delicately? "Do you usually forgo a condom?" He knew from the reports in her file that she saw a doctor regularly, and though the detailed results weren't included, the summaries had indicated no known diseases.

Two fingers sifted through the hair on his chest, circled his nipple, tugged gently.

Did that mean yes?

He'd opened his mouth to ask again when Elliot finally spoke. "The only time I was with someone, no, we didn't use a condom. I was a teenager, and the thought never even occurred to me."

But Elliot was twenty-four now. "Only one?" Did he want to know? He shook his head. "No, don't answer that. It's not my business."

"Only one," she said, ignoring his command. "When the people in charge found out, I was punished. I never saw him again."

Jesus. He remembered from her file that she was an orphan, which meant she'd likely been in the foster care system. He could understand removing someone, but it didn't sound as if Elliot had had a lot of affection in her life.

"Why no one since?"

She shrugged, the action rubbing her breasts against his skin. He fought back a groan. "I learned my lesson a little too well, I guess."

She had, though maybe not the lesson she thought she'd learned. She'd been punished for having sex, but what she'd learned was that giving herself to anyone led to pain. The thought gutted him. When Elliot shifted again, he realized he'd clenched his fingers into her hip. It took conscious effort to relax his hold.

But hold her he did, long into the night, wishing his arms around her could teach her a far different lesson than the one her teenage self had learned.

Chapter Seventeen

Elliot stirred the minute Deacon did. The room was dark, not yet dawn, but she could see the greenish glow of the monitor that still showed Sydney tucked safely in her bed. Normally Elliot's bedroom door remained open during the night; how could she have forgotten to open it last night?

Deacon's rough hand smoothed down her bare stomach, and Elliot closed her eyes tight. That was how she'd forgotten. Damn man. Not that it had been all his fault. Sex was no excuse for either of them. Yes, Saint would be patrolling the house, Fionn outside, but Elliot never left her charge to chance. Never.

Until now.

Deacon's palm pressed into her lower belly, right over the spot that had contracted so hard for him last night. The spot that tightened now in anticipation. His body curled around her, a protective curve she'd never felt before. It probably shouldn't feel as good now as it did, but oh, she wished she didn't have to move from this spot, from his hold, ever again. All hard muscle from head to toe and soft breath across her shoulder and neck. So very good.

But she couldn't afford to give in to the pleasure again.

Drawing her resolve around her, she eased the sheet from her bare body. Another mistake. She never slept naked on an op. Being ready at a moment's notice was a necessity. Not that a naked body would keep her from running into danger—she was more dangerous naked than most people were fully clothed and armed. Still, it wasn't her first choice.

Deacon's arm went steel-hard when she started to slide from the bed. "What's wrong?"

The gruff question sent tingles down her spine, memories washing over her of that rough voice whispering to her last night, telling her what to do, commanding her to come for him again.

"Nothing." She had to clear the husky tone from her voice before saying, "Just need to get to work."

"No, you don't."

Unfortunately Deacon knew their duty schedules as well as Elliot did. No hiding behind work then.

"I need to go."

"You mean you need to run." He pulled her harder against him, against the part of him that was growing harder with every breath she took. "Why do you need to run, Elliot?"

Just scared shitless, that's all. "I'm not running."

Deacon's fingers moved lower, lower, lower. "I think I know why."

She couldn't help it; her legs loosened, refusing to stay clamped tight against his seeking touch. And when two thick fingers slid down either side of her clit to discover her already creamy invitation, all she could do was close her eyes and pray he didn't call her on her lie.

"That's why you're running," he whispered, all husky and male, in her ear. "Because you're afraid."

Her spine went rigid. "I'm not scared of anything."

Deacon laughed, the sound rumbling along her spine. One finger slid deep, teasing her, tempting her. "Then stay here with me for a few more minutes. I can make you feel good, Ell; you know I can."

Feeling good; that's all this was about. And she hadn't lied. She wasn't scared of anything—except this being about more than pleasure. Did she want it to be? Did he? Both were equally terrifying options, and she couldn't risk them. Not now, not when she needed to focus on keeping him and Sydney safe from her father. Not when she knew he'd be walking away when Mansa was dead.

Not when today was her last day to tell him who her father was before Dain did it for her.

Maybe it was her inexperience making her feel this way. There had only been Josh for her. A rough, quick screw in a closet. Nothing like what Deacon had done to her last night. Nothing like what he'd made her feel.

But she had no illusions about his "intentions." There were none. She was convenient, that was all. Other men had come on to her during jobs, but she'd never been tempted to take them up on it, not till Deacon. And oh, what a temptation he'd been.

Still was.

She ignored the ecstatic reaction of her traitorous body and rolled out of the bed without a word.

The toilet had barely had time to flush before Deacon barged into the bathroom. Elliot was reaching to turn on the shower when the door opened.

"Deacon!"

"Elliot!"

His teasing tone didn't match the serious set of his face. When she didn't move, he reached past her and started the water. "You didn't think you'd get away from me that easy, did you?"

She opened her mouth to argue, though she wasn't sure how. A knock at the door cut her response off before it escaped.

"Otter?" *King.* "You got breakfast duty. Get a move on."

Deacon stared down at her, a lazy grin on his face, but at least his mouth stayed shut. That was all she needed, her team knowing what a colossal mistake she'd made. Although that wasn't what she'd been calling it last night after she'd climaxed…

"Be there in a minute," she called, not moving from her position next to the shower. Deacon's grin became a smirk.

She slapped his bare chest.

"You okay?" King yelled through the door. The handle started to turn.

Panic shot to a full boil in her belly. "I'm fine! Just fine." Any other time she could've come up with a million explanations on the fly for the sound, but between the panic and Deacon's silent laughter, she couldn't think of a single thing.

Damn you, she mouthed at him.

Before she could turn, his mouth was on hers, stealing any angry words along with any actual thoughts she might've had in her brain. She dimly registered the silence from the bedroom, the doorknob no longer turning, before Deacon's tongue slid between her lips and curled around hers.

What had she been arguing with him about?

Deacon lifted his head, and she stared up at him, her lips parted as if inviting him back inside. Would he take the invitation?

No. His hands on her waist turned her around to face the shower. "In, spitfire." He crowded behind her, his big body forcing her into the shower stall. And Elliot let him, her brain too empty to argue, even when a firm swat landed on her ass. Normally she'd have made him eat his fist, but now...

God, she was such a girl.

The warm water hit her breasts, her belly, but it was nowhere near as warm as the heat of Deacon's body behind her. That heat had seared her from the inside out last night. She'd never felt anything like it, doubted she ever would again. At least, not with anyone else. From the feel of Deacon's erection nudging her spine, she might very well feel that heat this morning if she didn't do something to avoid it.

Like the otter her team had named her, she closed her eyes to Deacon's crowding body and ducked her head completely under the water.

A moan escaped as the hard spray beat against the top of her head. Or maybe that was from Deacon's grip on her hips.

The water hid her, kept her emotions safe, if not her body. She tilted back until it rained down on her forehead, eyes closed to the force, the reality of Deacon surrounding her, his hands sliding around to cup her breasts. She turned her head away from his as he tucked it onto her shoulder. "Deacon..."

His warm breath hit her neck. "Tell me you don't want it, Ell." Rough fingertips gripped her nipples, hardened from the cool air and his touch. Her back arched instinctively. She let it speak for her—words were impossible when he touched her like this.

Deacon pinched and rolled and tugged, reducing her from a tough warrior to a quivering mass of jelly. Who knew breasts could have so much power over her? Men, yes, but women? She groaned as he rasped his palms across the hard nubs. When his touch disappeared, she cursed his absence.

Until he stepped in front of her, ducked his head beneath the spray, and sucked one tight tip into his hot mouth.

It felt so, so good, but it wasn't the pleasure that gripped her as she looked down at him. No, it was the welling tenderness in her heart that froze her in place, her hands cupping his dark head to her body. Something in her melted at the sight of his firm lips working her breast, his closed eyes with the long, dark lashes lying against his cheeks. Beautiful. Strong. Some might say the two didn't go together, but she knew they did. She might be a woman, but she had more strength than most men; men could have strength and still be beautiful, and Deacon was. She could see his daughter in his face, the traits he'd passed on to Sydney. She could see the subtle vulnerability, the passion that was sweeping over him. She could see emotion, where most people like them hid any trace of feelings. All of it was beautiful.

And mesmerizing. She didn't want to let it go any more than she wanted him to let her go.

When she stepped back, the pull of Deacon's mouth on her nipple sent a tingle of pain and pleasure through her core. She ignored it and urged him to his feet. Deacon growled at the loss, but he didn't protest when she went to her knees.

The heavy cock between Deacon's legs was already hard and throbbing. Elliot focused there, feeling her mouth water at the sight. She closed her mind to emotion and need and focused on the hunger to have him in her mouth. She'd never done this before. She wanted to. She needed to, if for no other reason than to protect herself.

A broad palm rested on her head. "Ell?"

She wished he wouldn't call her that. Without responding she leaned in, mouth open, and capped his cock in wet warmth. Deacon grunted.

The angle was wrong. Taking him in hand, she tugged down, leading him back into her mouth. Deacon bent at the waist, and she heard the slap of his hand against the wall before the adjustment registered and she realized his cock was aimed directly into her mouth. When she tightened her lips and slid down his length, they both groaned.

"God, Ell. That's it. Take me again."

She slid back, then forward. His length was a hard presence between her lips, on her tongue. Even this part of him was strong, steel, and Deacon wielded it like a weapon when he was inside her. He proved he could do the same now as he began a slow rhythm of advance and retreat that would've made her weak in the knees if she wasn't already on them. Careful not to push too far, he pleasured half his length with her mouth. His breathing quickened above her, cool blasts atop her head, telling her he was staring down at what she was doing. He watched, and it only made her want to please him more.

Her hand seemed so small on his thick erection, barely fitting all the way around. She gripped him anyway, using her palm and fingers to massage him down to the hilt while opening her mouth as much as she could, allowing him deeper access. When the soft tip hit the back of her throat, she swallowed against her gag reflex. Deacon cursed, the word harsh and somehow still beautiful. The thrill of knowing she affected him so strongly, that he might lose control because of what she did to him, had her repeating the move on the next thrust. They began a litany of sucking, swallowing, and cursing until Deacon's legs shook and his words became a sob. She cupped his balls lightly in her hand, and he cupped the back of her head, surging deeper than before as he went rigid and began to pulse down her throat.

Elliot choked, surprised. Deacon pulled out with a curse. She watched in fascination as he shot semen into her palm with each squeeze of his climax.

And then she did something she never thought she'd do: she brought her hand to her mouth and licked, tasting him, tasting what she'd done to him. His cum was salty, thick on her tongue, matching the taste at the back of her throat. She licked again, her gaze rising to meet Deacon's dazed eyes, and the roaring heat waiting for her there warmed far more than her skin.

"Jesus, woman."

As he hauled her up from the shower floor and back into the warm water, she wondered if he'd ever reacted like that to Julia blowing him, then immediately dismissed the thought. If he had, if he'd used those same words for the wife he'd loved, she didn't want to know. It didn't matter, anyway. He didn't love Elliot; he loved the sex, and so did she.

That's all this was. Nothing more, even if she might dream about more, deep down inside where no one would ever know.

Deacon used his big body to maneuver her back until her spine met the cool tile. She squeaked in surprise, glaring up when Deacon chuckled.

"You didn't think we were done, did you?"

Weren't they? He'd come, so...

A hand pushed roughly between her legs. Elliot opened to him automatically, a moan escaping when his fingers caught her clit between them and began a soft circling motion, dragging the hood over that sensitive spot in a way that crossed her eyes.

Okay, not done. She tilted her pelvis and thanked whatever god she'd pleased to be blessed with such a skillful lover her second time around.

This time it was Deacon who dropped to his knees. He worked fast, his mouth on her breast sucking hard, his fingers pushing deep inside her body, his palm pressing tightly against her clit. Elliot laid her head back against the tile and clamped down on a scream as he shoved her over the edge fast and hard. Her legs shook as she pulsed around his invasion. And even when it was waning, it wasn't over. Deacon's rough fingertips found her G-spot and rubbed, the feeling so good she dropped her weight onto his hand, pressing down to get more as she climaxed a second time. Only when the contractions eased and her ragged breath became a bit more even did he withdraw, and even then he kissed his way up her breast, her throat, her jaw. He took her mouth and her last sighing moan at the same time.

Elliot let him; she had no other choice. Her mouth opened to him, her tongue met his, and her leg even wrapped around his thigh so she could feel him against that satisfied, empty part of her. The part that wanted nothing more than to do all of this over again.

Not the only part, Elliot.

Because she was an idiot if she thought this was all about sex for her. It wasn't. And that's what made it so fucking dangerous.

Chapter Eighteen

Elliot opened her mouth. Deacon found himself anticipating whatever she had to say, his body tensing to argue, to convince her, cement their relationship—whatever it was—before this skittish woman had a chance to get away.

The sudden blare of an alarm from the bedroom cut the moment off. Elliot's eyes went wide. "Code Red!"

And then they were both running for the other room.

The alarm was emanating from Elliot's comm, a particular blaring pattern that signaled something more than the ghost visits they'd been getting; it signaled someone was hurt. Elliot grabbed for the comm and slipped it into the pocket of a pair of fatigues as she pulled them on. Deacon scooped up his fatigues from the floor beside the bed and dragged them on as he rushed for the hallway. A quick look showed Sydney still in bed, eyes closed—so, not her. Someone else then. He shouldn't be relieved, but God, he was. He so was.

Elliot hit the stairs before he did, her body now clothed in a tank top as well. The familiar calm of battle settled over him as he followed her down to the first floor. He could hear yelling coming from the vicinity of the kitchen. Dain. Saint. What the fuck was going on?

Elliot grabbed the banister about five steps from the bottom and vaulted over the side, landing on a run without pausing, Deacon on her heels. Their footsteps barely whispered on the hardwood floors as they slammed through the swinging door into the kitchen.

Inside was chaos. Dain was yelling, "Hold him still!" while men struggled with someone on the floor. Deacon paused in the doorway to count heads, figure out who was where. The only person he couldn't account for was Fionn. And then the thrashing reddish-blond head on the ground registered.

Shit!

Choking back his fear, he pushed around Elliot and through the crowd to kneel next to his best friend. Fionn lay on the hard tile, blood spreading across his gray T-shirt. He thrashed around, fighting the hard hands holding him down, biting out curse after curse as he struggled.

"Motherfuckers! I'm fine, a'right. Let me go."

"You're not fine. Settle now, soldier," Deacon barked.

Fionn went quiet at the familiar authority in Deacon's voice. It centered Deacon as well, pushing back the fear and anger and despair at the thought of losing another team member and, even more, someone he considered a brother. He wouldn't lose Fionn, not now.

"Saint, get his shirt off."

Saint grabbed a pocketknife from his belt while Deacon bent closer, forcing an eyelid open to examine Fionn's unfocused eyes. Fionn jerked his head, then stilled, his breathing choppy.

"Stab wound," Saint muttered.

Clear, cold rage rose. "How did this happen?"

"He was supposed to be patrolling close to the house," Dain said, handing Deacon a wet cloth.

Deacon cleaned away some of the blood to assess the chest wound. Not critical, thank God. The puncture was high on Fionn's left shoulder, in the hollow beneath the join of collarbone and arm. Not too deep. They'd had ten times worse out in the field without flinching. Fionn would never have passed out or panicked from a wound like this. But his friend's gaze too disoriented for Deacon's liking despite the compliance he showed with Deacon's commands. Compliance in itself was disturbing—Fionn might obey, but not without a smart-ass comment.

"Concussion, I think." Feeling along the back of Fionn's skull, he found a lump and a long, thin cut where the skin had been broken open. No cracks in the bone that he could feel, but he'd let a doctor rule that out. He shifted Fionn slightly onto his side to show Dain. "He was hit on the back of the head."

"We have a doctor on call specifically for JCL. We can get him out here without having to take Fionn to the hospital," Dain assured him. "Unless there's someone at GFS you want us to call."

"Discreet?"

"The most."

"JCL is closer. Do it." He tucked one of the dry clothes Saint handed him under Fionn's head, then used a second as a pad against the still-bleeding stab wound. "How'd you find him?"

"We didn't," Dain told him. "He stumbled into the kitchen a few minutes ago."

"Wound is fresh," Deacon muttered. "Couldn't have happened long ago. Anyone do a check?"

"I did," King said as he walked through the back door to join them. "No sign of an intruder, nothing out of place. Just a patch of bloody grass near the north side of the fence. I did find a trail of white powder at the fence's base, but no sign of any damage."

"Did you get a sample?"

King held up a small plastic bag. Deacon could barely see a white substance inside. "Yes."

"Was there another alarm?"

King jerked his head in a negative.

"Fucking Mansa. How the hell did he get inside without us knowing it?" And then another fear hit him—if Mansa could get inside the fence, could he have also gotten inside the house? He glanced over his shoulder. "Elliot, go get Sydney, bring her down here with us."

Fionn surged up, catching Deacon off guard, knocking him on his ass as a growl of rage erupted. "No!" Between one second and the next, Fionn had Elliot pinned to the wall, every ounce of his considerable weight seeming to rest on the hand around her throat. Even weaving, he was strong enough to keep her there, but Deacon noticed she didn't fight his hold. Her breath might be choked off, but her eyes were cool, calculating. Considering.

Deacon moved cautiously to his feet, something inside him going very still. "Fionn?"

From the corner of his eye Deacon saw Dain and Saint move in on either side. He held up a hand. Both men paused.

"Talk to me, Irish!"

Fionn shook his head as if trying to clear it, but again he responded to the command in Deacon's voice. "She's a traitor."

Deacon swore his heart stuttered to a stop at his friend's rough words. "What?"

More weaving. "She's…" He leaned his forehead against the wall, and Deacon took the opportunity to move a few steps closer. Fionn's eyes were closed, a crease between his brows—pain. "She's…" His eyes snapped open, his gaze boring into Elliot's. "He had a message for you. Called you by name. He said to be telling you, 'Hello, Daughter.'"

Shock hit Deacon like a kick to the gut. "What?"

"'Hello, Daughter.' That's what he said. 'I won't kill this one. He's my gift to you.'"

"Who?" Deacon demanded.

"Mansa."

But it wasn't Fionn who said the name. It was Elliot, her voice straining against the force of Fionn's hold. Deacon's gaze met hers. For a moment time stopped and the eyes he saw were the soft, shy blue ones reflecting back his pleasure as he'd slid inside her over and over last night. The eyes that had teared up when her climax hit. The eyes that had seemed to hold nothing back as she gave herself over to him just a few short minutes ago in the shower.

And then his vision cleared and he saw the blank slate that she had become.

A traitor. The daughter of the enemy, and he'd trusted her with his child. Trusted her enough to fuck her.

He hadn't realized he'd hurtled himself toward her until hard hands bit into his arms and shoulders.

179

"Wait, Deacon." Dain, intensely quiet, in his ear. "Just wait. There's an explanation for this, I promise."

"You knew?" Deacon jerked away from the man. Dain let him go, his gaze dropping to the floor. When it met his again, Deacon could see the mantle of responsibility in it.

"I did."

Saint made a disbelieving sound at Deacon's side. A glance told him Elliot's other team member hadn't known. King, too, seemed bewildered, his gaze shifting from Elliot to Dain to Deacon without settling on one.

So Dain and Elliot had kept secrets from their own team. "You—"

But he didn't know what to say. What to think. What to do.

The kitchen door swinging open decided for him. Sydney pushed through, her wide eyes taking in the arguing adults, the blood on Fionn and his half-torn shirt, the brutal hold he had on Elliot. Fear welled up, and Deacon could see her start to shake. "Daddy?"

Before he could respond, Fionn made a surprised noise in the back of his throat, his eyes rolling back in his head, and slid to the floor. Sydney cried out.

Elliot almost beat him to her; Deacon scooped Sydney into his arms just in time. "Keep your goddamn hands off my daughter." Carrying Sydney's slight weight, he went to kneel beside Fionn.

"Saint, contact that doc, and tell him to step on it." Fionn had likely blacked out from the concussion, but Deacon wouldn't take chances with his friend's life. Nor was he letting go of his daughter anytime soon. "King, when he's done, the two of you move him into the library for me."

"I can help," Dain said. He got no more than a step closer before Deacon's glare froze him in place.

"You are getting nowhere near him. You can take your team member and get the hell out of my house before I lose my shit. Ignorance I can forgive," he said, "but not lying. I asked you if there was anything else I needed to know, and you both assured me there wasn't."

Sydney lay quietly against his chest, her tiny hands clutching his bare shoulders. He laid a hand on her back and realized she was shaking. He should get her out of here, get her away, but his options were limited and he had to think about Fionn. For now the safest place for Sydney was in his arms where he could protect her from everything but the anger frothing inside him.

"I can explain, Deacon."

The resignation in Elliot's voice told him she held out little hope that he'd let her. She was right.

"Get. Out."

Saint came to his side. "Doc's on his way."

Deacon nodded, never taking his eyes off Dain and Elliot. "Let's go."

King and Saint maneuvered Fionn into a fireman's carry over King's shoulder. Dain and Elliot watched, unmoving, as they moved toward the door. Deacon knew both men gave their team members a look from the way they flinched. Dain's lips tightened as Deacon moved past them, Sydney on the hip opposite where they stood.

"You need to let me explain, Deacon."

Elliot. He pushed open the door, refusing to turn around and meet her eyes. "The time for explanations was five days ago in Jack's office, Ms. Smith."

"Even after last night?" she asked quietly, the words barely reaching him. "After what we—"

He rounded on her, and whatever she saw in his eyes shut her up. "Last night was a lie just like everything else about you, I'm sure. I'm done with your lies and with you. Is that clear enough?"

Elliot's blank expression revealed nothing. He wasn't sure if he was glad or not—part of him wanted to hurt her, wound her as much as she'd wounded him. Part of him wanted to choke her with his bare hands for putting his child at risk. And part of him, some deep, hidden, traitorous part, searched avidly for any sign of the emotions they'd shared for so few hours in her bed. He wouldn't give any of those parts freedom.

"Daddy?" Sydney whispered against his neck.

He rubbed a hand across her shoulders, at the same time drilling Elliot with his gaze. "I said, is that clear?"

Elliot's mouth pinched, then relaxed. "Yes, sir."

"Good." He turned and walked through the door, praying for once that Elliot Smith would do as she was told. Because if he saw her again, got his hands on her, he didn't know which part of him would win.

He was pretty certain, though, that either way, both of them would not be left standing when it was over.

Chapter Nineteen

He followed King into the library. No way were they getting all of Fionn's 220-pound frame up the stairs, not without jarring him unnecessarily. "Try and keep him steady. I don't want to aggravate the head wound."

Sydney kept her head tucked beneath his chin, her breath too fast against his bare skin, her tiny nails digging into his arm and shoulder. He hadn't realized how much he'd carried alone until someone—or more than one someone—had stepped into his life and lifted some of that load. Now the safety net of sharing his burdens had been ripped away, and his loyalties were torn: care for Fionn, keep Sydney safe. Deal with the traitor in their midst.

But no, he'd already done that. He'd thrown Elliot out. By the time his two charges were settled and safe, she'd be gone from his life. He'd never see her again.

He refused to think the hollow ache in his stomach was anything but a reaction to her betrayal.

Behind him he could hear Saint on the phone, presumably with the doctor. As Deacon murmured softly to Sydney, King knelt next to the couch, his lean muscles barely straining under his burden's weight, and rolled Fionn onto it, then arranged the man's head and limbs in a more comfortable position. Fionn didn't stir.

The rumble of Saint's voice faded. When Deacon turned, it was to see him exiting the library, phone still to his ear. Dain entered behind him.

"Why are you still here?"

The look Dain gave him was tired. "If you want me gone, call Jack. Until then, I'll be doing my job. You need backup."

"I need backup I can trust," Deacon countered.

"And this afternoon, Jack can have a fresh team out here—if that's still what you want. In the meantime…"

Dain's shrug sent the need to attack vibrating through Deacon's muscles. "This isn't—"

Sydney raised her head at his angry tone. "Daddy?" She glanced around, her gaze coming to rest on Fionn's prone form, and the color in her face paled. "Daddy, what's wrong with Fionn?"

Forcing himself to breathe, to temper his tone for his child's sake, Deacon turned his back on Dain. When he'd settled in the deep armchair near the foot of the couch, Sydney cuddled in his lap, he said, "Fionn got a bump on the head. He's gonna be fine, I promise."

"I'm scared."

Instinctively his body began a gentle rocking, the same rhythm he'd used when she was a baby and he'd held her in the rocking chair that now sat in her room. Soothing her. Soothing them both. "I know, Little Bit. It's scary when someone we love gets hurt, but it's gonna be okay."

"Is Fionn gonna die like Mommy?"

Deacon glanced up, his gaze connecting with Dain's. The man ran a hand over his face, his eyes.

"Listen to me, baby." Deacon wrapped his arms even tighter around his daughter, using the warmth of his big body to cocoon her. "Fionn is not going anywhere. He's hurt, but not like that. People get hurt sometimes, but that doesn't mean they have to die."

Wide green eyes stared up at him, faith and doubt mixing with tears. "I don't want Fionn to die."

"Me neither. He won't; I promise you, Syd."

"Where's Elliot?"

"She…" Shit. He couldn't believe he'd let his daughter get so attached to a traitor.

Dain broke in before Deacon could choke down the emotions closing off his air. "She had to go do some things, Sydney."

Saint reentered, a slightly built Indian man trailing him. From the stethoscope already around his neck, Deacon assumed this was the doctor. He rose to meet them.

"Deacon, this is Dr. Karak."

The man zeroed in on Fionn even as he reached a hand out to Deacon. "Nice to meet you." They'd barely shook before he turned away. "Move, King."

King grinned as the doc shoved him aside. "Nice to see you too, Roger."

The doctor humphed. Despite the razzing, the room went tense while he completed his exam.

"Blunt-force trauma to the head, needs stitches." Dr. Karak probed around the stab wound. "This one's a little more complicated." He turned to his bag and began emptying it onto the coffee table. "May want to clear the room," he murmured with a glance at Sydney.

But Deacon needed to know— "Anything else?"

Dr. Karak paused his unpacking to meet Deacon's gaze squarely. "Nothing else. He'll be fine... Well, except for one massive headache he didn't earn having fun." He gave Sydney a wink when she shifted to lay her cheek against Deacon's chest, looking his way. "He'll be giving you pony rides in no time, I promise."

Deacon felt the push against his breastbone as Sydney's cheeks plumped with a smile.

"Thanks, Doc."

Dr. Karak waved away the gratitude, returning to his equipment without a word. Deacon stood to leave. Dain shadowed him out of the library.

He ignored the man and the anger still seething inside him as he carried Sydney up to her bedroom, retrieved a set of clothes from the closet, and took his daughter into her bathroom. Sydney quietly followed directions, seeming as unsettled as he was after the morning's events. He brushed her hair and pulled it into a neat braid as he stared at her face in the mirror, seeing fatigue in the dark circles under her eyes. Sydney wasn't an early riser; she'd always been a good sleeper, and her night had been cut short a couple of hours. "Want some breakfast?"

She yawned. "No."

"Okay." He dropped a kiss on her head. "Can you play for a bit while I talk to Dain?"

A nod. "When will Elliot be home?"

He opened the door to the bathroom, hoping if he ignored the question, Syd would drop it. She didn't, just stood inside the bathroom, waiting. Even at four, she could be as stubborn as he was.

"I don't know, baby."

Her shoulders drooped, but she went obediently to her bed and grabbed Katie Kitty. Deacon walked over to join Dain at the window.

Beyond the drape of pink material Dain had pulled aside, a storm darkened the early morning sky. Appropriate considering how the day had started. And considering the SUV headed down the drive and into the storm. Red taillights brightened briefly as Elliot followed the curve. Deacon caught a quick flash of her stark white face in the driver's side mirror, and then she was too far away to see.

"She won't have any protection out there, no one to watch her back," Dain said.

"She's Mansa's daughter. Why would she need protection?"

"Mansa doesn't have family; he owns commodities." Dain turned to stare at him, shaking his head. "You should've let her explain."

Though his voice was quiet, Deacon couldn't miss the edge to the words. His own were equally hard. "She deceived me. So did you. Why should I listen to anything either one of you have to say?"

"Because she was going to tell you."

"Really?" Deacon snorted. "She got caught in a lie. Saying she would've told me anyway is irrelevant, if you could even prove it. Which you can't."

"No, I can't." Dain leaned a shoulder against the wall, his gaze going back out the window, back to the bit of driveway they could see. "Did you never wonder why we were late coming that first day?"

He'd wondered.

"I gave her an ultimatum before we left the office: five days. Either she told you or I did."

"If she could tell me after five days, she could've told me on the first, Dain."

"No, she couldn't have, but you won't believe that right now. The truth is, I believed it, and I made a tactical decision. We needed her more than we didn't, so I gave her a deadline. I told you I'd force her to reveal anything relevant, and that's exactly what I was doing."

"That wasn't your decision to make! My daughter's life is at stake. I keep her safe, and I invited you here to do the same. You knew she was dangerous, and you brought her here anyway."

"I brought her here because she is the absolute best chance you will ever have of finding that bastard and killing him," Dain argued, a red flush beginning under his dark skin.

"She's his daughter, damn it. You brought her into my house."

"Elliot has no loyalty to Mansa."

"Right. And exactly how do you know that?"

"Because Mansa enslaved her mother, raped her for years, and then blew her to goddamn bits!"

The words were low, too quiet for Sydney to hear, but venom dripped from each one.

"That personnel file you read?" Dain smirked, the expression holding zero amusement. "It's fake, all of it. No one knows that but me. No one would know because I'm good at what I do, and I made sure her background was airtight. Want to know why?"

No, he didn't, but he arched a brow anyway.

"Because if Mansa ever found out she was still alive, then there was every chance he would take steps to reacquire her. The only way we've kept her secret is by limiting the knowledge to two people: her and me.

No leaks, no risks. Coming here, revealing who she was could blow all of that to hell in an instant. But she still came. She knows what Mansa can do, what it's like to be his slave. She was born on Dhambi Isle, a product of rape. That tattoo between her shoulders?"

"Her what?" But he knew. The number fifty-seven flashed in his mind's eye, the feel of the inked skin beneath his fingers this morning. He'd wondered, but he hadn't asked. His mind had been on other things.

His stomach knotted.

Dain nodded, confirming Deacon's sick intuition. "That's her product number. Mansa breeds children—boys and girls—for sale, and when he kidnapped her mother from a Peace Corps convoy, he knew he'd gotten something special. Small, delicate. Blue eyes and white-blonde hair." Dain's voice choked off. He swallowed hard. "He knew her children would be worth a fortune, and he did everything he could to make sure she bred quickly. Elliot was born eleven months later."

And somehow her mother had escaped. Something clicked in Deacon's brain. "The 'case' from early in Elliot's career."

"Very early. She was thirteen when Mansa caught up with them."

"What happened to her then?"

Refusal tightened Dain's expression. "Anything else is for her to tell."

"That doesn't seem to be her strong suit."

"Not her strong suit?" A choked laugh escaped him. "You have no idea what you've done to her, do you?"

"What *I* did?"

"That's right." Dain pushed away from the wall. "You. You slept with her, but you didn't trust her."

Deacon felt his eyes go wide.

"What, you think I couldn't tell?" He dared to lean forward, a finger jabbing close to Deacon's chest. "I know her better than you ever will, lover or not."

Red sheeted Deacon's vision. He moved closer until that finger hit his sternum. "I'll just bet you do, *Daddy*."

The anger building in Dain's eyes satisfied something dark in Deacon's soul.

"That's beneath you. Elliot sure as hell doesn't deserve it, but I'll spare your teeth since I think that's how she would want it."

Probably. If he knew Elliot—and that was a big *if*—she'd rather punch them in herself.

"I know what her childhood was like," Dain was saying. "I know everything she hides—because she trusts me. Because I've earned it. I know exactly why she is the way she is, why she couldn't bring herself to claim that bastard aloud and see the look on everyone's faces when they found out. On your face."

"If you know so much, then maybe you should explain it to me, because right now all I know is I'd like to do a little punching of my own."

"You don't get that piece of Elliot from anyone but her. I'll tell you one thing, though. You want Mansa to come to you?" He jabbed at the window now. "Your biggest piece of bait just drove out that gate. You want the bastard? You better get her back."

"We can outwait Mansa."

"You can? Think Fionn agrees with you?"

Fionn. His best friend, lying on a couch downstairs getting holes in his body sewn closed. Mansa's message rang in his ears: *I won't kill this one. He's my gift to you.*

Fionn hadn't ended up like Trapper because of Elliot.

Dain smirked. "You might want to think that one over. And if you decide I'm right, meet me downstairs at"—a glance at the thick black watch on his wrist—"1900 hours."

"Why?"

Dain turned to leave. "Because I'm the only one who knows where she's going."

"No way. I'm not leaving my daughter here with just your team."

The team lead stopped at the bedroom door. "Like I said, Jack will send a backup team. I wouldn't risk that child any more than I'd risk my own. And Deacon…"

He crossed his arms over his chest, squaring off with Dain across the room.

"When I say think it over, I mean it. You'll only have one chance to rebuild that bridge. Don't blow it."

Chapter Twenty

Elliot Smith left Walsh's property just as Mansa had intended. Kivuli ordered his driver to follow her, first to JCL, then to her apartment, but she did not stay at either place, nor did she give them opportunity to approach without warning her. Instead she drove to a shopping center just west of her home. Kivuli watched as she exited the small black sports car she'd retrieved from the company garage and sauntered down the row of vehicles toward what appeared to be a combination bar and restaurant.

"What now?"

He glanced first to the driver, then to the two men in the rear seat, all three staring expectantly at him. They were of average intelligence, the requisite "muscle," but not hunters. If they had been, they would know their prey had detected their presence.

He pointed to the man in the seat behind the driver. "Scout."

The man flashed him a cold look, reluctantly opening his door. Before he could slam it shut, Kivuli warned, "Do not go near the woman, *ja*?"

The chill spread from his eyes to his mouth. "You're the boss."

Indeed he was, but he ignored the man's insolence for now. If they considered Kivuli exacting, they did not know his employer well.

He returned his attention to Elliot Smith. The location she had chosen—a sports bar, his driver informed him—contained a traditional restaurant portion to one side, adjoining an area that resembled a garage, complete with garage door. The door was currently lifted to create an open-air patio. His prey entered the open area, weaved through multiple high tables to disappear at the back, then reappeared a few minutes later with two beers in hand. She settled at a table near the sidewalk.

Meeting someone?

No. Smith drank both beers, sitting in the sunshine, in plain sight of their SUV, surrounded by an ever-changing crowd that nonetheless did not ebb nor give them an opportunity to move closer.

Ja, Smith knew she was being stalked. She was taunting him.

The hunter in him rose to meet her challenge, peering from his eyes, scenting the air—the spirit of his ancestors saturating his bones. This was worthy prey, the spirits assured him; that was why she did not run. She had no need to. She was unafraid.

Not like Mansa's other victims. The difference stirred a faint unease in his mind.

Their scout returned.

"Report," Kivuli ordered.

The scout dared to roll his eyes at Kivuli's command. "It's—"

Aikona! Before the man could blink, the hand with which he gripped the driver's seat was pinned in place by Kivuli's knife. He opened his mouth to scream. Kivuli reached him first, laid a long finger against the man's open lips. "We do not want to do that here, no?"

The man sucked in air, choking on his pain as he stared death in the eyes. "No."

"Good." Kivuli yanked his knife out. A thin red line between two metacarpals rapidly spilled blood, but Kivuli had ensured the man would still have use of his hand. "Now-now, describe the location to me while your friend wraps your wound."

Tense silence filled the vehicle—the driver and third man deciding what they should do. Gradually the driver's fists loosened on the steering wheel and the third man dug in the back for a first-aid kit. Kivuli's stare never left his victim.

"It's a typical strip mall," the man said, voice breathy with pain. "Several large buildings, all one-story, lining the block. Alleys on either side of the sports bar, leading to a central loading area accessed from the rear of each building."

"Very good." He turned back to watch Smith enjoying her third beer.

The cell at his belt beeped, demanding his attention. He clicked to accept the call and silently brought the phone to his ear.

"Report."

Kivuli listed Smith's actions for his employer.

"Has she shown any awareness of you?"

"No." Nothing he could pinpoint definitively.

Mansa grunted, in response to Kivuli's denial or something else, he didn't want to know. His employer's…tastes…were repugnant.

"Flush her out," Mansa commanded.

Kivuli didn't agree, but neither did he argue. The cell beeped when he ended the call; he returned it to his belt. Next to him, the driver raised an eyebrow in inquiry.

"Are we still dripping?" Kivuli asked without glancing toward the backseat.

"No, sir."

The words were firm. Good. Kivuli jerked his head toward Smith. "Let's go."

They exited the van. Kivuli gave each man a once-over before assigning their positions with a silent nod. Only when each one was in place did he make his approach down the long aisle, flanked by parked cars. He didn't bother to hide; there was no need—the woman did not glance his way, nor did her body tense. She seemed unaware, but instinct, the spirits' whispers in his ear, told him she was not. When he came to the end of the row and walked into the drive fronting the restaurant, and Smith swept the landscape, finally settling on him, he knew that the spirits were correct. Those eerie blue eyes caught him in their trap, absorbing how he moved, how he stared, the trajectory of his path. Recognition dawned, lit an eagerness for battle within him, an eagerness he could not surrender to.

Smith did not rush to flee. Instead she lifted her bottle and took a last long swallow of the amber liquid before setting it down precisely next to its siblings. She even took the time to place a tip beneath it, ensuring the bills would not blow away in the light wind. Only then did she slide from her seat and make her way unhurriedly toward a side door of the restaurant, at a right angle to his position.

Smart; he had sensed that. He had also planned for such a contingency.

She was small, he realized. In the surveillance photos she'd appeared delicate, but this close, in person, she looked too fragile for the kind of work she did. Perhaps her male teammates assisted more for a female than they would for each other. Such a small woman would bring out a man's protective instincts, especially if she allowed them to fuck her.

Knowing two of his men were even now circling the building to flank the woman, he signaled the driver into the narrow alley Smith had entered. A lascivious grin stretched the man's face, roughening his already hard features, his sharp eyes fastening onto Smith's small form. Kivuli followed, barely able to see around the man's thick neck, but he caught a glimpse of Smith pausing to glance over her shoulder, tracing his subordinate's body first before meeting Kivuli's eyes directly. Assessing her opponents.

Yes, she was nothing like Mansa's usual victims, but then, she was Mansa's offspring. Mansa was intelligent as well, though Kivuli suspected he had relied on other men to protect him for far too long. He was no longer sharp. This woman did not suffer the same problem.

Smith continued on. Kivuli's subordinate picked up speed, but before he could reach her, the alley opened into a loading area. Plain walls with a series of doors, each store's name clearly emblazoned, marched down the space. Smith beelined toward the opposite side, only coming up short when one of Kivuli's men appeared directly in her path. A turn to the right, her last chance of escape, but his third man had already stepped from the next alley, blocking the final line of their triangle.

"It appears the time for our meeting is finally at hand, Ms. Smith."

The woman turned to face him, backing rapidly until her spine met a wall. Kivuli and the driver were before her, one of his men closing in on each side, just in sight. Nowhere to run, though he had no doubt this bit of prey would surprise him.

He stepped forward.

"You know my name," she said. Planting her feet in a fighter's stance, Smith cocked her head to the side. "How about yours? Or should I just call you fuckhead?"

Her language was nothing like her father's—she was hot, fierce. Anticipation set off the beat of ceremonial drums in his head, as close to a sexual high as Kivuli came. The spill of blood was what excited him most, the hunt. It had been long since such a worthy opponent had faced him.

"You should come with us, miss."

Her mouth formed a slow *oh*. Her bow was half-formed, an insult more than a compliment. "The ghost, I presume."

His solemn nod confirmed it, though he did not give her his name. Names had power.

"Well, ghost"—she took a sidling step away—"I'm not going anywhere with you."

No, he did not expect that she would. A good hunter did not allow the prey to surprise him, but he did use all the weapons available to him.

A sharp gesture signaled his men to close in.

Smith lifted her hands as if to ward them off—a weak, feminine gesture. "Hey, wait, guys! I've got nothing against you." She sidled along the wall again, placing her closer to the man who'd entered the loading area farther down. "Can't we talk about this?"

Such succulent prey. The men couldn't resist, and though Kivuli saw her intent clearly, he did not warn them. They would wear the woman down before Kivuli took her himself. These men were expendable, and if they were so easily drawn in, he knew Smith would agree that they deserved whatever she dished out, as they said here in America.

The closest man lunged forward, a hungry grin baring the depravity within him. Smith cowered back against the wall, making herself small, and then, with a block and swing that slipped right between the man's reaching hands, landed a punch to his jaw, to one side of his chin—a knockout point. He dropped immediately to the ground, eyes closed, unmoving.

Smith shook out her fist. Fragility fell away as she turned to face her remaining opponents. "Down to two. Who's next?"

Both remaining subordinates charged the woman. Kivuli stood back, watching, assessing, waiting for Smith to tire herself out with the fight. He'd expected a trained fighter but not a warrior, and a warrior she was. She kept the men lined up, one between her and the other at all times, paying no attention to Kivuli's position off to the side—or at least, not appearing to. No doubt she surmised his intent to wear her down. Her size allowed her to get under strikes and move lightning-fast around her bigger, slower opponents. By the time they'd turned to find her, she'd already struck—a blow to the kidney or the base of the skull, a kick to the side of a knee or the ribs or, even worse, a too-close hand; Kivuli counted a half dozen broken fingers. One of his men hesitated a second too long, allowing Smith to whip around him, drop down, and deliver an uppercut to his unprotected groin from behind. He hit the concrete face-first, hands cupped over his most sensitive anatomy, and immediately began vomiting.

Smith's laugh was filled with exhilaration, her expression more alive than he'd seen it before. A feeling of kinship rose inside him as he watched. A worthy opponent indeed.

After an incredulous look, Kivuli's final subordinate took the bull's approach and bore down on the woman, no doubt hoping to use his greater weight to control her. Instead she gripped his massive bicep between her small hands, flipped to put her back to his stomach, and dropped to her knees all in one movement. The man flipped over her head. He barely had time to groan before a boot to his jaw ended in a shattering sound that assured Kivuli the man would not be speaking anytime soon.

Smith rose to her feet. Pivoted to face him squarely. One delicate finger lifted to her mouth, to a thin trickle of blood, and swiped it clean, depositing the life-giving fluid on her own tongue. And then she smiled. The heart of a warrior, a predator, was in that smile. "That was short," she said. "Too short. I'd've thought my father could afford better help."

The insult meant nothing—Kivuli recognized it for what it was, just as he recognized the woman for what she was: a hunter who shared the spirit of the warrior within him. He would not crush that spirit, but he would prevail. Purpose settled in his breast as he stepped forward into battle.

Without warning, a door behind Smith slammed open. A large man, heavily bearded, carrying a full trash bag, took one step through, glanced up, and jerked to a stop at the sight of the bodies littering the ground. "What the hell?"

Kivuli reached for his waistband, for the knife he kept there. The hilt was between his fingers for no more than a second before he threw it.

Smith traced the faster-than-sight movement for a split second, then lunged toward the man, shoving him back. Kivuli's knife slammed point-first into the door.

"Get inside!" Smith growled as the man instinctively fought her. "Call 911!" She shoved him once more, back far enough that she could slam the door shut. Shouts filtered out, assuring him he would not make it more than a foot inside the building.

His prey had outmaneuvered him.

It would not do for the American police to find and detain him here. He retrieved the keys from his unconscious driver and hurried back down the alley toward the van.

Chapter Twenty-One

The impotence of an unfinished fight roiled in Elliot's gut for the rest of the day. She'd baited her hook, reeled in her fish, then been cock blocked by a civilian taking out the trash, for fuck's sake. She'd been forced to allow the ghost's escape in order to protect the noncoms around her, had been unable to follow him, trace him back to her father and finally finish this. She hated the feeling of helplessness, the growing urgency to engage Mansa before he could engage her team. She couldn't find him, couldn't do anything but wait.

And so she'd ended up here, in the ring at an underground fighting match, getting the shit pounded out of her. It sounded strange to say she was loving every minute, but she didn't know how else to express the deep sense of ease every kick, punch—hell, even bites and hair pulling—gave her. It pushed away the world when it became too much to bear, allowed her to leave it all behind for a short period of time. It fed the part of her that hungered for punishment.

She deserved it, though she didn't think anything could erase the memory of Deacon's face as he left the kitchen this morning, Sydney tucked safely in his arms, protected. From her.

The punch hit her cheekbone like a bomb, setting off a starburst of pain that satisfied something deep inside her. *Focus, Ell. Where's your head?*

She knew exactly where it was. Staring down the man in the ring with her, she allowed a grin to stretch across her face. The bunching of the skin made her face throb, rubbed in the pain of multiple blows. Every breath sent twinges through her ribs. Her bare knuckles screamed.

Elliot savored it, grinning wider.

Her opponent blanched beneath his dark olive skin.

She turned her head, offering him the opposite cheek. "How about another?" she asked, blinking innocently up at him.

His lips pulled back from his teeth. A growl escaped. She could almost see the calculations going through his brain.

He lunged, his fist shooting out.

She took the punch half on her cheekbone, half on her brow. *Black eye—nice.* But it didn't stop her from catching his wrist on the withdrawal, whipping sideways to stretch him off balance, and planting her heel in his groin. The man's body lifted half a foot off the mat. Even the cup he wore wouldn't save him from that kind of impact.

He dropped like a sack of potatoes and gagged.

That's number three down. "Who's next?"

The referee—to use the name loosely—blew the whistle dangling between his fleshy lips. "Take ten."

She gave the man an impatient look, but his back was already to her. Probably couldn't take another minute without a drag. Elliot pivoted toward the opposite corner.

And came face-to-face with Dain. Over his shoulder, Deacon stared enigmatically down at her.

She looked back at her boss. "Are you here about Kivuli?"

Dain cocked his head. "No. Should I be?"

So they didn't know. Good.

"What do you want then?"

He looked like he wanted to question her further, but something stopped him short. "It's time for everything to come out in the open, Elliot."

So he was keeping his promise, then. If she didn't spill, he would. Except her personal demons—and what she chose to do about them—hadn't been part of the deal.

From the fact that Dain had brought Elliot's lover into her personal hell, she gathered they were now.

"Fucking bastard."

He shrugged, though she couldn't miss the way his gaze cataloged her body. No doubt he already had a list of injuries in his head. It didn't matter, though; she wasn't his problem anymore. Time to move on.

The agony that ripped through her at the thought was worse than any blow she'd taken today, but she managed—barely—to tuck it beneath the rest. She wouldn't put her team in the line of fire just because she wanted to be with them. She wasn't meant for a family.

"What do you want, Dain?"

"You won't be fit to come back to duty if you keep this up."

She dropped her focus to the tape on her wrists, picking at a ragged edge. Anything to keep from seeing Dain's disappointment. "I'm not coming back."

A heavy sigh. "Of course you are, little Otter. And I'd rather it be while you can still walk."

"Oh, this is nothing." She peeked up, barely catching his expression. "You should see the guys I fought this afternoon; now that was some serious damage."

"You fought someone else today? Who?"

Dain's tone was more exasperated parent than real concern. Wasn't he in for a surprise. "Kivuli."

"What the hell?"

But Elliot was already plowing on. "Well, not Kivuli himself. His goons. Kivuli booked it when witnesses arrived."

"Elliot—"

Deacon broke in. "What the hell happened, Elliot?"

Was his voice hoarse? "What do you fucking care? I don't work for you anymore, Mr. Walsh."

A string of ugly curses left his mouth, low and angry and, Elliot had to admit, more inventive than her usual go-tos. She preferred vulgarity over variety.

Tilting her head playfully hurt like hell, but she managed. "What's that, Mr. Walsh?"

The curses petered out as Deacon glared down at her. Elliot grinned, ignoring the shaft of pain through her lip.

"I'm not the one in the wrong here," Deacon said.

And he wasn't; she knew all too well that she was to blame, for everything. Still, "Again, I don't work for you anymore, Mr. Walsh."

Something volcanic ignited in his expression. "You weren't calling me Mr. Walsh last night, were you? Or this morning in the shower."

Elliot reached for a towel hanging over the ropes and used it to wipe her face, used the motion to wipe every ounce of expression away, every thought. It was the only way to stay upright. She turned toward the ref's assistant, a slinky blonde in a costume more suited to pole dancing than a boxing ring. A quick slash of her hand across her throat told the woman she was done for the night.

Deacon didn't step back when she slid her leg through the ropes to climb out of the ring. She didn't let it intimidate her. Her ass brushed his thigh, her sweaty arm knocking his away as she moved past. She didn't look back on the trip to the locker room.

Unfortunately the swinging door had no lock. And her male companions had no qualms about waltzing in behind her. Guess it really didn't matter; both of them had seen her naked, though in very different circumstances—assignments didn't always allow for privacy. But Dain and her team didn't really look at her body; they assessed her strength and ability to work, her health if she'd been injured. Deacon didn't look at her like that. There was something squirm-worthy about having her lover and the man she considered her father figure together in the room she was supposed to strip in, even when she was clothed.

"You didn't answer me, Elliot. What happened?"

"Not much. They trailed me, cornered me in an alley, got their asses kicked, and Kivuli ran." She shrugged. "I need to shower. You can go now."

"No—"

She caught the slash of Dain's hand from the corner of her eye, his own *we can discuss that another time.* Deacon rubbed roughly at his face.

Yeah, I get that reaction a lot.

"All right, then, how about another question." Deacon surveyed her wounds, something akin to horror in his eyes. "What the hell where you doing out there tonight?"

She sat on the bench to one side and began to slowly unwrap the tape from one wrist, anything to keep from seeing that look on his face. "It's called fighting."

"It's called punishing herself," Dain countered.

The burn at the backs of her eyes had her tugging particularly hard on the tape. She bit back a curse as several layers of skin went with it.

"It's what she does," he continued. "Beat the emotion out of herself."

Better that than let it kill you.

"You don't deserve punishment any more than the rest of us, Elliot."

She raised her head, staring beyond Deacon to the man who meant far more to her than anyone still alive on this earth. "I quit."

"I don't accept."

Elliot shrugged.

"You see, Deacon," Dain continued. "Elliot was raised on the run. Her mother escaped when she was three, on a boat with a captain she later married. For ten years they kept moving, kept hiding, always isolating themselves and their daughter in order to avoid Mansa's vindictive reach."

She balled the used tape up, tossed it toward an overfull trash can, and started on her other wrist.

"Except when she was thirteen, Mansa caught up with them. You guessed right," Dain said. "The couple was Elliot's mother and stepfather."

A fireball of the hottest red and orange and yellow she'd ever seen. Screams ringing in her ears—her own. Her mother hadn't had time to scream.

"And then Elliot followed the instructions her mother had ingrained in her. She traveled to the Colorado wilderness, where she was taken into a survivalist camp run by an acquaintance of her stepfather's."

She stood, threw the second ball, and turned to her locker. The slap of metal against metal rang through the room when she pulled the door a little too forcefully.

"A survivalist camp?" Deacon asked. He was still facing her, watching her; she could tell by the sound of his voice, the heat of his gaze. The skin between her shoulders, right over her tattoo, crawled like she was a bug under a microscope.

Dain wasn't letting up. "A militia group run by an ex-general from Africa. See, Elliot has more real-life training than any of us—she was, quite literally, raised to it. Having emotions beat out of her is second nature. And when the general threw her out at the age of eighteen—"

"Stop it, Dain! Shut up. Just shut up." She snatched her bag from the locker and rounded on the two men. "You don't get to analyze my past. I'm not some psych experiment, and you're sure as hell no therapist, so get the fuck out."

Deacon took a step toward her. "Ell, don't—"

Her glare was filled with all the rage boiling inside her, the hell of hearing that name again, the name he'd called her while he was inside her. Deacon blanched.

"Don't you dare call me that. Don't pretend you give a fuck. You hate me now; fine. I did what you wanted. Now leave me alone."

"I—" Deacon clamped his mouth shut. The muscle in his jaw jumped as he seemed to fight with whatever words he wanted to say. "I don't hate you, Elliot."

"Really?" she scoffed. "You should. I put Sydney in danger. Just by being born, I put my mother in danger. She ended up dead. You should keep me as far away from your daughter as humanly possible."

"I can't!" Deacon shouted. "I can't, no matter how much I want to—because Mansa wants you, not just her."

All the anger deflated, leaving her body a hollowed-out balloon with nothing to keep it afloat. No wonder they'd come to find her. She didn't know why she hadn't seen it earlier: they needed bait.

She looked at Dain, but whatever he was feeling, she couldn't tell. "So that's why you're here?"

Dain's sigh sounded like it hurt. "I came because you belong with us. You need to come home, little Otter."

She barely managed to turn away before a tear escaped. She was scrubbing it into oblivion with her fist when the creak of the door opening registered.

Her boss had said his piece, apparently. As she spun to stare at the closed door, the weight of the silence in the room threatened to choke her.

Deacon advanced, his wide shoulders blocking her view. He didn't stop until her back was to the row of lockers and all she could see was his angry face and tense body looming over her.

Why the hell did that make her the tiniest bit hot?

"I need you to come back."

"I'm a liar, remember? You can't trust me. I might be working for the enemy."

This time it was Deacon's turn to sigh. "Okay, explain it to me. Why did you lie, Elliot?"

"I didn't lie. I omitted things."

His fists landed on the lockers behind her with a jarring bang. "Don't play games. This is too important. Now tell me, why did you lie?"

She tried to swallow, but every drop of spit had dried up. Not because of Deacon; his anger she could handle. It wasn't him she was afraid of.

"Dain gave me the basics, and I get it; your childhood was a nightmare. You were raised to secrecy and raised to believe trust would get you killed. That doesn't mean I can forgive you for withholding information that would affect my daughter."

"But you still want me in the same house with her."

"I don't have a choice."

Right. She should be used to being a commodity. Maybe she had gotten soft staying with Dain's team.

And yet she couldn't stop herself from rubbing salt into the wound. "And what about us?"

She was staring at Deacon's broad chest, right in front of her face, but she didn't need to see his expression to interpret his shrug or the disdain in his voice. "What about us? The sex is good, we've had it, and now we're done."

She had to laugh. She'd been such a *girl*, reaching for something she had no business wanting, then hurting when she didn't get to keep it. Stupid. Fucking stupid.

She looked at the floor, her gaze catching midway down. "Done. Really?"

Without thought her hand came up to cup Deacon's cock. His erect cock. When her fingers folded around his length, he grunted.

She glanced up from beneath her lashes. "You were saying?"

She had just enough time to watch his brown eyes go black before his mouth slammed onto hers. The back of her head hit the locker behind her, but she didn't care—all she cared about was the hot, angry taste of him in her mouth, the bruising pressure of his hands as they wrangled hers above her head, the heavy push of his thick thigh as he forced her legs open around it.

"I was saying"—he bit down on her bottom lip, sending a zing of pain through her—"we're"—another bite, this one to her jaw—"done." His teeth caught the sensitive join of neck and shoulder and clenched. When Elliot arched into the sting, her hard nipples dragged across his body. Deacon shook his head, worrying her skin like a dog with a bone.

She lifted her chin, giving him access to more. A hard suck on her neck pulled a whine from deep inside her.

The sound sent Deacon into a frenzy—she couldn't tell if he needed her to hurt more or simply couldn't take holding back any longer, but either way, the foreplay ended there. No sweet caresses, no whispered endearments. That wasn't what this moment was about. It was about muttered curses and heavy breathing, the rough jerking of zippers and tearing of material and then finally, finally, the hard entry of his body into hers. Only when he hit the end of her and a cry of pain escaped did Deacon still. Elliot hung there, pinned to the metal lockers by his cock, his hands, the force of his weight against her. She panted through the minute it took for her vagina to soften, for her body to accept its too-full invasion. Tears tracked down her cheeks, but they weren't from the pain—they were from fear. She could finally admit it: she was afraid. Of revealing herself, of Deacon's rejection, all of it. She didn't want to have this taken away from her. She didn't want to go the rest of her life without knowing Deacon, without knowing love, without knowing what it really meant to be a family. She didn't want to lose him or Sydney or Dain or anyone else.

She didn't want to lose this.

"I—" She closed her eyes, needing to keep some small part of herself hidden when her entire body, her very soul was being invaded. "I didn't tell you because…I…I just can't. I can't talk about it. About him. You don't understand."

The death grip on her wrists loosened the slightest bit. Deacon shifted his hips, pushing her thighs out until it was the most natural thing in the world to raise her legs, hook her knees around his waist. Hold him like he was holding her.

She kept her eyes closed.

"I was born dirty, Deacon. You can't understand what that's like. What he did to her just to conceive me…it was…ugly. I'm ugly."

A soft brush of his breath on her skin, then his mouth against her neck. "You could never be ugly, Ell."

Her body clenched around his cock when he whispered her name.

"I can never be clean," she argued. "But I could pretend...if no one knew."

Deacon lowered his arms, taking hers with him. At her hips he released her wrists, his hands moving down, down until he had her ass cupped in them. She opened her eyes when he lifted her away from the lockers.

The dark brown depths of his eyes drew her in, drowned her. Nothing else registered until he settled on a bench, his back to the door. The shift allowed him in deeper, if that was possible. Elliot moaned at the back of her throat as the base of his cock pressed against her clit.

Deacon held her steady, a hand at her lower back, one at her nape. His grasp wouldn't let her hide her face, wouldn't let her do anything but stare up at him as her body grew wet and his shaft pulsed inside her.

"You don't need to pretend, Ell." His lips brushed hers. His tongue stroked into her mouth, then withdrew, but he didn't. His words were spoken into her mouth, into her soul. "Nothing he did can make you dirty any more than it made your mother dirty. You've been clean since the moment you were born. You've been worthy. You've been a gift. He can't change that. Only you can. Don't give him that power."

And then he tipped her backward, arching her spine to bring her breasts to his face. He sucked a nipple right through her clothes.

Elliot lifted toward the touch, needing it, needing him.

They both groaned at the slick slide of her up his cock.

"Again," Deacon muttered, then sucked her harder.

Elliot did it again, lowered, lifted, beginning a slow, rolling rhythm as she stared at the bright fluorescent light over her head, blind to everything but Deacon—his mouth, his thrusts, his gravelly curses. And her tears. Deacon was shattering her, breaking apart everything she was, and afraid or not, she wanted it. So much. So she kept going, kept moving, even when it felt like the coming explosion would leave nothing of her behind. Even when it felt like she'd never be put back together again, she continued. Again and again and again.

And finally, when she stood on the edge, looking out over the precipice toward the unknown, she clutched him to her and prayed.

Then let herself go.

Chapter Twenty-Two

Elliot came home with them. After forcing a few more details about the afternoon confrontation from her tight lips, Dain had handed over pain meds and water and lapsed into silence. Elliot thanked Dain, then went back to staring out the window with the eye that didn't have an ice pack over it. Deacon watched her, trying to get it, trying to wrap his head around what he'd seen, what she'd told him. He had witnessed her sparring session with Dain, had seen her in the ring tonight, but the reality of her injuries— he'd only seen men out in the field ignoring injuries like that. And yet, other than a slight stiffness to her movements, Elliot didn't show it.

She was a fighter, no doubt about that. And yet the vulnerability she'd shown in his arms had wrecked something inside him. She'd handed him her innermost secret, trusted him in a way she'd never trusted anyone else except, perhaps, Dain. The question was, did he trust her?

Elliot's intel on Mansa made so much more sense now. If a killer might be tracking you, you'd make certain to know everything you possibly could about their movements, their associates, their business. But Elliot had not only been protecting herself; she'd been tracking her mother's murderer as well. And she didn't do anything half-assed.

No, it really wasn't about trusting whose side she was on anymore. It was about trusting that she wouldn't lie to him again.

Two black SUVs were parked in the drive outside the house when Dain pulled up. One belonged to the backup team Jack had sent out this afternoon. Mark and T.C. and Christopher were all good ole boys with laid-back manners, but Deacon had interviewed each and every one of them carefully, could read the quality in them just as he had with Dain's team. Sydney hadn't taken to any of them, though, asking repeatedly when Elliot would return, clinging to Saint or Dain when Deacon wasn't available. Hopefully with Elliot's return, his daughter would calm.

Dain nodded at the second vehicle as he put their SUV in park. "Jack's here. He wanted a strategy session as soon as we were all together."

"Does he know?" Elliot asked quietly from the back.

"He knows."

Dain was done with holding anything back apparently. Deacon exited the SUV and moved to open the back door for Elliot, noting that the blank expression she'd worn when they first entered the locker room had returned—well, until he held out his hand to help her from the car. The look she gave him then was full of disgust.

Stubborn woman.

"Stop glaring at me and let me help. You're too short not to jar those ribs getting down," he pointed out. "Save your fortitude for when Sydney slams into you in a few minutes."

"Good point." Elliot wrapped an arm around her ribs and placed her free hand in his, easing carefully to the ground. When she would have let go, he refused to release her.

Elliot kept her eyes on the ground. Deacon growled impatiently. A firm grip on her chin forced her to meet his gaze.

He expected her to snap at him, but the fact that she didn't told him everything he needed to know about her emotional state. She'd put too much of herself out there; now she was pulling the scattered pieces back behind a wall, trying to rebuild her sense of safety, of self. Maybe that was a good thing. After all, he didn't know his own feelings at the moment. And yet something inside him wouldn't allow her a retreat.

What he really wanted was to ask her if she'd ever lie to him again. If he could trust his daughter with her. But asking was ridiculous if he couldn't trust the answer. And so he stood there, staring down at her obscenely blue eyes, and said nothing.

"People are watching," she finally said.

"Let them watch." He wasn't going to make the decisions he needed to make, do what he had to do, based on anyone but himself and his daughter. "Sydney...she missed you."

A hint of navy darkened the outlines of her irises. "Did you tell her I quit?"

"We told her nothing of the sort," Dain snapped over his shoulder, striding toward the front door. "Now stop mooning at each other and get your asses in gear."

Deacon felt a corner of his mouth curl up in a grin despite the heaviness of the night. "Guess we've gotten our orders, huh?"

"Yes." Elliot's gaze dropped to his mouth as if fascinated.

"Then let's stop mooning, Ell."

Her voice went husky. "I'm not the one holding me here."

Right. He dropped his hand.

"'Bout time," Dain called as he pulled the front door open.

Inside, Dain split off toward the library. "I'm sure you want to see your girl first. Join us whenever you're ready, Deacon. I'll fill the others in on Kivuli and sons."

Deacon nodded and walked toward the stairs, surprised to realize Elliot was right behind him. He was even more surprised to find Sydney's light on and the door open. He moved into the doorway but stopped to lean against the frame, suddenly wishing he had a camera. No one else would believe him otherwise.

Saint had Sydney duty. The muscular guard sat cross-legged on Sydney's rug, waving pink-tipped fingernails in the air as casually as if he were doing jumping jacks. Sydney, already dressed in her pajamas, sat opposite, mimicking him, her grin wide and happy and unmarred by the worry Deacon couldn't seem to escape every time he looked at her. For his daughter's sake he buried it as deep as he could before crossing the threshold of her bedroom. "Isn't it past your bedtime?"

"Daddy, look!" Syd splayed her polished nails out for him to see. "Saint painted them."

"Very nice." Deacon pretended to inspect her tiny fingers, then looked to Saint's. "That color becomes you, bro."

The man's grin held no embarrassment. "I have half a dozen nieces and nephews; I'm used to it. Pink happens to be my favorite shade, *bro*."

Deacon detected a glint in Saint's eyes that said he probably wasn't talking fingernail polish. "Me too." He bent to kiss Syd's hand. "Why are you still up?"

"I was waiting for Elliot."

"I'm right here, Syd," Elliot said from the doorway. She crossed the room, but for once Sydney didn't jump up and squeal and tackle her favorite person. Her smile was subdued, her gaze tracing the bruises already forming on Elliot's face. A knot formed between her brows.

Elliot sat on the floor next to Saint, who eyed her face too, but not with surprise. More an analysis, trying to determine how incapacitated Elliot might be.

He'd seen this before, then. Dain had said as much, but the confirmation in Saint's look had him cursing silently. And aching. This woman made him ache, and not just for sex. What would it mean to his family, to Sydney, to bring someone so broken into their lives?

"It's okay, Sydney, I promise." Elliot traced the puffy area around her eye. "It looks bad, but I'm okay. You don't have to worry."

His daughter had done too much of that lately. This morning she'd asked him if Fionn was going to die like Jules. Did she think Elliot might die too?

He couldn't let her carry that fear. "Sydney—"

Without warning his daughter launched herself at Elliot. A faint groan left Elliot's lips, but then she was cradling the child in her lap, her eyes bright with tears she would never shed and would probably deny if anyone dared to mention them. Sydney tilted her head to the side, settled a cheek against Elliot's plumped breast.

His gaze met Elliot's. She gave him a faint smile, then tucked her chin down to nuzzle Sydney's head.

The sight struck him like a blow to his chest, forcing out every bit of air, every thought except one: how right they looked together. Madonna and child.

Saint reached for the nail polish, breaking the moment. "Gotta clean up after ourselves if it's bedtime."

His daughter's pout was about the cutest thing in the world—not that he'd ever tell her that. No need to give the kid ammunition. "Daddy? Elliot just got home."

Home. Out of the mouths of babes...

"And Saint promised to paint my toes too."

"He can tomorrow, I promise." The man's teammates would love the chance to rag him about his prowess with pink polish, no doubt. "Right now it's bedtime."

"How about I stay with you till you fall asleep?" Elliot offered.

That had his daughter up and running for the bathroom to brush her teeth. Deacon was surprised to feel a chuckle rise in his throat. "I think that's a yes."

Saint had gathered the supplies in his arms and followed Sydney into the bathroom. Deacon could hear him joking with Syd to the accompaniment of bottles rattling and the cabinet door shutting.

Elliot didn't speak.

"I'll be in the library if you need me," he finally said.

Elliot looked up at him from her position on the floor, so small she reminded him of a child. "I'll keep her safe, Deacon. I promise."

"I know you will." That much, at least, he had no doubts about.

Elliot stood and went to the bathroom to help Sydney finish getting ready. Deacon didn't call her back, didn't tell her good night. He'd save that moment for later. Maybe by then he would have figured out what to say.

The library was a massive jumble of testosterone and aggression, most of which seemed to be directed at the stack of pizza boxes on the long table. Deacon made a mental note to get Elliot some before she went to bed as he walked over to grab a plate. King and Dain stood with Jack, surrounding the chair Fionn was seated on. Across the coffee table, the new team from this afternoon crowded onto the couch. A lone man stood near the pizza, holding a glass of iced tea. He held out the other hand when Deacon approached.

"Deacon, I'm Conlan James."

Jack's partner. He'd been out of town the day of Deacon's initial meeting, so they had yet to meet. Deacon eyed him as they shook hands, thinking that, aside from a bit more bulk and height, he looked enough like Jack that they could be brothers.

"Conlan, I hadn't expected to see you here."

The man turned to pick up an already filled plate of pizza, but not before Deacon caught the change in his expression. Work mode; he recognized it all too well.

"Call me Con, please. We take our clients' safety seriously, especially when there's a child involved."

Deacon had to clear his throat before he could respond. "Thank you."

"That's what we're here for." He nodded his head toward the group around the coffee table. "Let's talk."

They'd barely sat before Jack called for everyone's attention. "Deacon, we've gone over feeds, worked with your contact at GFS. We found no evidence of tampering in the footage or at the site of Fionn's attack, only the powder King collected." He held up a paper. "It appears to be some kind of herbal mixture, but we don't know what it's for. Since the suspect is African, we've reached out to an expert, but that takes time."

"So that gets us nowhere."

"For now. Honestly, we're at a loss as to how your ghost got in and out without being caught on surveillance."

Deacon's heart thumped into his throat.

"There's also no trace of any contact between Elliot and Mansa—or Elliot and anyone but the people in this house. We have records of her online chats searching for information, her Internet searches, even her dark Net forays. There is no indication whatsoever that she betrayed you or her team."

"Of course there isn't," King muttered. "And just for clarity, I took a few minutes to call one of my contacts on the APD while we were waiting, and he did confirm an altercation at the location Elliot gave you. Three men, all severely injured—"

"That's our girl," Saint threw in.

"All insisted they'd been fighting each other and refusing to press charges."

Deacon rolled his eyes. "Of course they did."

Jack cleared his throat, bringing attention back to him. "Deacon, because we can't find any leads, we feel it's better to be safe than sorry, so we're recommending that you move yourself and your daughter to the GFS campus. It's safe, more secure—particularly with the antidrone tech they have—and though it may take us longer to find Mansa, working together, I do believe we can make it happen."

It wasn't what he wanted to hear, but he knew Jack was right. Having Mansa come to them was the best-case scenario. Unfortunately, sometimes you had to go with something less than best. Right now, best had to be keeping Sydney safe.

"How soon?"

The tension in Jack's shoulders eased the slightest degree. "Tomorrow morning if that's all right with you. That gives GFS time to prepare quarters and you time to pack what you need for an extended stay."

"And what about tonight?" Dain asked.

"Tonight we're hunkering down," Con said beside Deacon. "All patrols inside only, and all members active on two-hour rotations. Jack and I, as well as Mark's team, will be here to provide additional bodies and eyes." He shifted to face Deacon. "Nothing's going to happen to your baby on our watch."

Deacon wasn't too proud to admit the relief he felt. If he could, he'd surround his daughter with an army, but he trusted these men to do what they said. And he and Elliot would be with Sydney constantly. If anyone made an attempt to take her tonight, they'd die.

And Deacon would dance on their soulless corpses without remorse.

Chapter Twenty-Three

Elliot spent the night on Sydney's bed, lying curled near the little girl that had somehow managed to steal a huge chunk of her heart. Deacon slept on the floor on the opposite side of the bed. Every time she shifted in her sleep, the pain in her ribs would wake her, and she'd find herself listening for his breath, wondering if he was asleep. Dawn seemed to come far too soon and yet, honestly, not soon enough.

Careful not to wake Sydney, she slipped downstairs to the kitchen in search of coffee and pain meds. The kitchen was quiet, empty. She breathed a sigh of relief, quick to cross to the coffee machine while the reprieve lasted. The light was still on, the half-full pot still hottish. She didn't think she'd ever been so grateful for who-knows-how-old coffee in her life.

The cup had barely been warming her hands for a minute before the door swung open and King walked in. A quick, hot swallow smothered the groan on her lips.

"She returns," he taunted quietly, following in Elliot's footsteps from door to coffeemaker to retrieve his own morning caffeine.

A shaft of something very close to regret made her squirm. It was too early in the morning to deal with this—she hadn't even had her ibuprofen yet. She reached for the jar she'd left on the counter last night, poured a couple of pills into her palm, and swallowed them dry. "You know why I couldn't tell you, King. Couldn't tell anyone."

"Dain knew."

And that bothered him, she could see. Like any family, the dynamics varied among the members. Dain was their father figure and the one Elliot was closest to, but King...he was her brother. They related to each other in a way the open, grounded, family-oriented Saint couldn't. King, more than any of the others, would see this as a betrayal.

"If it makes you feel any better, he had to get me falling-down drunk to drag it out of me."

King took a sip, his chiseled face hard as granite. "It doesn't."

"King."

Another sip.

Moving close, Elliot dared to lay a hand flat on her teammate's broad chest.

He refused to look at her, staring intently into the black depths of his cup instead. Elliot thanked heaven for being short for once and ducked under his chin, interrupting the view. "I'm sorry. I wanted to keep you safe."

King's light blue eyes narrowed. "You wanted to keep you safe."

The words hurt. They were true to a certain extent, but not totally. She fisted her hand in the soft fabric of his T-shirt and gave it a jerk. "I watched my mother and stepdad get into a car and get blown into a billion pieces. Coming from the man who plays most of his past very close to his chest, you don't have much cause to judge." She knew he came from wealth, knew his family was in the upper echelon of society somewhere, but had never cared enough to look them up—King was important, not his past. She'd certainly never dug into his secrets. He told what he felt comfortable telling, and that didn't include why he'd left his old life behind. "We all have secrets, but I care about you. I care about all of you; you're the only family I've had since I was thirteen years old. I'd be damned if I saw you murdered like I saw my mother."

King closed his eyes. For a moment she thought the grinding of his jaw meant he would continue to argue, but then his hand rose to cover hers, forcing it hard against his chest. "We love you too, little Otter. We'll do anything to keep you safe."

She didn't want them risking their lives for hers. The fierce glint in King's eyes when he opened them warned her not to argue.

And damn if she didn't feel tears stinging at the back of her nose *again*. Was all this emotion never going to go away?

King dropped her hand and raised his cup to his mouth, but he didn't drink. "I didn't think I'd ever hear an apology cross your lips."

Something in her relaxed at his words. If he was okay enough to tease her, then they would be okay. Eventually. "And if you tell anyone you heard it now, I might have to kick your ass."

"Language," King reminded her. The word was echoed perfectly by Saint as he walked into the kitchen.

"Great, surround sound." Elliot retreated to lean against the counter.

Saint retrieved a cup from the cabinet. "Where's my apology, then?"

Elliot buried her face in the faint steam still rising from her coffee. "I'm sorry, all right?"

Saint stopped, coffeepot lifted to fill his mug, to gawk at her. "That is the sorriest 'sorry' I've ever heard. My three-year-old niece does better than that."

She glanced over at him from beneath her lashes. "Maybe the next time you manage to win a sparring match against me, I'll give you a better one."

King hooted. "He's never won against you."

She lifted a brow at him. *Exactly my point.*

Saint started to respond, but the kitchen door opened just in time to stop him. Jack and Conlan entered. Both men's dark eyes zeroed in on her like junkyard dogs who'd sighted a particularly annoying trespasser.

And the morning just keeps getting better.

She threw King and Saint a look, wishing they were anywhere but here, witnessing the set down she knew she was about to receive. There was no hope for it, though; she always took her fucking lumps. After setting her coffee regretfully on the counter, she turned and brought herself to attention.

Jack came to stand in front of her, Con to one side. "Elliot."

His tone shot steel through her spine. "Yes, sir."

He shook his dark head, expression unreadable. "You always have been unusual."

She couldn't really argue with that

"You've done a good job for us, always, despite your…idiosyncrasies."

"Like putting clients on their asses?" Saint asked.

"Yes, Saint, like putting clients on their asses." Conlan's words were slow, sarcastic. Saint grinned.

"Seems to have worked well for her in the long run, at least in that case," King added.

What did that mean? King could not be insinuating that Deacon cared about her. It couldn't be true. Deacon enjoyed the sex; that was all. He probably felt some affection, sure, but he'd loved his wife, and Elliot was nothing like Julia Walsh had been, at least as far as she could tell. Deacon would want that again, not some fucked-up warrior woman who'd never even had a tea party before.

You have now, remember?

And it was a memory she'd cherish long after Deacon and Sydney forgot her name.

"Do you two mind letting me handle my own reprimand?" Jack barked.

"No, sir."

Elliot swore sometimes that Saint and King were twins. How they managed to synchronize comebacks so often was beyond her. Or maybe great minds really did think alike.

She glanced at the two men, leaning back against the countertop, matching smirks on their faces. *I wouldn't quite go as far as "great minds."*

She had her own small grin under control when Jack turned back to her. One look and she was swallowing more than amusement, though. She hadn't realized until this moment what it would mean if Jack fired her. Yes, her team had accepted her back into the fold, but ultimately they worked at the pleasure of their boss. If Jack dismissed her, none of them would have recourse.

The kitchen door opened, admitting Deacon and Fionn. A hot wash of shame filled her as she looked at the two men. Fionn wore a loose-fitting button-down, probably to avoid lifting his arm and aggravating the stab wound below his collarbone. When he turned his head to survey the room, she saw the bandage at the back of his skull. He'd had stitches there, she knew. He had a mild concussion too. And when their eyes met, the lingering awareness of his hands around her throat, him pinning her against the wall, stared back at her.

Fionn's injuries might or might not have occurred if she'd been honest. And Deacon…well, he might or might not have continued to be with her if she'd been honest with him too. She'd taken those choices from them—for the best of reasons, but still, she'd deceived them all. And that was something she couldn't get away from, no matter how many punches and kicks she took trying to erase it.

She brought her focus back to Jack. "If you feel I need to go, sir, then I will," she said quietly.

Deacon's attention snapped to her. A frown gathered around his mouth.

"I—we—want you to realize what you did wrong, Elliot." Jack crossed his arms over his chest. "A team is only as strong as their weakest link, and though I never thought I'd say it of you, *you* are their weakest link right now."

She flinched.

"You're also part of the glue that holds them together," Con added. "We recognize that, but it doesn't mean you're off the hook."

"We're demoting you," Jack said flatly. "King will move up to Dain's second. You'll be on probation for six months. I want details of every moment of your life, everything—names, dates, actions—in writing. I'll be verifying all of it personally."

And nothing would fool him now that the suspicion had taken root. Jack's tech skills were legendary.

"I want to know what you ate for breakfast yesterday and who you talked to on the phone last week. Every. Thing. You've. Done. Is that clear?"

Wonder what he'll say when he sees Deacon on the list of things I've done. "Yes, sir."

"And because of Dain's complicity, he will also be receiving a review," Conlan told her. Her chest went so tight she could barely suck in a breath. That she'd brought her team down was almost too much to bear, but to put Dain's integrity at risk?

And all because you were afraid. Was it worth it?

"He was trying to keep me safe."

"Elliot." Jack sighed as he ran a hand down the back of his neck. "When are you going to realize that Mansa doesn't want to kill you; if he did, you'd've been dead when the first surveillance photo was taken. He wants you, no doubt about it, but not like he did your mother. With you, he's retrieving a commodity. And if there's anyone that can keep herself out of his grasp, it's…guess who? You." He leaned in until they were eye to eye. "Your mother trained you for this moment. Trust the gift she gave you. It comes with some side issues, but when push comes to shove, it'll get you through."

Would it? Elliot could do no more than nod. When Jack and Conlan moved toward the coffeepot, she allowed herself a full breath, then grabbed her own cup on the way to the door.

Fionn stepped into her path. "Elliot."

She couldn't look at him. She knew she should, knew she needed to apologize *again*, ask how he was, if there was anything she could do—all the polite shit people did when someone was hurt. But raising her eyes off his boots was impossible.

"Elliot, I'm wanting you to know, I get it," Fionn said, quiet enough that the words were just between them. "Deac explained. I get it."

But he was still wary; she'd seen it in his eyes. That was the consequence of her choices.

"Thanks, Fionn." Without waiting for a reply, she brushed past him and into the hall. If only she could leave the roil of emotions inside her behind as easily.

Chapter Twenty-Four

"GFS has a dorm that contains a few private quarters, mostly for clients," Deacon explained as they watched the interstate pass outside the blackened windows of the SUV. He and Elliot occupied the middle bench seat, one on each side of Sydney's booster, buckled snugly between them. "Commander Alvarez has been kind enough to invite us stay until we have further intel."

"What's 'intel,' Daddy?"

He tugged playfully on the ponytail gracing the top of his daughter's head. "It means intelligence. Information."

"What do you need infernation about?"

Elliot chuckled across from him. "Well, it does help you infer things."

He waited until she looked his way to mouth, *Smart-ass.*

Elliot raised her eyebrows at him. *Always,* she mouthed back.

God help him, but he really did want this woman, and not just in his bed. She was nothing like Jules had been, but still fit him just right—

Except for the unfortunate trust issue.

The reminder wiped his amusement away.

"Commander Alvarez is…?"

Deacon cleared his throat. "He's the owner, CEO, COO—you name it, he's in charge of it at Global."

The skin around Elliot's eyes tightened.

"What is it?"

She turned to look out the window. "I don't have much positive experience with people giving themselves ranks that aren't their own."

Dain had said the group she'd been sent to as a teen was run by an ex-general. When she'd told him the story about losing her virginity, he'd assumed she was in a foster home. What kind of punishment had the general enforced that would cause a teenage girl to swear off sex for years?

His stomach turned at the possibilities running through his mind.

"Where you grew up...what was the head honcho's name?" The bastard needed investigating.

A shiver traveled down Elliot's body, the small tell quickly suppressed. "General Ingram."

"What was his first name?"

She blinked. The fog of memory cleared from her eyes. "General."

He searched the side of her face that he could see. Dead serious. "You know I can find him, don't you?"

"Then you'll find I'm telling the truth. If he had any other name, we never knew it." She shrugged. "We had a running bet that he'd had his name legally changed."

That was when her lip twitched. No more than a millimeter, but he caught it. Wondered what she would do if he pulled her over Sydney's seat and nipped that lip in punishment.

Luckily their arrival at GFS rescued him from his own instincts. All three SUVs were vetted and inspected before security allowed them through, a fact that eased some of the tension that had run continually beneath the surface for the last few weeks. It wasn't an ideal location for a child, and Sydney would be confined more than he would like, but she would be safe. He just had to figure out how to make sure she stayed that way. They couldn't live here on the compound forever.

Dain parked in front of the main office. Saint and Jack pulled their respective vehicles in on either side of his. As they exited, Deacon told Dain, "I want Fionn's wound checked out, make sure it's healing properly. Can you take everyone inside? Amelia will be at the front desk. Everything is all set up; she'll show you to our quarters."

"Sure."

Jack and Con got out just long enough to shake hands. Deacon thanked them both for the escort. There was no way to know if Mansa would resort to taking out one or more of their vehicles, so the logistical support was greatly appreciated.

Elliot came up beside him as he lifted Sydney out of her seat. "Go with Ell, okay?" he told his daughter. "I'm going to take care of Fionn, and then I'll be right over." He also wanted to check in on Trapper, make sure his teammate was up to speed on the latest. If Trap was well enough, they'd bring him onto the team in a support capacity while they were here. It would be good for the man to have something to occupy him besides therapy.

Elliot held out her arms to Syd. "Ready, baby?"

Sydney flung herself willingly into Elliot's arms, no hesitation, no concerns, just pure acceptance. He envied her in that moment, the innocence that she possessed—would possess for a long time if he had anything to say about it. He leaned close, breathing in the combination of her almost-baby scent and Elliot's heated femininity. When he lifted his head from kissing his daughter, his gaze met Elliot's, and he could read the echo of his desire to kiss her in those blue depths.

How could this woman affect him so deeply? He wanted to kiss her, wanted to see her laugh, wanted her lost to desire beneath him—and still didn't know if he could forgive her, if the trust they needed could be restored. The warring parts of himself threatened his equilibrium when he needed it most, which was why, instead of giving in, he stepped back. "I'll be over in a few."

The disappointment in Elliot's face followed him across the compound.

"Trapper, then the doc," he said to Fionn as they walked toward the medical building.

"You know I'm not needing any more docs poking at me," Fionn groused.

"Do it anyway." Deacon used his commander voice, the one that brooked no argument. Fionn was still mumbling curses under his breath as security watched them swipe their badges and place palms on the fingerprint scanner. No more than thirty seconds and they were waved through.

Inside, many of the offices were empty, the usual clutter of rushing humans absent during the lunchtime pall. Fionn led the way, giving Deacon time to assess the way his friend held himself, observe any unconscious concessions to pain. His appraisal was cut short by a small figure hurtling around the corner of the T-junction just ahead of them and slamming into Fionn's side.

"Bat Girl?"

"Fionn?" Owlish eyes blinked up at Fionn, then switched to Deacon. "Sir, um…" Again the side-to-side glance. "What are you two doing here?"

Fionn cocked his head. "What's the story, Sheppard?"

"Nothing. Just…you know…nothing." Her shrug reminded him of a marionette getting jerked around. "What brings you guys back so soon?"

"We're having to change base camps," Deacon told her absently. Behind the glasses, Sheppard's eyes were red, her hands were shaking, and her normally pale skin was vampire-white. Her voice was high and strained. Something had definitely upset the little tech. "We wanted to stop by and see Trapper and Doc Hicks."

Fionn tried to pass, but Sheppard fluttered her hand out, almost touching him before drawing back. "Oh, Trapper isn't in his room. He's in the cafeteria. It's Edward's birthday—you know, cake and stuff. Balloons." A pause. "You can catch up with him there."

An unpleasant tingle tripped up Deacon's spine. "Sheppard, are you sure you're all right?"

"Oh. Yeah." Again with the hand waving, such a typical Sheppard gesture. "Just…stuff." She drew a deep breath. "I think I'll join you. I hear the cake's chocolate." She cut between them to walk back the way they'd come, toward the cafeteria at the other side of the building. With a roll of his eyes, Fionn followed.

Weird. But then Sheppard strayed pretty far from the center of the normal spectrum.

She was also in a hurry. Her short legs had carried her halfway down the hall. As he came alongside him, Deacon noticed Fionn's attention wasn't on the floor or the hall ahead; it was centered on the slim lines of Sheppard's back. He'd have to remember to rag him about that when they had some privac—

The world exploded around them.

One minute he was midstep, looking forward to giving Fionn as good as he normally got, and the next he was slammed onto his face, the sting of a thousand tiny pieces of shrapnel hitting his back. His ears went hollow like someone had pulled their plug and taken the power with it. His eyes clamped closed at the pain of impact, then blinked open to the tan uniformity of utilitarian carpet and something gray. Wispy.

He blinked.

Smoke? Dust?

Shit. A bomb.

Alarms began to sound. That, he could hear; apparently his ears had juice after all, but now he wished they didn't. Shouts and running registered. Fionn…where was Fionn? Deacon told himself to turn his head, to find Fionn—and Sheppard! God, Sheppard had been with them. It seemed to take forever for the command to leave his brain and travel the relatively short distance to his neck, but it eventually happened, and then he saw Fionn, prone, unmoving.

The shock jolted him to his hands and knees. "Fionn?"

Fionn rolled slowly, carefully to his side. "Could you please not be talking s'loud? I think someone mistook my skull for the home of the Liberty Bell."

A sharp laugh escaped, mostly from relief. "You can joke. You're okay."

"I'm wrecked!" Fionn groaned. "Just a concussion and a stab wound and stitches and... Shit!" He jerked up, a move that had his eyes rolling back in his head. "Where's Sheppard?"

Farther along the corridor, huddled against the wall, lay a rag-doll bundle of color. Deacon crawled toward it. Sheppard had been thrown against the drywall, her body leaving a huge dent. She lay facedown, but it was Fionn who got to her first, Fionn who ran his hands over her small body. Fionn who gently rolled her over. "Deac?"

"I got it." He forced his resisting legs to gather under him, push his body upright. Calling for security, he stumbled down the hall, damning the fact that he had no radio or earbud to call medical, get them on the scene fast.

"Mr. Walsh!" One of the security guards from the door—Deacon knew him, George or Greg or... He flagged the man down.

"Get a doc here asap. We've got a woman unconscious."

The guard nodded and turned back toward the building entrance, radio already in hand. His partner passed him, coming toward Deacon, radio at his ear. "Can you pinpoint the blast?" he asked Deacon.

"Down near the long-term medical wing." Trapper's wing. A few more seconds and...

That unpleasant tingle returned, snaking up the back of his neck.

"Call the cafeteria and have them get a head count," he suggested.

"Will do." A quick relay through the radio. "I think most of the building is over there. I'm not sure who might've still been in their rooms or offices."

"Pray there aren't any," Deacon said, voice rough from the smoke and dust and the heavy dread settling on him. "Radio the front office right now and make sure my daughter and her guards are in place. Have every building swept for bombs." When the guard hesitated, Deacon growled at him. The radio returned to the man's mouth the next instant.

Deacon waited until he heard directly from Dain that Sydney was safe, then returned to Fionn and Sheppard. His friend continued to hover over the girl on his hands and knees. Deacon thought he heard a soft crooning sound, and then Fionn looked up and the sound cut off. "Well?"

"They're on their way, I promise. How is sh—"

Sheppard turned her head. "Fionn, what…?"

"Shh." He eased the broken glasses from Sheppard's nose, then cupped her head carefully. "You need to be still now, Bat Girl. We're no' too sure what all's going on with you yet."

"Hate that," she murmured, eyes closed.

"Hate what?" Fionn asked. Deacon leaned closer to hear her reply.

"Hate when you call me that."

The grin that tugged at his lips felt obscene in light of what had just happened.

"So sorry."

Fionn frowned down at her. "Sorry about what?"

A wave of her hand toward the far end of the hall, the area where the explosion had occurred. "Sorry. Couldn't stop it."

"Of course you couldn't, sweetheart." Fionn glanced at Deacon, his gaze beseeching. Deacon tensed, ready to blast the hovering security guard with a barrage of "where the hell are they's?" He turned in time to see the first EMT jog into the hall.

"Never would've hurt anyone. Tried," Sheppard was saying. "Had no choice."

"What?"

"The bomb…had no choice…"

Fionn jerked back onto his heels. Ugly certainty congealed in Deacon's chest as he moved out of the way to allow the EMTs to take over Sheppard's care. Fionn sat motionless, eyes wide and unbelieving, until one of the medics barked at him to move.

"Deacon." Fionn joined him farther down the hall, stumbling like a drunk, hand rubbing hard at his chest. Reeling to a stop against the wall, he bent over double. "Deacon…"

There was really no response. For the second time in two days, they'd uncovered a betrayal that shook the foundation of everything they'd held to be true. Only this time it wasn't just about a connection to their enemy. This time, it was about doing the enemy's bidding. Setting a bomb.

Trapper could've died. A helluva lot of people could've died, including Deacon and Fionn.

A dull roar came out of nowhere. Deacon jerked his head up in time to see Fionn's fist shoot out and slam into the drywall, punching right through, a primal shout tearing from his lungs.

Deacon stood and bore witness—it was all he could do. They'd felt safe here, felt in control. But they'd been compromised, again, this time by one of their own.

Chapter Twenty-Five

They'd heard the bomb, even four buildings away, felt the shaking, saw the windows rattle. For a moment Elliot had been thrown back in time to another bomb, a car, and a little girl without the safety of multiple concrete walls between her and danger. That's when the realization set in.

This couldn't be a coincidence, not right now.

GFS personnel wouldn't allow her team near the scene, wouldn't tell them anything more than that Deacon and Fionn were alive. Dain relayed every word through Elliot's earpiece. As much as she needed to see Deacon, to know he was safe, she refused to leave Sydney with anyone else. Deacon would want them together. Deacon would want...

Fuck. Fuck fuck fuck! She couldn't imagine her life without him in it. Didn't want to.

He's fine.

But for how long? Her father had done this; she didn't know how, but she knew it was the truth. And he'd failed, which meant it wouldn't be long before he tried again, and again, until he either succeeded or died. How long would Deacon be safe? How could she keep him alive when her opponent was a phantom she couldn't find?

The question consumed her, the tightness in her chest strangling her even more when Sydney came to snuggle in her lap. So trusting, so affectionate.

Nothing would change that, nothing. Elliot vowed it even as fear grew in her mind.

A couple of hours after the explosion they were taken to a large conference room in the central building, the one where they'd met Amelia, the woman assigned to escort them on arrival. Elliot made herself look around, assess the location when all she really wanted to do was run to Deacon, touch him, assure herself that he truly was all right. She couldn't, not now. If she did, there was no way she could hide the emotions breaking her apart inside, and there were too many people here watching. People who could read her too well.

And so she set Sydney on the ground and let her go instead. The child threw herself across the room. "Daddy!"

From the corner of her eye Elliot caught a glimpse of Deacon scooping his child into his arms, the slight grimace of pain he couldn't quite control. The knot in her gut twisted even tighter.

"Going in?"

She moved to let Fionn by, her gaze traveling up his body. "Oh."

"Mm." Fionn's grin was halfhearted and didn't reach his green eyes. "Oh."

New scrapes and bruises decorated what she could see of his skin. From the size of the bandage on his temple and the careful way he placed his feet as he entered, his concussion was likely worse as well. But it was his expression that worried her: not remote, not blank; more like a lid had been placed over a boiling pot of water and was tipping constantly to release small bursts of steam. Only the steam looked far more like fury in Fionn's case.

A second man followed him into the room, walking almost as carefully as his teammate. Trapper. She recognized him from the initial intel on their case. Trapper's scarring was significantly more horrific in person, the stiffness of his movements and the wary way he held his body—part afraid someone might bump into him and cause pain, part afraid his skin might not hold all of him together for much longer—bringing home the fact that this man had been tortured and somehow survived. Elliot reached a hand out to shake, refusing to flinch or baby him. He didn't need that; he needed a warrior's acceptance, and she gave it willingly.

Everyone gathered around the conference table: Dain, King, Saint, Mark's team, Fionn, Trapper, Deacon, and Elliot. Sydney went happily with Amelia to the far end of the room to play. Elliot found herself sitting in a chair directly opposite Deacon, and when she glanced up, their eyes locked naturally, irrevocably into place. She stared, cataloging his bumps and bruises more closely than she had Fionn's, searching for any hint of pain. All that stared back at her was…

No. It wasn't love. She wouldn't recognize love if it hit her in the face, and besides, it couldn't be; it was too soon, too ridiculous, too…everything.

But the longer she looked, the more she realized she wanted desperately for it to be love. And in that moment, all the emotion she'd kept locked away, everything she couldn't bring herself to say welled up in her eyes. She tried to stop it, tried to hide, but Deacon's gaze wouldn't let her; it bored into her, digging up everything, stripping her naked in a roomful of hardened soldiers—

None of whom mattered when Deacon gave her a soft smile. She hadn't seen a smile like that since their shower together. No bitterness, no anger, no mistrust. Just...

Fuck. She couldn't breathe.

Later, he mouthed and turned his head to look down the table, starting the meeting. But the sense of connection lingered, so foreign and yet exactly right, like pieces of a puzzle falling into place.

"The bomb appears to have been set by Lyse Sheppard," Deacon announced. The words were quiet enough that Sydney couldn't hear them at the other side of the room, but firm nonetheless.

"Did she build it?" Dain asked.

"Sheppard?" Trapper shook his head. "That girl knows computers, not bombs. She's scared of her own shadow."

"Computers have the Internet, which has plans for bombs. Most anyone can make one," Dain argued.

"I have to agree with Trap in this case," Deacon said. "I can't see her actually making the bomb."

"Just placing it," Fionn said bitterly. The words—and the tone—shook away Elliot's distraction.

"Fionn says you think I was the target?" Trapper flattened his scarred fingers out against the conference table, fisted them, spread them again. Stretching the too-tight skin, more than likely. "I don't get it. Why go to the trouble?"

"We believe Mansa is here to finish the kill on Deacon in person," Dain explained.

"But the other team members are expendable." Fionn rubbed the back of his head near his stitches. "We're now oh for two against."

Elliot fought the instinct to hunch her shoulders, make herself small and unnoticeable. Trapper had been tortured, but Fionn had not—and they all knew why.

A tap on her arm. Elliot turned to accept the sheaf of papers being passed around. King added a wink to the pile. Of course he'd know how she was feeling in this moment.

She buried her face in the paperwork.

The file on Sheppard was thick. Elliot flipped to the back, to the employment contract and intake information. Typical family unit—mother, father, one brother, all normal. Sheppard was the same age as Elliot, but with a different expertise. GFS had scooped the woman up straight out of intelligence training, which she'd finished at eighteen. Sheppard wasn't simply an intelligence expert; she was a fucking genius.

No flags on the background check. Nothing suspicious other than the speed with which she'd flown through her training. And yet the fresh-faced nerd staring back at Elliot from the profile image had jumped aboard the terrorist bandwagon?

Elliot wasn't buying it.

"Here's what I don't get," Deacon was saying. "Why would Sheppard do this? What's her motive?"

"Money?" Saint asked.

"The woman's a hacker," Elliot pointed out. "She could earn her weight in gold every year if she wanted to." And if she had no scruples. Scruples had a hard time coinciding with the things terrorists would ask a hacker to do.

"Any signs of excess in her lifestyle, any debts, anything like that?" Dain asked.

Elliot flipped to the front of the file, but the last annual review was clear—and holy shit, the woman made a lot of money. That cleared up more than one thing, even while it left others murky. "No."

"There has to be something," Fionn argued. "Some reason."

Elliot stared at the image of Sheppard. From all accounts shy and unassuming. Awkward. Why would a girl like that help a terrorist blow up the people she'd worked with for years?

Except she hadn't, had she? The birthday party in the cafeteria had been her doing. She'd tried everything she could to clear the area, including leading Deacon and Fionn away. So…hurting people hadn't been her goal. That put her at odds with the enemy, but she'd done their bidding. Why?

Because she'd been trying to protect someone. A friend? Or maybe family? No, her family was clean, according to the file. So who?

Elliot looked up, skimming Fionn before coming to rest on Deacon. Worry darkened the brown of his eyes as he stared at his friend. Of the two of them, Fionn seemed to be taking this harder, though Elliot wasn't sure why. Some subtext she wasn't privy to, obviously. Something Deacon hadn't shared.

They all had secrets.

The door to the conference room opened, admitting Commander Alvarez. The rest of the table stood, so Elliot did as well.

"Gentlemen." The commander nodded in Elliot's direction. "Ma'am."

Elliot frowned, sitting when the others sat.

"Anything from Sheppard yet, sir?" Deacon asked as the commander took an unoccupied seat.

Alvarez's mouth tightened. "Not as yet. Hicks says she's in and out of consciousness right now. I've called in a team to go through her office and computers, get what data we can."

Another knock. "I ordered some lunch for you all," Alvarez said as the door opened again. Outside, a line of wheeled carts stood at the ready. Alvarez gestured them in.

The team members staggered from their seats. Elliot was the last, her mind still turning over the information about Sheppard, needing to fill the voids and wrap the woman's motives up nice and neat in a pretty little box. She wasn't aware of Deacon until her arm brushed his hard stomach.

A glance up showed a question in his eyes. "Hmm?"

"Would you mind taking Syd a plate? She keeps eyeing you like you're the last doughnut and she can't wait to get you all to herself. I'd rather not show her cannibalistic tendencies here."

It was stupid to feel special because he'd asked her to care for his daughter. He'd trusted her with Sydney over and over again, and yet every time it took her by surprise, filled her with this zing of pleasure. "Sure."

She would've stepped past him, but Deacon moved into her path, the wide spread of his shoulders blocking out everything but him. Here. Alive. Right in front of her. She couldn't resist the urge to lay her palm on his heavy muscles, spread her fingers wide to soak in every bit of his heat, feel the thump-thump-thump of his heartbeat beneath her touch.

Deacon covered her hand with his, pressed it hard against him. Their gazes locked.

I'm glad you're okay. I almost lost my mind when I couldn't see you. I don't know what I'd do without you.

The words ran through her mind, but she managed to keep them off her tongue. Deacon helped when he bent to take her mouth. The room dropped away—her teammates, the commander, Deacon's friends—and it was just the two of them and the heat that flared to life as he delved between her lips.

If this isn't love, I don't think love is what I want. This, Deacon kissing her, holding her, feeling something for her, no matter what it was—this was everything.

This was what she would lose if her father succeeded.

Deacon lifted just enough to allow her to breathe. "If you don't get that dazed look off your face," he murmured against her mouth, "I might have to sweep you away and have you all to myself."

"What?" She licked her lips.

Deacon chuckled. "Maybe that wasn't the best threat I could come up with."

She shook her head absently, arrested by the look in his eyes, the happiness. How could he look like that when life dealt him one blow after another? When his daughter was in danger and a madman threatened his life? He wasn't like her, would never be. Their lives—hers chaotic and terrifying, his stable and supportive—had shaped them. She stared into his amused gaze and knew, suddenly and painfully, that she didn't just want him, she needed him. Needed to understand him and, God help her, learn from him. She'd never wanted to hand that kind of control over, ever, to anyone, but with Deacon? He could teach her so much, about how to live instead of just surviving. How to love. How to be normal, a family.

Her heart clenched. She brought a hand up to rub her breastbone.

Deacon's fingers curled around the hand he still held against him. "You okay?"

She couldn't choke out words, just a nod. Her attempt at a smile was probably as pitiful as it felt, but she tried. Before he could read far more than she was comfortable revealing, she walked toward the food, leaving him behind.

Chapter Twenty-Six

A soft *click* echoed through the room as the bedroom door closed behind him, but Deacon didn't turn to see who it was. He couldn't. All he could think about was what might've happened if he'd taken Sydney with him to see Trapper. He'd pushed the thought away all afternoon, refusing to let the downright terror gain a foothold, but now there was nothing to distract him. If he'd been carrying her in his arms, would Sheppard have warned them sooner? Would she have spared his child?

Just imagining it made him shake. He didn't really care what Sheppard's motives had been; she'd put his daughter in danger. There could be no mercy for that.

Sydney slept deep, unaware, in the small second bedroom attached to his. Standing in the doorway, he lingered on the sight of her, the sweet face so like her mother's, the easy breathing, the small hands wrapped around Katie Kitty. Did Elliot see the same things, catalog Sydney's features the same way as she stopped at his side? She wasn't Sydney's mother—maybe Elliot didn't know how to be a mother—but the look in her eyes when they rested on his child… She cared about Sydney, and she cared about him. There was no other way to interpret that look.

He felt her ease close to him. Elliot didn't speak, even when Deacon reached for her without looking, wrapped his arm around her waist, and pulled her against him. If he could freeze this moment, stay here forever, his family safe and sound, he would. But life didn't work that way.

That's what he needed right now: life. He needed to soak in it, drown in it. He needed to drown himself in Elliot.

A glance assured him the second door in Sydney's room was bolted securely. No windows, no closet, nowhere for anyone to gain entry except the door connecting to his bedroom. The door he quietly closed. A flick of the lock guaranteed Sydney wouldn't walk in unexpectedly, though she'd been so exhausted he didn't think she'd stir if a bomb…

He clenched his eyes shut. *Damn.*

She wouldn't stir.

Elliot watched him turn toward her, blue eyes unreadable in the dark.

"I need you."

His words were gruff, raw, but Elliot didn't flinch, didn't question. She simply walked backward toward the bed, step by quiet step, as she grasped the hem of her T-shirt and pulled it over her head.

Thank fuck.

"I need you too."

There was something in her voice, something he couldn't quite name, but he brushed it aside. This room had a window, the shades angled downward, allowing in the faintest bit of light from the street. It painted stripes across the defined muscles of her arms, her flat stomach, the graceful curve of her shoulders. Where he really wanted to see it was on her breasts. He hadn't spent near enough time with her beautiful breasts. His mouth watered at the thought, and he moved closer, ducked his head, and drew one cloth-covered tip between his lips.

The faintest cry escaped Elliot. She arched into him, her arms crossing over the back of his head, her fingers digging deep into his hair to force him closer, force him to take more. He opened wide, laving and sucking and moaning around her flesh, but it wasn't enough. He needed skin. He needed nothing between them but air, and that only long enough for him to erase it.

Elliot seemed to need the same thing, because she reached behind her and unsnapped her bra. Deacon jerked the offending material away, but he didn't go back to feasting. Instead he knelt at her feet, bringing his face in line with her nipples, and looked his fill. Breathed her in. Imprinted this moment in his brain to carry with him forever.

When his breath washed over a hardened tip, Elliot moaned his name.

"Strip for me, Ell."

He caught the hint of uncertainty as she hesitated, but her nipples peaked even harder. She began to undress—belt, boots, pants, socks. The slide of her silky underwear down her slender legs had him swallowing hard. He stood.

"On the bed."

"Deacon."

Her voice was no more than a breath, but she was climbing onto the bed, gracing him with an up-close view of her perfect ass and the pretty pink slit beneath. The ache of need in his body coalesced in his groin, lengthening his cock, tingling in his balls. God, he needed her.

Elliot turned to lie on her back, her shaggy hair almost as white as the pillowcase it rested on. He cupped his erection, squeezing down. "You have no idea how beautiful you are."

He swore he caught sight of a flush creeping over her pale cheeks. "I want to look at you too."

He reached for the bottom of his T-shirt. "Open your legs for me, Ell. Let me see all of you."

The uncertainty was clear this time. Elliot had so little experience, and what he was asking her to do took a measure of confidence she probably didn't feel in the bedroom. But he let the heat and hunger of his gaze reassure her. Slowly her legs eased outward, matching the rise of his shirt inch for inch, but Elliot was no coward; she didn't stop there. Her hands framed her breasts, presenting them, flicking her nipples to keep them hard. For him. The sight took his breath away, but it was the pinch of a jutting nub that broke his control. He shucked the rest of his clothes and joined her on the bed in seconds.

He lay on his side and pulled Elliot to him, his chest against her smooth belly, his stomach against her mound, his mouth at the perfect height to draw the breast he hadn't tasted yet inside. He licked across the pebbly areole, loving the texture of her need, feeling the hard nipple reach for him. Elliot begged him with her body, arching into his mouth, and clamped down, sucked hard, savoring his treat, refusing to give it up. He devoured her; there was no other way to describe it. Every pull, every rough abrading of his tongue on the tip of her nipple was delicious, satisfying something inside him he couldn't put a name to but had no desire to deny. He only wanted more.

As he sucked, Elliot parted her legs, one moving to rest at his hip. Opening herself to him. Giving herself. The strong scent of her call filled his nose, and suddenly he needed her climax more than he needed his next breath. With two sure fingers he parted her shyly closed lips and slipped through the wetness to fill her to the hilt.

"Deacon." His name was strangled, a mix of agonizing pleasure and the need to stay quiet—perfect. He pulled his fingers back and shoved them in again, grinding his palm against the hard nub of her clit. This time she choked on the first syllable of his name. The third time there was no sound, only the hard clasp of her body on his invading fingers as she tripped over that last hurdle and tumbled into pleasure.

Deacon sucked and nibbled and gloried in her spasms—and knew his world to be as perfect as it could be in this moment.

Elliot didn't stir for long minutes, nor did she protest his attentions. He switched breasts, leading her from softened satisfaction to the firming of renewed need, and she clutched his head closer. When he withdrew his fingers and began to trace that most feminine part of her—the creamy lips, the now shyly hidden nub, the open slit waiting to be filled—she tipped her knee out, giving him all the access he wanted. And oh, did he want.

He used his weight to push her onto her back.

Elliot's fingers tangled in his hair, but he ignored the pain as he moved down her body, his intent obvious. She gave a single questioning, "Deacon?" before subsiding. His Elliot, so strong and tough on her feet, but willing and pliant in his bed. He showed his pleasure with a long lick from the bottom of her opening to the top.

Another choking sound. He savored her taste on his tongue, savored the privilege of Elliot's surrender, but there was a tinge of heartache too. Each new taste of pleasure seemed to startle her, unknown and unfamiliar, underlining what she'd denied herself all this time. But no more. He licked her again, set up a rhythm, and brought her to release once more with only his tongue and lips and breath.

And love. Too fast or not fast enough, dangerous or not, he was in love with the woman beneath him. He remembered what it felt like, recognized what was in his soul—the feeling was the same even if the woman and the circumstances were different. He knew his heart, and his heart wanted Elliot. Needed her. Needed to be deeper than he was right now.

He waited until she was once again breathing hard, her fingernails digging mindlessly into his skin as she lost herself in the pleasure he was giving her, and then he moved up her body and drove himself deep in a single move. His kiss smothered the cry rising to her lips. He could feel the tension in her body, the conflict of pleasure and pain warring inside her, and then all of her softened beneath him—her mouth opened, her breasts cushioned him, her muscles melded with his, and inside...oh, inside, she melted around him until he couldn't tell where he ended and she began.

Slender, strong legs lifted to grip his waist. Strong arms encircled his ribs, eager fingers gripping the thick muscles lining his spine. The cuts on his back protested with a zing of pain, but they didn't matter because Elliot surrounded him in every way possible.

When he drew back slowly, then pushed inside again, her chin tilted up, exposing the quivering muscles of her throat. He ducked to nibble the sensitive skin along the side.

"Deacon, please. Please. I need… I… Please!"

He couldn't tell if she was begging for mercy or begging him to move. They were the same thing in the end. Needing to surround her as she did him, needing her closer than he'd ever held her before, he forced one arm beneath her hips and one beneath her head to brace her exactly where he wanted her, then drew his knees up to start a heavy rhythm of advance and withdrawal that neither could deny and certainly couldn't stop. Didn't want to. Elliot curled into him, the huff of her breath filling his ears every time he hilted. Then there it was, the rush of warmth around his cock that signaled her rise to orgasm. The feeling freed the animal instinct inside him, taking her hard and rough and exulting in his woman's equally wild response. When she dug her heels into his thighs and forced her pelvis against his, seeking that final push over, he gave it freely and joined her on the downward slide.

"Elliot, God." He shuddered for a long time in her arms, unable to break away from the feeling of complete peace she'd given him in the middle of this insane day. He would stay here forever if he could, inside her, her body keeping the world at bay. But already he could feel sleep swamping him, stealing him away, and he clutched her harder to try and stop it. "God, I love you."

His brain shut down and he drifted off, but somewhere in the transition, faint and far away, he swore he heard the sound of tears.

Chapter Twenty-Seven

Deacon's weight went heavy on top of her, the day and the emotion finally catching up with him, it seemed. Or maybe it was just that he finally felt safe enough—and felt Sydney was safe enough—to relax. Either way, Elliot savored the struggle to breathe and the overwhelming peace that settled deep inside her. She'd never known real peace, not till Deacon and Sydney came into her life.

And in the next few hours, she would probably lose any chance at keeping it.

When Deacon groaned and rolled off her, onto his side, she braced herself. Sliding from the bed was harder than she'd thought it would be, the need to stay tugging her back even as she pulled her clothes on. But the night was passing, and she had a lot to do before dawn woke them all.

The outside room was dimly lit, King reading in one corner, Trapper and Mark playing poker in another. Fionn and T.C. would be outside the suite door, she knew. With the barest nod she crossed to the bathroom and locked herself in for a quick cleanup. Her duffel waited under the sink, and she grabbed fresh underwear and socks. Dressed, hair pulled back from her face, she returned to the living room to put on her boots.

"Where are you going?" King asked.

"Commissary." She'd scouted earlier and knew the store was open 24-7. "I need supplies."

King seemed ready to argue, but when she lifted her brows and waved a hand toward her crotch, his mouth clamped shut. One thing about King being a loner like her: he'd never been truly comfortable with anything related to her biology. At the first indication that her period had come, Dain would give her an understanding smile and immediately offer to go to the commissary for her. Saint, with the overabundance of women in his family, would fearlessly make a joke about that being what was wrong with her mood. Not King. He clammed up and even blushed—she could see it in the low light of the room.

She was lying, of course. But this was the easiest way to get out without suspicion. Using her team's idiosyncrasies against them. Yes, she was a bitch, and yes, they'd probably never forgive her, but it was far past time that this was finished. No one else would be hurt on her watch.

Outside the door, Fionn immediately straightened away from the wall. "And what would you be needing? Want me to call down for something?" His finger went to his earbud.

"Tampons?"

Fionn choked. T.C. cracked up—quietly, of course; it was one a.m., after all.

"Yeah, I didn't think so." She waved a hand over her shoulder as she walked down the hall. "I'll be right back."

She wasn't going to the commissary—she was going to the infirmary. GFS had outfitted them with general badges that allowed entry and exit, providing Elliot with a quick trip across the compound to the temporary medical wing that had been set up this afternoon. Once inside, she simply asked the nurse to let her sit with Sheppard. The woman confirmed via computer that Elliot was associated with the case, searched her, and allowed her into the room. The door had barely slid closed before Elliot was shaking Sheppard's shoulder.

"Lyse? Lyse!"

The woman looked fragile, as if she would fall apart at the slightest word. If she hadn't read it in Sheppard's file herself, Elliot would have a hard time believing they were the same age. But weak or not, the girl's thin eyelids fluttered open at Elliot's insistence. After several long blinks, recognition flared in her eyes, determination settling in the tired lines of her face. "Elliot Smith."

"Lyse." She squatted until her face was level with Sheppard's. "You made it."

A slight shake of her head. "That's not necessarily a good thing." Her chin trembled. "What's important is, did everyone else make it?"

"They did."

"And…" Sheppard licked her cracked lips. "Fionn?"

"Is that why you did this?"

Tears leaked as Sheppard's eyes closed. "Fionn was attacked. I never believed… I couldn't figure out how they got to him, couldn't keep him safe. He's on Mansa's target list, and Mansa never stops." She choked on a sob. "I don't know how they found out, I really don't. But I got a message saying if…if I helped… They would spare Fionn."

The girl was in love with Fionn. How had she not seen it sooner? Sheppard hadn't asked about Deacon, though both men had been with her in the hallway, and her eyes— This wasn't mere concern for a colleague. She'd traded Trapper's lives and the lives of anyone else caught in the blast...to save the man she loved.

"I couldn't do it," Sheppard whispered. "I couldn't hurt anyone. I thought..."

"So you got everyone away."

"Why go through with it, right?" Sheppard shook her head. "But I couldn't figure out how to get back out once I was in. Maybe I should just tell them to stop treating me, walk out the gates, and let Mansa take care of my punishment. That would make everyone safe."

"No, it wouldn't. Not with Mansa."

Sheppard's stare was as hopeless as they came. Sympathy tugged at Elliot, but she couldn't indulge it; she needed to get her intel and go.

"Lyse, Fionn is all right, but he won't be for long. Where is he?"

A slight frown through her tears. "Fionn?"

"No, Mansa. I know you've figured it out." Sheppard wasn't one of those geniuses with no common sense; she'd had to know this could all backfire. She'd expected to die, had been willing to do it if it meant the people around her were safe. The only way to ensure that it wasn't all for nothing was to dig up the dirt on her opponent, create a weapon that could be used after the fact. "Now tell me."

"I don't know..."

"You do; I know you do. And you're going to tell me, because Fionn? He's not going to be okay, and neither is Trapper or Deacon or Sydney or *you* if you don't help me kill that bastard; you understand me?"

Sheppard's eyes went wide, startled. "You plan to kill Mansa?"

"I'm the only one that can get close enough—and before you ask, yes, I'm perfectly capable. I've trained my whole life for this." Jack Quinn had been right about that.

Sheppard gave her a wary nod.

"Tell me where he is so I can finish this once and for all."

The uncertainty faded. "USB. My desk, *Star Wars* bobblehead."

A touch of amusement sparked in Elliot's chest—where else would the little tech nerd hide something important?

And then the spark faded. "Got it." She turned to leave, but a surprisingly strong grip on her wrist pulled her back. "What?"

Sheppard's desperation shone from eyes sunken with pain and fatigue and defeat. "Make sure he's safe. Do what I couldn't. Please?"

Elliot felt the hollow pit inside her, the one that had appeared the moment she'd realized she had to lie to Deacon one last time—and that the betrayal would kill anything he still felt for her. If Sheppard felt anything like she did… "I will. Fionn will be protected, I promise."

She hurried out before the woman's emotions could force her own any closer to the surface.

Sheppard's office location had been in her personnel file. Elliot was in and out in under five minutes, the thumb drive securely in her pocket. The SUV was parked where they'd left it that morning in front of the main building. After checking to be certain the tactical supply chest was still in the back and fully stocked, she backed out and drove toward the gate.

The guard at the post shone a light in her eyes. "Ma'am?"

She bit off the curse that jumped to her lips. "Sir."

The man had to be twice her age—if the gray in his beard didn't prove it, the condescending look did. He didn't appear to catch the sarcasm in her response, unfortunately. "Where are you going?"

"To the store to get tampons." Deliberate emphasis on that last word. "The commissary was out, and I can't wait."

Red tinged the rough skin of his cheekbones. He cleared his throat. "I see. Badge?"

She handed it over. The man wouldn't meet her eyes on the return pass, simply gave a nod in her general vicinity and opened the gate.

Shaking her head at the squeamishness of the males of the species, Elliot hit the gas. Time was wasting, and her father awaited. After pulling onto the blacktop, she floored it.

If Mansa had a home base, it would be somewhere near his most important target: Deacon. Elliot took the interstate toward Deacon's property but exited at the first rest stop, pulled the SUV between two 18-wheelers, then raided the chest in the back. The laptop inside powered up quickly, and Elliot accessed the USB even quicker. Sheppard had been smart, hacking a back door into what Elliot figured was probably that prick Kivuli's cell phone to access location services. Mansa wasn't used to hiding his whereabouts too hard—everyone knew where he lived. Elliot blessed the girl's ingenuity as she powered down the laptop as fast as possible. She was on the move mere minutes after stopping.

The darkest part of the night had hit by the time she reached Mansa's current location, a lodge deep in the hills about half an hour north of Deacon's house. She took the SUV off-road, through the woods and down into a valley between two hills. After unscrewing the dome light, she climbed into the back and suited up. Essentials only: gun in her equipment belt, extra clip, phone. She left the cell powered up, ringer off—GFS needed a way to pinpoint her exact location if Mansa moved them. The vehicle had its own tracker, but there was no guarantee Elliot would be on the property by the time Deacon's team found it.

What else? Two knives, one in her boot, one strapped to the inside of her thigh. The equipment on her belt would be taken immediately, so they were mostly for show, but the knives…those she might just get a chance to use.

The dim moon helped hide her as she made her way toward the lodge, the details of her plan running through her head. Well, really only one detail: *get caught.* The men working for Mansa, with the exception of Kivuli, were of no importance and would likely scatter when their master got his head bashed in. If she could take one or two out, it might help Deacon when he arrived, but the real objective was to get in the room with her father and Kivuli. That was the part of the battle that mattered, the part she would reserve her strength for.

The building sat atop the tallest hill in the area, strategically placed to give Mansa and his men the advantage. More than likely they would be looking for obvious targets. Elliot approached low and slow, angling toward a back corner of the house. Two guards paced the back balcony, two the front, and she counted at least six more walking the perimeter. None of the men were Kivuli. When Elliot reached the tree line, she crouched amid a thick patch of bare elderberry bushes and waited, breath easy, eyes vigilant.

The first guard passed within two minutes. She counted down the time, another three minutes before guard number two walked by, smoking a cigarette. She marked the scent and restarted her count. Three-minute intervals brought each guard back around. The casualness of their movements, the lack of glances out into the woods, told her they'd reached the part of the night where boredom made them lazy. When one decided his bladder needed emptying just as he came even with her, she smothered a grin and shifted silently into a position that allowed for easier movement.

The guard walked a few feet into the woods to face an old, thick oak. A zipper whizzed down. Rustling cloth. A steady stream began, accompanied by a sigh of relief. Elliot approached from the back.

Tall bastard. She didn't want to kill him—these men weren't from Africa, probably hired mercenaries, but she had no idea of their pasts. Still, she needed to take them out. Since she couldn't reach the guy's neck, she waited till he was in midstream, then hit the back of both knees with a solid roundhouse.

The man stumbled, balance lost. His head hit the tree. Not enough to knock him out—Elliot did that with a choke hold. After he was unconscious, she tied his wrists with zip ties and left him lying in his own urine.

Her second chance came with the cigarette-smoking guard. As he rounded the corner, she saw a faint orange light arc from his hand toward the grass. He ground the butt out with his toe, already retrieving his half-empty pack from a back pocket. She was in front of him before his lighter flared, killing his night vision. Her kick to the groin bent him over, evoking a rough gagging sound that cut off when her fist connected with the point just behind his ear.

Two down.

Unfortunately the bastard was too heavy to move quietly to the woods, so she zip tied him, then rolled him against the side of the house, buying herself a few minutes, hopefully. She started the countdown as she searched him, looking for keys. Front right pocket. She was approaching the shadows of the back patio when the next guard appeared.

"Hey!"

Game up.

She sprinted for the woods, just to make it look good. Thick arms yanked her off the ground before she took four steps. This one was fast. And strong, if the protesting in her ribs was anything to go by. Elliot fought him, but he carried her easily to the patio. Bastard wasn't even breathing hard when his partner arrived.

"Where's Peters and Cragen?" the new arrival asked.

Her guard dropped her on the concrete. Before she could scoot away, his booted foot landed on her back, forcing her prone. She let a few choice words loose.

More arrivals, more discussion. Elliot rolled her eyes and rested, waiting, knowing the moment would come. And then it did: Kivuli walked from the house to the patio, white teeth and eyes gleaming against his midnight skin. Tall and lean, there was still no doubt that the man was lethal.

Every guard around her went rigid.

Kivuli ignored them, coming to stand directly in her view. "So, you've arrived."

"Surprise!"

A spark of amusement actually lit in the enforcer's scary eyes. "No, but you are welcome. We've been waiting." He nodded to the guard whose boot still rested on her back. "Bring her."

Chapter Twenty-Eight

The hard fingers biting into his shoulder shook him wake. On instinct he gripped the palm, twisting it backward, using the leverage to jerk the attacker onto the bed beside him and scramble to drop a knee on their chest. Only then did he come awake enough to realize it wasn't an attacker beneath him, but Fionn.

"Be gettin' your hairy-ass balls outta my face, would ya?" Fionn growled.

Deacon released him in favor of finding his underwear. "What's going on?" Sydney's door was still closed, locked, but otherwise the room was empty. "Where's Elliot?"

"That's the problem."

He paused halfway to the floor, reaching for his fatigues. "What?"

Fionn scrubbed a hand across his forehead. "Come in the living room."

Fuck. What now?

He dressed quickly. Before leaving his room, he unlocked Sydney's door so she could exit if she needed him. He hadn't intended to leave it locked, but after he and Elliot...well, he'd passed out harder than he'd intended. The worry was wearing him down, obviously—unacceptable on an op, but it wasn't going away until his daughter's safety was guaranteed.

Careful to be quiet, he eased her door open, needing to see her, to remind himself that, no matter what shit was hitting the fan, his daughter was secure. Sydney lay curled around Katie Kitty, the blanket twisted around her body, a frown pulling at her mouth. As he walked closer, he could see the frantic movements of her eyes beneath the closed lids: a dream. Good or bad? He did his best to keep her waking hours calm, but the chaos of the past few days was enough to disturb the calmest adult, much less four-year-old. Was it finding an outlet in her dreams?

Helplessness was a twist in his gut that he was becoming very familiar with lately. He was a warrior, not a mother. How did he soothe his child and fight off her tormenters at the same time?

In the end all he knew to do was lay his hand on her head, hoping against hope that the warmth and reassurance of his presence would soothe her. When she quieted beneath his touch, his stomach unknotted a little, but still he left her door cracked open so he could hear her if she called out.

And then he turned to face whatever awaited him in the living room.

The three-man team he'd left when he went to bed was doubled when Deacon exited the bedroom and cracked the door behind him. The increase in numbers made his heart jump into his throat. "What happened?"

"Elliot's gone."

It took a moment for the meaning of the words to register. His immediate reaction was denial—no, she wouldn't do this to him, not again. Something must've happened. "Where? We need to find her."

"I don't think she wants to be found," Dain said as he entered through the main door. Alvarez followed him inside.

The weary look on Dain's face threatened to tear through Deacon's disbelief, but he clung stubbornly. He'd made love to Elliot just a couple of hours ago, held her in his arms, connected to her on a level that he'd only ever shared with Jules. She wouldn't walk out without telling him where she was going—and besides, there was nowhere for her to go; they didn't have Mansa's location.

"She wouldn't leave without—"

"Deacon." The guttural tone of Dain's voice hit harder than a shout. "You and Fionn almost died yesterday. Your daughter could've died if she'd been with you. Elliot cares...a lot, for you and your daughter. I'm not even sure why I'm surprised."

King grunted an agreement.

Deacon opened his mouth—to argue or simply scream, he wasn't sure—but Dain forestalled either reaction. "If Elliot thought what she was doing would keep you both safe, she sure as hell would walk out that gate and never think twice about it. And she wouldn't tell you because she wouldn't want you following her and putting yourself in jeopardy."

"That's not her fucking choice to make!"

Dain scoffed. "And we both know how much that matters to her."

"You— Damn it, Dain!" He channeled his fury, his frustration into a hard growl, forced himself to turn away, pace it off instead of strangling the man in front of him. Dain was right, Deacon knew it even if he didn't want to, and taking this out on him wouldn't do them a fucking bit of good.

Dain gave him a moment, long enough that Deacon could gather the tattered remnants of his control. Still pacing, he forcibly turned his mind to tactical mode. Maybe if he could lock away the emotion, the memories, the fear…that was the only way he'd get through this. Focus on the details, the op. What had happened to the soldier who'd taken Andre Diako out with a single steady shot?

He fell in love, dumb-ass.

"How do you know she's left instead of just going out for a run?"

It was King who answered. "She told me she was going down to the commissary. When twenty minutes passed and no Elliot, I started making calls. She left through the front gate almost half an hour ago."

"Where would she be going?" Deacon argued. "We don't know where Mansa is."

Alvarez spoke up for the first time. "We do now." Deacon noted absently that the man still wore his suit, still unrumpled, tie still knotted, hair perfect. Did he never sleep? "Not long after Smith left, I received a call from medical. Sheppard became agitated after Smith went to her room. Started kicking up a fuss, demanding to speak to someone associated with the case, fighting off the staff when they tried to sedate her to calm her down. They called me." His grin was more shark than not. "Seems our intrepid little techie had more than one secret. She gave Smith the location."

Fionn cursed under his breath. "Why didn't Sheppard give it to us?"

Alvarez shrugged. "I don't know, but I can guarantee you I will, sooner than later."

Because they'd force her. Deacon wanted to be okay with that, yet the thought of the woman they all referred to as *girl* being tortured twisted him up inside. A common state for him lately, it seemed.

The thought brought a grim smile to his face. He wanted to storm after Elliot and put her over his knee, make sure that every step she took for days would remind her not to run off half-cocked with no backup. He wanted even more to knot his fists in her hair and fuck her until the desperate fear in his gut finally dissolved. The first wasn't happening, and the latter would have to wait—he had an op to prep. "Do we know the location?"

The commander started talking back doors and algorithms and Deacon stopped listening. The answer was no. Except…

He dug in his pants pocket—empty. "Did she take the SUV?" It made the most sense. They had brought one of GFS's vehicles and one of JCL's with them, but Deacon had been carrying the GFS keys.

Alvarez brought his phone to his ear.

She stole the keys while you were sleeping. After you had sex. After you told her you loved her.

He remembered drifting off and thinking he heard tears, and the truth hit him: Elliot had been planning this then. She'd been planning, and hurting, and he'd fallen asleep. His woman had needed him, and he'd fallen asleep.

Damn it.

"What the hell could she be thinking?" Fionn asked. "Mansa isn't alone. She cannot be believing she can take them all on her own."

Deacon looked at his best friend, watched him rub a hand over the bandage covering the wound on the back of his head. Beside him was Dain, the man who'd saved Elliot before she'd even realized she needed saving. Then Saint, his crucifix shining in the dim light. King, anger and frustration and fear mixing in his expression. And Trapper, whose scars and pain could not be missed. "She's not trying to take them all," he said, the pieces coming together in his mind. "She's only going for Mansa. He wants her alive. It's a given that she can get in the same room with him." The rightness of the plan settled in him, right alongside the gut-wrenching fear. His woman, on her own, with a madman.

His woman. Maybe spanking her ass wasn't totally out of the question.

He met Dain's troubled gaze. "She just might succeed."

Dain nodded. Deacon saw his throat work as he swallowed hard.

"She has our SUV," Alvarez finally confirmed.

"Good. Get her tracked, Commander." He didn't care if Alvarez was the boss or not; on this op, Deacon was in charge. "And get me a small army." His heart wanted to focus on Elliot, but he had to step back and look at the bigger picture: this was the opportunity they had been waiting for, the possibility of taking the fight to Mansa instead of waiting it out. Their scout was already in; now they needed to save her ass and take the target.

"Already on it," Alvarez said. "You'll know logistics as soon as I do."

"Suit up," Dain said. His men went to work.

Fionn and Trapper looked to Deacon.

"Get prepped."

They didn't blink, just moved to get ready.

Deacon had turned to grab his weapons when a wail rose up from the bedroom. *Sydney.*

She was sitting up in her bed, rocking, Katie Kitty still clutched in her arms. Her eyes were unseeing, but hysterical cries poured from her lips. Deacon's heart nearly stopped at the sight of her. "Little Bit, it's okay. Daddy's here."

His voice seemed to break whatever hold her terror had on her. Frantically she reached for him, sobbing his name. Deacon swept her trembling body into his arms to hold her close. Pet her. Comfort her. He closed his eyes tight.

God almighty, he didn't know what to do. He needed to be out there, finding Elliot, helping her, killing Mansa and Kivuli and anyone who stood between him and them with his bare hands—and he needed to be here, holding his little girl, keeping her safe, taking away her nightmares. But one of those nightmares had Elliot too. How could he protect them both? How could he make this right for all of them?

His struggle must've been obvious, because the next thing he knew, Dain's hand squeezed down on his shoulder. "You don't have to do all this alone, you know."

But he felt like he did. He'd felt like that since Jules took her last breath and left them behind, he and their daughter, to face this world alone. He'd been responsible for Andre's death, and he'd needed to fix the consequences. But he couldn't, not by himself. He needed help.

He'd think about how much that sucked ass later.

"Can you run point, get us ready?" he asked Dain.

The man was already walking toward the door. "I'll try not to feel insulted that you had to even wonder that, much less ask."

At least his smile this time was genuine, if small. He listened to the sounds of men preparing for battle outside his door while inside, his baby girl curled in his arms and slowly calmed, her body no longer rigid, her tears dying away. When shivers racked her, he tugged up the blanket, cocooning her in warmth, and rocked her quietly. By the time Dain returned, she'd drifted back to sleep.

"We're ready to move."

Deacon gave him a nod and stood. After laying Sydney carefully on the bed and covering her once more, he followed Dain into the main bedroom. "Dain."

The older man turned, one brow lifted.

"You're staying here."

"No, I—"

"You're staying here," Deacon repeated. "I'm not arguing with you about it. Sydney feels safe with you. We don't know what we're walking into, and I'm not willing to risk the only man on your team with a child on an uncertain mission. We'll have enough men to make your ass redundant."

Thunder gathered in Dain's expression. "You have a child too."

"I know." And it was tearing him apart to leave her behind, but Dain would take care of her as if she were his own. Deacon had spent a lot of years saying good-bye to his wife so he could do his duty, both in the military and with GFS, and now was no different. Besides... "I have to go to Elliot, Dain. I…"

"You love her."

Surprise jolted up Deacon's spine. He'd known it, had said it aloud to Elliot just a few hours ago, but how had Dain…?

274

Dain arched a brow in his direction. "You're not going to try and deny it, are you?"

Deacon squirmed, unable to get past the feeling that he was a teenage boy facing some girl's father and being asked his intentions. "No."

The approval in Dain's expression made the teen-boy feeling even stronger. "Good. She needs you. Elliot...she loves as fiercely as she fights, Deacon. If she chooses to let you in? You couldn't ask for a better gift. And you couldn't ask for anyone better to help you raise that little girl."

He just had to make sure Elliot was around to do that, didn't he?

"Mansa will know their location is blown," Deacon said. "The element of surprise is gone."

Dain's shrug said maybe, maybe not. "You don't need surprise."

"We need everything we can use to our advantage."

"That's true of every fight, but we take our advantages where we can find them. Or make them." He clapped Deacon on the shoulder, urging him toward the living room. "That's what Elliot is doing right now. Don't let it be a waste of effort."

Chapter Twenty-Nine

Kivuli divested her of the knife in her boot and the one on her thigh—hadn't that been fun—but he didn't tie her up before leading her inside. She'd read the man's file, faced off with him in the alley, but being this close, feeling the menace that practically radiated off him, made her mouth go dry. She endeavored not to show it as he walked her ahead of him through the back patio doors, the chilled air kissing her skin where her pants leg had been torn open.

The lodge was a warren of rooms and passageways. The room Kivuli led her into was three stories high, open, lined with windows looking out onto the valley, like a sacrilegious church sanctuary in the middle of the Georgia woods. Especially with the men lining the walls, maybe twice the contingent she'd run into outside. And there, on a raised hearth in front of a massive fireplace, sat the devil himself, Martin Diako.

For a moment a sense of unreality made Elliot dizzy. All these years, all the things she'd imagined about this man, this monster, and here he was, in the flesh. Just a man. He was reclined on a tall, wide chair that could be called a throne without too far a stretch. His Afrikaner heritage showed—light brown hair swept back from a high forehead, and equally light brown eyes stared down at her, set in paler skin than she'd imagined. Not the gray of a security still, but the tan of a man who spent his time on indoor pleasures instead of out in the harsh African climate. No wonder he'd gambled that her mother's unusual coloring would pass to her daughter.

He'd been right too.

Mansa had his long legs extended, utterly relaxed, smoking a cigar while wearing clothes of the finest silk and wool she'd ever seen—all he needed was a scepter and crown and he'd be set. A woman knelt to one side of his feet, a thin white shift barely covering her, a collar around her throat attached to a chain Mansa held in his fist.

The sight sent bile up the back of Elliot's throat.

"Fuck me." She shook her head. "I knew you were an egomaniac, but really, did you have to take 'pirate king' quite so literally?"

The flaring of Mansa's nostrils was his only reaction, but it gave her a distinct kick of pleasure. She doubted anyone defied him, ever, although she had to wonder about Kivuli—he didn't seem the type to follow blindly. But she might as well prove right off she wasn't like anyone else; she'd never cower before this man, ever. She'd die first.

Which is totally possible, Ell.

She shrugged off her common sense and gave Mansa a smirk. The way he examined her, eyes lingering on the bare skin of her thigh, the roundness of her breasts, made that feeling of being dirty, the feeling Deacon had done his best to exorcise, surge up.

"Welcome, Daughter."

"I am not your daughter."

"No, you will always be number 57." The words sent a jolt through her, one she couldn't hide, and satisfaction sparked in his narrowed gaze. "I remembered. The minute I saw you, that hair... Nora was my favorite cherry."

Elliot blinked, refusing to give him the satisfaction of a reaction again. Her mother was one of the reasons she was here, and the reminder only served to strengthen her, but Mansa wouldn't get that. He saw her as a number, a commodity, something to own and use and torture, like a helpless animal. He didn't see her as a person—and that would be his downfall. If there was one thing Deacon had taught her, it was that emotion could make you stronger, could push you farther than any detached resolve to win, any sense of duty. Without emotion, she'd be just like Kivuli. That wasn't how she wanted to live, not anymore. "Can we get this over with?"

Mansa shifted, his free hand settling on the head of the slave at his side. The way he stroked her hair, as if he gave a shit about the poor woman, made Elliot's skin crawl. "Kivuli tells me you are a true warrior, a gifted fighter. I find myself intrigued by his claims, wanting to see them for myself."

You'll see it—up close, I promise. Her heartbeat ticked up. "You want to see me fight?"

"*Ja.* I want to see you fight Kivuli."

Fuck. Not good. She looked at the enigmatic bastard standing next to her. "He must not value you much if he's that eager to lose you."

Kivuli didn't react, not even the flutter of an eyelash. Mansa, however, laughed. "You think you are that good? Kivuli is my strongest warrior, but perhaps you can distract him with your...feminine wiles. Like your mother did me." He smiled down at her, but those eyes—they weren't amused. More like hungry.

"And perhaps, if you win as you say you will, I could be convinced to use you for more than just breeding."

There was a perverse eagerness in his words. She made sure her smile matched it. "You don't want to use me for breeding."

"Oh?" An arched brow. "Why not?"

Elliot stared deep into Mansa's eyes, her father's eyes. "Because if you do, you'll never breed again. I'll guarantee it."

Kivuli shifted next to her, the movement grasping her attention. When she turned to look, she could see the tiniest hint of amusement in his expression. "She is indeed your daughter," he told Mansa.

Mansa laughed, full and hearty. "She is, indeed." And then the laughter stopped. "Proceed."

Kivuli gave Mansa a slight bow, then backed away from the throne. Elliot found herself wishing she hadn't been through a night in the ring and the confrontation with Kivuli's men in the past two days—her body felt like shit already, and she had no doubt Kivuli would make her hurt much worse. Mansa hadn't spelled out any limits, but he didn't want her dead; that, at least, was to her advantage.

And looking into the inscrutable face of her opponent, she knew she'd need every advantage she could get.

Stuffing away the emotions rioting in her head, she let her body settle naturally into a fighting stance, her hands coming up. She couldn't stop her heart from beating too damn hard against her aching ribs, but she could breathe through it. Kivuli's gaze met hers, and he stared for the longest moment, not a flicker of emotion or intent in his eyes.

And then he attacked—or, rather, flew. One minute he was on the ground; the next he was in the air, his long leg sweeping toward her face. Elliot ducked, feeling the rush of air as his shin passed over her head. She followed with a hard elbow into the back of his knee, the impact increasing his momentum and toppling him toward the ground. He avoided her kick to the face and used a quick grab to pull her leg out from under her.

That wasn't the last time she hit the ground either.

She had no idea how long they fought, the minutes blurring into the next kick or the next stab of pain in her ribs or the next breath of air knocked out of her lungs. The men around them circled closer, catcalling, egging them on, filling the air with shouts and bets and curses when they didn't move out of the way fast enough. A few even attempted to grope her as she passed. That stopped the first time she broke a guard's fingers. Kivuli actually grinned.

Then he tried to kick her teeth out. A girl just couldn't get a break.

"I doubt Mansa wants me damaged," she reminded him, a bit too breathlessly for her liking.

"He will do far worse damage, warrior."

Warrior? Was she supposed to feel flattered by the…what could she even call it? Professional approbation? *Yes, you're a great fighter, but my boss is a practiced rapist, so don't count on winning.* Really? Where did men like them come up with this shit?

She thanked him with a fast whip around his back and a drive-by back fist to the base of his skull. Kivuli jerked forward just enough to minimize the impact.

Bastard.

The enforcer had seen her fight, knew she was fast and able to duck under blows and around kicks, but he didn't know the endurance she'd forced her body to learn for years. Elliot allowed herself to lag, let him think her strength was waning—and it was, damn it, but not as much as she let on. Just how far would they take it before her father called a halt?

How far could she take it?

When she barely managed to avoid a kick to the head, she knew she was slipping too far. Time to end this.

Kivuli inched closer, seeming to sense a change in her strategy. A flurry of punches and kicks assured him of her aggression, but her true objective was the leg sweep she managed to sneak in. Kivuli grabbed her shirt before he fell, and she let him take her down with him. Even let him flip her so he could claim the upper position.

She'd spent so much time grappling with her teammates that Kivuli's leanly muscled body felt weirdly light atop her. She managed to draw one knee to her chest before he closed the distance, and planted her heel in the crease of his hip. A hard shove of her foot forced him onto his opposite hand, his body off balance. That's when she went for the knife at his belt.

Kivuli twisted his hip out of her reach. Still grasping, her fingers settled around a pouch attached to his belt. Elliot clamped down instinctively on the leather bag.

"No!"

But it was too late for him to stop her—the strings broke and the pouch came free in her hand.

When Kivuli lunged for the bag, a panicked look in his eyes, she used his momentum to turn him completely over onto his back. Her knees clamped at his hips brought her with him.

His hard buck up almost displaced her, but that wasn't his objective: he was frantic for the bag she held. Elliot had no more than a moment to wonder what the hell was so valuable before her free hand landed on his throat and she used the power of her feet, planted on either side of his body, to shove him backward.

Kivuli's head hit the floor, his eyes still trained on the bag.

Elliot's weight landed on his throat. Cartilage disintegrated beneath her palm.

As he choked, Kivuli gripped her hand, turned it, and dumped the contents of the pouch through the small hole in the top. White dust fell onto his face.

She didn't know what it was—some kind of drug, maybe?—but the stuff had an immediate effect. Kivuli's eyes rolled back in his head, his body jerking with convulsions. Elliot threw herself to the side, desperate to get away from whatever could cause such a reaction. The room fell silent at the sight, only the sound of slowly dwindling wheezes filling the vast space.

Kivuli, struggling for every last breath he could get. Elliot held her own, counting the seconds until the final rasp left his lips.

The rattle of a chain and scraping of boots came from near the throne. Mansa stood, his body quivering with rage. "Bring the bitch to me."

Elliot cringed away from the burly guard who came for her, keeping up appearances, but his grip on her biceps was impossible to resist. He dragged her most of the way across the room as she scrambled to get her feet under her. When he deposited her on the stairs of the dais, in front of her father, she sank to her knees, one arm wrapped around her screaming ribs.

"And that is exactly where you belong, cunt," Mansa taunted. "On your knees."

Elliot kept her head down, refusing to give him what he craved: a response. Instead she focused on breathing, on replaying every one of the coming seconds over and over in her head to be sure she had it right.

"Have you nothing to say to me, Daughter?"

Not in this lifetime, asshole.

Mansa nudged her with the tip of his boot. "Perhaps, now that you've deprived me of my soldier, you will take his place."

A harder nudge threw her off balance. She slapped a hand down to keep herself upright.

"Or perhaps breeding more warriors like you is the best use of my prize." Mansa bent closer. "Are you untried, like your virgin mother was, Number 57? Do not worry; when I am finished with you, you will suck cock like a *haker*."

She didn't know what *haker* was, but she could guess—and she had no intention of sucking anything. She took a deep breath, holding in her response as she tightened her grip on the knife she'd slipped from Kivuli's belt, the knife concealed against her stomach.

"Are you sure you want her that close to anything important? After that fight?" a voice asked from the back of the room.

Shock quivered through Elliot's body. *Damn it, Deacon, why did you come?* He was supposed to be back at the compound, safe with his daughter, not here in a roomful of men armed and ready to kill him.

Mansa straightened above her. "Well. Deacon Walsh. Welcome."

Footsteps traveled toward the dais from behind Elliot. "Fuck you."

Men rushed to take him down—Elliot could hear it, but she didn't turn to see. Her moment would arrive; it had to.

"Stop!" Mansa shouted. "Let him come."

Deacon chuckled. "You're not rolling out the welcome mat, are you, Mansa? 'Cause you've got to know I'm here to kill you."

"Of course I am not." Mansa shifted, and Elliot dared to glance up. A flash of light glanced off the gun in his rising hand. "I simply want a clear shot."

It all happened at once: Mansa's aim. Elliot surging to her feet. Deacon running behind her. The burly guard lunged, but the slave next to the throne was there first, tripping him up. Elliot watched in slow motion as her fist came up, connecting with the underside of Mansa's arm as a shot went off. The blast reverberated in her ear, her heart, but there wasn't time to worry about Deacon because she was tackling the pirate king to the ground, listening to the smack of skull hitting stone. Mansa looked up at her with dazed eyes.

She crouched above him, and something in her soul settled into place, as if this moment had been preordained from her birth. "I finally get it, you know."

A frown pulled at Mansa's lips, and Elliot realized with a shock that his mouth was shaped just like hers. "What do you finally get?"

"You. I get you." Nausea churned in her belly. "You murdered your family, destroyed lives, used people as product...because they were weak."

Pleasure sparked in his dark eyes. How had she not gotten those eyes? How had the darkness in him not been dominant in her genes? "And I am strong," he said. "Only the strongest survive."

"True." Maybe his genes were dominant, just not on the outside. "I guess you passed on one trait after all."

"And what is that, Daughter?"

"I'm definitely not weak."

All the anger she carried, all the pain and terror and grief of the last twenty-four years coalesced in her as she lifted the hand that held Kivuli's knife. She didn't aim for his throat or his chest, though. No, she wanted him to feel it, to hurt, to realize his life was draining from his body before he finally died.

She aimed for his groin.

The strike hit true. Kivuli hunched forward, mouth gaping, his hands automatically covering the wound as she pulled the knife away. Blood poured through his fingers.

She smiled into his incredulous eyes.

"I told you you'd never breed again, didn't I?"

This time she made it a gut strike. Mansa grunted, eyes sliding closed.

Elliot brought her face down until her mouth was at his ear. "That was for my mother, you son of a bitch. I hope you rot in hell."

One more strike, this one merciful: the jugular.

The room behind her was filled with the noise of men fighting, shouting, sounds of pain and anger and fear and triumph. Elliot knelt beside Mansa's throne, watching the life flow from his body, his blood hot and sticky on her hands, and felt a strange void slowly swallow her. The man who'd fathered her was dead. Deacon and Sydney were safe. Her mother had been avenged; all of Mansa's victims had been avenged.

She'd finally accomplished her life's objective. Mission complete. So why did it suddenly feel like it wasn't enough?

Leaning back on her haunches, she stared down at her bloody hands and couldn't hold back the hot tears rushing to her eyes, the whispered words escaping her shattered soul.

"I love you, Mama."

Chapter Thirty

A small stack of paper slapped down on the table next to Elliot's hand. The number of sheets was deceptive—that stack meant a minimum of two hours more work. "Really, Dain?"

Her boss shrugged. "You create the problem; you complete the paperwork."

She'd gotten herself beat to shit, killed two men, and what thanks did she get? Fucking paperwork. "Dickhead."

"You've always been my favorite little headache," Dain countered as he moved toward the other side of the room.

"You didn't have to kill him, you know," Saint said mildly. "That always adds to the paperwork."

The remembered feel of Mansa's blood on her hands, of knowing her mother was finally at peace, filled her mind. "Yeah, I did have to kill him."

A heavy hand landed on her shoulder, making her jump. King gave her a quick squeeze and moved on, but not before she read the understanding in his expression. It was echoed by her other team members when she looked at them, the knowledge settling something inside her that she hadn't realized was a worry until that moment.

They got it. They understood, teasing or not.

She released the breath she'd been holding.

"You still have to do the paperwork," Dain told her, "even if you are one scary woman."

And don't you forget it. "Dain?"

"Yeah?"

She raised a hand and gave him a middle-fingered salute. Laughter came from every corner of the room, at once reassuring and somehow incongruous. The strangeness would pass, she knew. She'd been here before, but hopefully never again.

Her demon was dead. And now all she wanted to do was tie up the loose ends and get the fuck out of here before Deacon showed up again.

Mansa's shot had gone wide, thank God. While the men with him had wreaked havoc on the guards, Deacon had fought his way to the throne, toward Mansa, but it had been too late by then; his enemy was beyond his reach.

He hadn't spoken to her since.

Granted, there hadn't been much opportunity. Between subduing Mansa's hired guards and dealing with the local police, they'd all had their hands full. Elliot's injuries had made it perfectly believable that she'd killed Kivuli and Mansa in self-defense. There'd been hours of questioning, followed by a trip to the hospital. King and Saint had brought her back to GFS for more prodding, more X-rays, and then finally to Dain, but after two hours of sitting in this office she was beginning to think her fears had been right on target: Deacon didn't want her anymore, not after she'd kept the truth from him again.

If only those damn words didn't echo in her mind every time she thought of him. *"God, I love you."*

She squeezed her eyes shut against the pain.

"You okay?"

Dain pulled out a chair and sat. Elliot forced herself to look at him, to not hide what she was feeling like she'd tried to do all her life. She needed him to see the truth.

"Can't I do this back at JCL?"

"Alvarez said they needed us here to tie up loose ends with them."

Right. Sure. "This delay tactic isn't going to work, Dain."

"I have no idea what you're talking about."

His confusion could've fooled anyone else, but not Elliot. She knew him too well. Leaning in close, she dropped her voice until only the two of them could hear her words. "Look...I hurt all over. I've faced about as many of my mistakes as I can tonight. I can't take much more; I need to get the fuck out of here."

And he knew why; she could read it in his eyes. He'd opened his mouth to respond when the door behind them opened.

Elliot's muscles went rigid. Only when she saw Alvarez and Trapper from the corner of her eye and realized they were alone was she able to relax.

Dain ignored her tension. "Commander."

Alvarez gave a hearty bellow as Elliot stood with the rest of her team. "There's the woman that saved the day." Crossing the room, he held out a stack of papers. "Here."

Elliot stared, disbelieving, at the pile. *You have got to be kidding me.* "This is the thanks I get?" Hopefully the man never discovered her birth date; she'd hate to see what he gave her then.

Alvarez chuckled. "Test results, Smith. Just test results." He gestured to the table and waited while they all took seats, then sat next to Elliot. She forced herself not to scoot toward Dain. "We figured out at least one riddle. The white substance Kivuli left at Deacon's place. It's the same stuff that was in the pouch you poured on him at Mansa's."

Elliot shuddered at the memory.

"Knowing the man was likely a native, we called in an expert." Alvarez reached a hand out, and Elliot passed him the papers gratefully. He shuffled through until a particular page caught his eye, then passed it around. "It's a substance called a *muthi*, made of herbs and animal parts. Usually for medicinal purposes, but some criminals obtain them from so-called witches for the purpose of black magic. This particular mixture is supposed to render the user invisible to the people he targets."

"So you're saying he lined the fence with the powder, and that's why we couldn't see him on surveillance?" Dain asked, eyes wide.

"Bullshit," King barked. Saint looked thoughtful.

Alvarez shrugged. "I'm just passing along what our expert told us; I can't attest to its viability. If you have a better explanation, I'm all ears."

Elliot wanted to scoff like King did, but she couldn't, not when she remembered the look on Kivuli's face when the powder had hit him, remembered him sucking it into his mouth with his last breaths, seizing, choking. Another shudder went through her, and from the looks on the faces around the table, she didn't think she was the only one.

More shuffling through the papers. "The woman Mansa was holding was able to give us her name," Alvarez said. "She'll be sent back to her family after she's stabilized."

"Were her injuries extensive?" Elliot asked.

Trapper spoke for the first time. "From the fight, no. Those were minor, some bangs and bruises." His hand flexed against the table. "There were other long-term issues though." He didn't say what those were, and Elliot found herself grateful. She didn't think she could deal with any more guilt right now, any more if only's. There was no possible way she could've gotten to Mansa's hideout sooner, and she had to live with that. It was far easier than living with the knowledge that her mother's killer had been walking around free.

Alvarez tapped the edge of a paper against the table. "We've made sure she's getting top-notch care, and we've found a group that has agreed to take over follow-up and counseling when she arrives back in Spain, where she's from. Everything we can do to help her, we will."

"Thank you." There was really nothing else Elliot could say. Memories of her mother waking with nightmares, screaming, uncontrollably crying, crowded in. Hopefully with help, this woman would be able to heal in a way Nora had not. No one deserved to live with that kind of pain.

"Absolutely. We wouldn't—"

The door burst open, jerking everyone's attention toward the noise as Fionn rushed through, eyes wild, hair and clothes a ragged mess. "Where's Deacon? We've got to be getti—"

"Whoa, whoa!" Alvarez was on his feet and crossing the room before the rest of them could stand up. "What happened, Irish?"

Fionn opened his mouth but was interrupted by Alvarez's phone going off, then Trapper's. The commander answered his cell, his look grim.

Fionn shoved a hand through his hair. The desperation in his eyes as he fumbled for his own phone kicked Elliot's heartbeat into overdrive. A couple of taps and he brought it to his ear.

Trapper limped toward his teammate. "Tell us, Fionn."

"Sheppard is gone."

A shock wave went through the room.

"What?" Dain asked. "How is she gone? The woman had a concussion, for God's sake. Security—"

"She invented half our security," Fionn growled. His call must've gone unanswered, because he jerked it away from his ear and threw it across the room. "Where is Deacon?"

Dain was tapping on his phone already. "We'll find him."

Were they worried about Sheppard attacking Deacon and Sydney? As soon as the question entered her mind, Elliot knew the girl would never take that step, not even if Mansa hadn't been out of the picture. And now—well, Sheppard would know he was dead; no one could've missed the chaos in the makeshift medical wing all night. Elliot's mind replayed Sheppard's begging as she stood next to the young woman's bed. Her reason for planting the bomb no longer existed.

No, Elliot bet Sheppard had run for a far different reason, a reason that nothing to do with Deacon and everything to do with the desperate man pacing in front of her right this minute.

A man who was done waiting, apparently. "I need to go."

Fionn rushed the door, but it opened before he could reach it. Deacon walked through, Sydney secure on his hip. The sight of them hit Elliot like a blow to the chest, so hard she found herself sitting abruptly back in her chair.

Deacon zeroed in on the movement immediately. She couldn't read his gaze, and honestly, she didn't want to. Some things were better left alone.

"Where've you been?" Fionn was asking. "We need to be gettin' you someplace safe."

"No, we don't." Alvarez walked toward them, the phone still to his ear as he talked. "Cameras picked up Sheppard leaving through the west gate forty-five minutes ago."

"That gate's closed," Deacon said, eyes narrowed. "How did she—"

"She's Sheppard." Alvarez sighed, a heavy sound that seemed to come from his very toes. "There's not much our girl can't hack, and you know it."

"Damn."

Fionn's response was a bit more volatile than Deacon's; he marched through the door, slamming it so hard the impact vibrated the table beneath Elliot's hand. She focused there, praying Deacon would follow his friend.

He didn't.

For a moment the men stood silent, seeming stunned. All except Deacon, who watched the door with a worried look. It was Saint who finally broke the gridlock.

"Well, if he needs an assassin, Elliot's available."

Dain groaned. Elliot swore she heard a snigger— either King or Trapper, she wasn't sure which, but she didn't blame them. Sometimes gallows humor was the only way to push through the shit.

Alvarez had a questioning look in his eye like he wasn't sure if that was a joke or not.

"I'm not gonna kill Sheppard," Elliot assured him.

A chorus of noes and of course nots echoed in the room. Elliot gave them all a narrow-eyed glare.

Deacon cleared his throat. "Commander, could I borrow Elliot for a few?"

"Certainly!" Alvarez beamed at her.

Elliot didn't move. She couldn't.

"Ell."

It took a few moments to turn her head, but she finally managed to meet Deacon's eyes. Could he read her fear? She didn't want him to, but the way his expression softened said he had anyway.

"Come talk to us," he repeated, jostling Sydney a bit as if to assure her that he wouldn't jump down her throat with his daughter in his arms. Which…right. Yeah. Of course. Elliot's brain was obviously addled at this point. "Please."

"Pleeeease," Syd added.

That pulled her to her feet. She kept her eyes on the ground, trying desperately to ignore the hot flush creeping into her cheeks. Trying to ignore the silence as every man in the room watched her walk out the door. Whatever they were thinking, she didn't want to know. This was a moment she had to face alone.

Funny that doing so now seemed unusual, like an old suit that no longer fit just right.

Sydney was oblivious to the emotional undercurrents. The little girl chattered away as they moved into the hall and down to an empty office Deacon shut them into. Elliot let the sweet voice wash over her, but she couldn't bring herself to respond, not until the voice went silent.

She turned to face them. They looked so right together, so perfect, almost…complete. How could what they shared ever have room for someone like her?

"Where were you, Elliot?" Syd asked. "You were gone forever."

And Sydney had a fear of people disappearing, Elliot knew. Instinct had her reaching for the little girl, arms aching not from her injuries but from longing—she wanted Syd in her arms, cuddled against her. Almost as much as she wanted Deacon to hold her.

Deacon pulled Sydney away. The move hit Elliot like a hammer blow.

"Daddy says you can't hold me right now," Sydney informed her.

"Oh."

"I don't want anything aggravating your ribs. You've done enough to aggravate them as it is." Deacon's head tilted, a frown settling on his mouth. "Why else wouldn't I let you hold her?"

"I—" Elliot shrugged. "I don't know."

More silence. Elliot's nerves felt like they'd snap any minute. "So…you wanted to talk to me?"

"I did." Deacon rubbed a hand along Syd's back, seeming to search for words. "Are you okay?"

He already knew about her injuries, knew she'd been looked at, but she was standing here, so he must mean something else, something not physical. She had just killed her mother's murderer, after all.

"Fine. I'm fine."

His look said he didn't believe that but wouldn't fight her over it, not right now.

Elliot shifted, leaning a hip against the desk at her side.

Deacon cleared his throat.

A shot of knowledge hit her as she looked at him. She'd been so caught up in her own fears that she hadn't taken the time to notice his, but the silence, the way he kept rubbing Sydney's back...he was nervous. *Of her.*

Well fuck. Was it possible she hadn't completely screwed herself after all?

"Look..." Deacon laughed a little. "I don't have a lot of experience at this."

And I do?

"But I...we..."

"We what?"

He shifted again.

"We want you to be our girlfriend," Sydney burst out.

Elliot felt her eyes bug.

"You want me to what?"

This time Deacon's laugh was full, happy, without the strain of before. Sydney grinned up at him.

"Well that's one way to ask a woman out, I guess." Deacon swiped at the tears at the corners of his eyes. "Thanks, Syd."

"You're welcome." That spot where she'd lost her tooth made an appearance as she flashed her father a grin.

Then Deacon's deep brown eyes met Elliot's and all the laughter died, replaced by something richer, deeper, something that took her breath away. His stare seemed to drill right to the heart of her, the part that was fluttering with panic and fear and a whole helluva lot of aching need—for a family, for him. For all of it.

She'd been too scared to name that look the last time she saw it, but Deacon hadn't. He'd named it without fear as he'd fallen asleep, cushioned by her body.

"God, I love you."

"Elliot."

She sucked in a breath.

"I said something last night, something you probably think I regret. But I don't."

"You don't?"

"No." He seemed about to say something else but glanced at Syd and reconsidered. "I meant what I did and what I said then, and I mean this now: all we want, all *I* want, is for you to give us a chance."

As if they had to beg her? They'd be the one taking a chance, not her. "Deacon, I…"

I care. God, I care so much—and it scares the shit out of me.

"Don't you like us, Elliot?"

She looked helplessly into Sydney's eyes. So much trust shone there. What if she couldn't live up to that look? What if she failed? She'd never had a family before, people depending on her, expectations to live up to.

Except she had, hadn't she? With Dain. With her team. She'd loved them and protected them and lived with them, and she hadn't let them down.

You can do this, Ell.

Deacon reached for her, his calloused fingers rough on her cheek. "Don't be afraid, Ell. Just tell us."

"Of course I"—a glance at Sydney—"like you." *Love you.* "A lot. I like you both." She knew she should step away from Deacon's touch, but her feet wouldn't move. "But I—" Oh God, what did she do? "Deacon, I'm too…broken. I don't want to be, but we both know that I am." She ignored Sydney's frown, knowing the little girl didn't understand. Maybe someday…

No, there wouldn't be a someday here. She had to stop wishing on stars and get back to reality. She had to make Deacon understand. "You deserve someone so much better than me, someone whole."

Deacon continued to stare her down, not a hint of surprise on his face. "We deserve to be loved, and we get to choose who we want it from. We choose you."

Her heart thumped hard, a bass drum in her ears. "I—"

Deacon came closer, close enough that it almost seemed Elliot was holding Sydney as much as he was. Two parts making a whole. His broad hand cupped her flushed cheek. "Trust me, Elliot," he said, and this time it was a command, not a request. She could feel the iron strength of his will wrapping around her even as his thumb stroked, soothing her heated skin. "Trust me. You've asked me to trust you this whole time, to believe you. Now I'm asking you. Trust me. That's all we need."

Was it?

Trust. In him, in herself, in the two of them together.

That's all we need.

She looked into the brown and green eyes staring back at her, wanting her, needing her, and realized she was letting fear win. She hadn't let it win at thirteen, and she hadn't let it win when she'd joined Dain's team. Was she going to let it win now, in the most important battle she would ever fight?

Fuck no.

"Yes." *Yes, I'll trust you. Yes, I'll be with you. Yes, I'll love you both—always.*

A tear slipped down her cheek to wet Deacon's thumb. *Always.*

Deacon smiled. She saw it as he leaned closer, felt it when his mouth met hers. The kiss was chaste, sweet, but the look he gave her as he eased back promised that later, when Sydney was asleep and they were alone, he'd give her a better, longer, more adult version. Desire warmed her belly at the thought.

"Daddy!"

They both blinked out of their daze. Deacon raised an eyebrow at his daughter.

"I want a kiss too."

He kissed her cheek.

"Not you. Elliot!"

"Of course, Little Bit." He tipped his daughter toward Elliot for a kiss as well. Elliot reveled in the baby-shampoo scent Sydney always carried, the sweet innocence of her kiss on Elliot's cheek, the way her fragile arms wrapped around Elliot's neck, and prayed like she'd never prayed before, for one thing: courage.

She'd faced her demons and won. Now it was time to face life.

Deacon held out his hand. "Let's take my girls home."

Elliot put her hand in his, held on tight, and let him lead her toward the door.

Epilogue

One month later

"Looks like your ribs are finally healed. Not back to a hundred percent though."

Elliot glowered at Deacon, following the look with a quick jab-sidekick combo. Her breathing was heavier than she'd like. No, she wasn't fully back to normal—she'd fought for her life, for fuck's sake, more than once—but that didn't mean he had to point it out. "You know I've been working all day, right?"

"And what have I been doing, sitting on my ass?" Deacon raised an eyebrow. His elbow strike–back fist landed a light blow to her temple. "Running after a four-year-old isn't sitting, ya know."

He was taking it easy on her. Elliot threw a punch at his face. When he blocked, she targeted his ribs. He growled at the contact.

"You're getting slow is what you're doing."

"No, I'm getting distracted by the scenery."

Elliot gave him a perky smile. Her breasts bounced behind her sports bra as she pivoted on her toe and shot another side kick at him.

Fuck. Me.

He tackled her to the mat.

"Deacon!"

"Elliot." He buried his face in the damp cleft between her breasts. One hand cupped her nape, the other her ass, holding her right where he wanted her. No more fighting. "I think it's time for a shower." And not because they were sweaty from their workout.

When he traced a line of sweat with the tip of his tongue, Elliot melted into the mat beneath them, her legs opening, knees coming up to cradle him against her. When they were like this, when she surrendered to the alpha in him, let the warrior fall away and became all woman…fuckin' A, she blew his mind. It had been weeks since the first time he'd made love to her, and every day he wondered if it was possible to ever get enough.

"It's late already. I have to be up early if I'm going to get Syd ready and into town in time to meet Livie."

He nudged his already hard erection against her clit. "I doubt this will take long."

That was an out-and-out lie, but he didn't care. He'd waited all week for her most recent assignment to end, spent five days aching for her in his bed, and now that he had her, he'd take his time and then some. She'd sleep deep tonight, no matter how late he got her head on the pillow.

Yes, he was a selfish bastard, but he didn't care. Turning his head, he traced the edge of her bra with his tongue.

Elliot moaned. He hid his grin against the creamy skin at the top of her breast.

She usually stayed with them on the weekends, but though tomorrow was Saturday, she and Sydney had plans. They were meeting up with Dain's wife,

Livie, to do a bit of pre-baby shopping. The couple's little one was due in two-and-a- half months. Sydney had talked of nothing else all week, but Elliot…his woman hated shopping unless it was to add to her arsenal, which rivaled his in both size and scope—and that was saying something.

Elliot's thoughts seemed to be running parallel to his, proof he wasn't doing his current job well enough. "I could stay home tomorrow. I'm not much of a shopper."

"You did pretty well last time."

Elliot blushed, the fiery color reaching all the way to his lips on her skin. He'd wondered if her blush extended to her breasts; he knew now. He'd really known when she'd shown him her purchase last week. The memory of her in the deep blue lace bra and panty set was enough to make him harden in ways he really shouldn't in an athletic cup—and fighting with Elliot, the cup was a necessity.

No, not on the mat. In the shower, though…

He hauled Elliot to her feet.

He'd kept the room down the hall from Sydney's, just enough space between them that he didn't have to worry about any sounds he and Elliot might make waking his daughter. He led her straight into the bathroom now, his hands shaking with the need to have her against him, have her surrounding him. After locking the doors, he turned on the water, then turned to Elliot.

His mouth watered.

She was dragging her sports bra over her head, workout shorts and underwear already on the ground. Totally bare to him, totally unguarded. Deacon's gut clenched. There was no guile in Elliot—last week he'd commanded her to keep the lingerie on, only pulling the cups down to bare her sensitive breasts for him. She'd given him a confused look, one that faded into shock, then a heavy surge of hunger when he'd sat her atop him, pulled her panties aside, and feasted on her nipples while she gloved him tight. Her open pleasure stood in sharp contrast to the secrets she'd held inside for so long, like her soul could finally let go. And every time, the hunger seemed to surprise her—his and hers. He didn't think he'd ever lose that hunger. If not for Sydney, they'd spend days in bed instead of a few hours on the weekends.

He stalked toward her now, loving the way she shivered, the way her bright eyes darkened with desire as he went to his knees in front of her, kissed his way across her damp skin to the turgid nipple just waiting for him. When he nudged her with his nose, the tip of his tongue, Elliot's fingers clenched in his hair.

He pulled the nub between his lips and suckled.

They both groaned.

"Deacon, please."

He released her with a lick. "Please what?"

"Please stop teasing."

He chuckled, his breath blowing against her wet nipple. The tip crinkled up hard.

"Bastard."

"You love it; you know you do."

"I do." Her hands slid down to his jaw, tugging upward until their eyes met. "I love you."

She had no idea what a gift those words were—or maybe she did. The glint of tears in her eyes confirmed the emotion behind them, the same emotion that burned at the backs of his. Elliot had come such a long way in such a short time. He thanked God every day for the gift he'd been given, to love again, to show her how to love, how to be a family. And someday soon, when she was ready, he'd ask her to make it official, to marry him, to move in with them.

But in the meantime…

Standing, he took her hand and led her toward the shower.

Steam surrounded them as the door clicked closed. Elliot gravitated toward the hot stream of water, her head tipping back beneath the spray just like her namesake. His cock jerked at the sight, and he couldn't resist reaching for her, following the tracks each droplet made on her skin, exploring every hill and hollow, every place that made her breath catch and made his balls ache for release. He traced the graceful curve of her neck, the shoulders too delicate to carry the weight of her past, her training, her job. Those full, beautiful breasts with tips so sensitive she hissed as his calloused fingers moved over them. Narrow ribs, full hips. The light patch of curls between her legs.

And God, her legs…he wanted them wrapped around him—now, not later. Wanted to know again the power that surged inside him when she opened herself and let him in, trusted him with her body and her heart, trusted him enough to be vulnerable in a way she'd never trusted anyone before.

"Open for me, Elliot."

Without hesitation one leg slid out, giving him access. He brought a finger up to open her shyly closed lips. Elliot whimpered at the glide of his touch along her most vulnerable place, tilting her hips to get more as he pushed a long digit inside her. So wet. So right.

Elliot went to her toes.

"You're ready, aren't you, spitfire. So ready for me."

"Yes! Deacon, please…"

He added another finger, the tight fit making him sweat. Elliot's G-spot was puffy, swollen, shouting her need clearly. He rubbed the pads of his fingertips against it. When his palm pressed up, adding pressure to her clit, she detonated with a loud cry.

"That's it, love." He ground his hand against her, inside her. "Let go for me."

Aftershocks spasmed through her muscles, one after another, squeezing his fingers. Elliot stuttered his name.

When she finally stilled, he pulled his fingers free. Elliot grasped his wrist, tugging until he stood, and guided his hand to her mouth. Full lips surrounded his finger, her tongue laving him, collecting the essence of the pleasure he'd given her.

The last strap on his restraint snapped.

Fuck slow. He'd meant to savor, to take his time, take her over, but he couldn't, not with that look on her face. Not with his cock throbbing like a son of a bitch with the need to be inside her. He couldn't wait, and he didn't; he grasped her hips, lifted, and impaled her on him all in one movement.

Elliot choked at the tight fit. He barely held on long enough for her body to soften, for her creamy invitation to ease the way, and then he was pounding her against the wall with every ounce of the desperation filling his very soul. The catch of Elliot's breath, the ragged sigh of his name, the scratch of her tight nipples against his chest drove him higher and higher until he thought his head might explode—he certainly hoped one of them did. Elliot's legs pushed wider, trusting him to hold her, her pelvis straining against him, and the rising pitch of her cries told him she was right there with him. A tiny shift of his angle, enough to pound the base of his cock against her clit, and that was all either one of them needed.

They shattered together, so hard Deacon couldn't breathe, couldn't think, wasn't even certain he'd survive. Everything disappeared but the pleasure clenching his gut and the sense of being one soul, one body. He took Elliot's mouth, gave her his tongue, savoring the moment for as long as he could make it last.

Finally, minutes later, he helped Elliot to stand, holding her tight until her legs were solid beneath her, then tugged her back under the water. Her skin felt soft and slick beneath his soapy hands as he washed her, reveling in the way her eyes closed and a smile tugged at her lips. Content; his woman was content. His chest actually puffed up at the thought—yes, he was that Neanderthal.

Elliot was practically asleep on her feet now that the last of her tension was gone. He rinsed her off, then gave her a nudge toward the shower door with a firm hand on her ass. "Go get in bed. I'll be there in just a sec."

She didn't argue, which proved exactly how tired she was. It took him no more than a few minutes to clean up before getting out, drying himself, and wandering into his bedroom to change.

Elliot was nowhere to be seen.

Boxers on, he went into the hall. Downstairs was still dark, only the slight glow of a night-light showing faintly at the top of the stairs. The same was true for Sydney's room, but he heard the slightest movement in that direction, so he followed, his footsteps stumbling to a halt at the door. The sight before him was arresting—there was no other word for it. Elliot, dressed in her normal nighttime tee and shorts, lay on one side of Sydney's bed, her body curled around his child, their hands linked together.

Sound asleep, both of them.

He found himself leaning against the doorjamb as his knees went weak and his heart melted. He'd spent his life fighting for what was right, bringing justice to the world, but nothing he'd accomplished compared to moments like these, when the healing of Elliot's heart became so damn obvious. She was theirs, and they were hers—and Elliot had been courageous enough to let it happen. They might be taking it slow, might be feeling their way through this thing that had hit them both out of the blue, but when he saw her like this, when he saw the two of them together, he knew. With everything inside him, he knew.

His family was complete.

∞

Did you enjoy DECEIVE ME? If so, you can leave a review at your favorite retailer to tell other readers about the book. And thank you!

To find out all the latest news on Ella's upcoming releases, sign up for Ella's newsletter at ellasheridanauthor.com.

Before you go...

Some mistakes don't deserve forgiveness.

DESTROY ME
Southern Nights: Enigma 3

Lyse Sheppard planted the bomb that almost killed everyone close to her, including the man she loved. Now in hiding, she spends her days making amends the only way she knows how—using her genius computer skills to save women enslaved by the bastard who blackmailed her. And every night she punishes herself by watching the man she lost live his life without her.

Fionn "Irish" McCullough can't let go of the rage Lyse ignited the night she betrayed his team. Betrayed *him*. After months of searching, he's no closer to finding his prey—until a mysterious message points him toward Ireland and a deadly threat against the only family he has left.

Caught in the twisted web of his past, Fionn must choose between revenge and keeping his mother safe. But the one weapon he needs—and the one touch he craves—may be the woman he can never forgive.

∞

Chapter One

These are not the droids you're looking for.

One of the most overquoted lines in all geekdom, probably because it fit so many situations, including this one. Or rather, Lyse Sheppard had only found one "droid" she was looking for, but he wasn't alone.

She shifted in her hard chair, the one from the dinette set that she'd snitched for a computer chair because all her focus had been on equipment, not comfort. She'd arrived in Ireland with nothing—no surveillance capability, no protection, not even a place to stay. The past two months she'd been able to establish her home base, but she forgot about padding until nighttime arrived and she was consigned to this damn chair. To aching hips and watching her former team live their lives without her.

Watching Fionn McCullough live without her. Not that he'd ever lived *with* her.

And why would he? She was just Bat Girl, right?

Pat the nerd on the head and give her a cookie.

Even knowing Martin Diako was dead—*go, Elliot*—Lyse hadn't stopped watching over her friends, making sure they were safe from repercussions. Deacon and Elliot and Sydney. Trapper. Alvarez. Even Elliot's team at JCL—King, Saint, Dain with his heavily pregnant wife.

And then there was Fionn.

Her heart sped up as he appeared on her computer screen. The image was grainy, rough. CCTV wasn't the best source if you wanted clarity. It allowed her to follow her target with ease, though, watch his back.

This time his back—and backside—was being watched by a slender woman with long dark hair.

Lyse's hands began to shake.

No, not this time. Turn it off. Don't do this to yourself.

It was sound advice; she knew that. Just as she knew she wouldn't take it. Not because she didn't want to. She wanted with everything inside her to reach out, click the button, and turn the monitor off. But there was no button to shut her brain off. It would follow the path of Fionn's sexy Lexus with the gleaming navy paint into the night, maybe to his house, maybe a hotel, who knew? It would follow him and the woman inside, and even if they were out of camera range, it would imagine exactly what happened the minute the door shut behind them.

Because torturing herself was her specialty—and no more than she deserved.

Two months later and it still killed her inside to watch him. That was the point, after all. You didn't try to blow your friends up and get away with it scot-free. Fionn might not be here to punish her, but he did just fine half a world away, whether he knew it or not.

His car was parked at the very back of Milligan's lot, just out of range of the camera. The same place he parked every time he came, which was frequently. Milligan's Pub was a favorite of Fionn's. A couple clicks of her mouse and she'd switched to the surveillance camera used by the car dealership directly behind the bar. The one pointed in the direction of the chain-link fence and Fionn's car on the other side. Under a streetlight. Perfect view for surveillance.

Fionn led the woman to the passenger-side door. He didn't kiss her; Lyse never saw him kiss the women he was with. Instead he opened the door and ushered her in. His lips moved without sound, his cocky grin telling her all she needed to know about the conversation she couldn't hear. And then he closed the woman in and circled the back of the car.

She squeezed her eyes shut, her lungs doing the same. *Turn it off. Turn it off, Lyse. Stop punishing yourself for something that happened months ago.*

Two months. Eight weeks. The night her life had ended. The night Fionn could've died.

She opened her eyelids, forcing herself to watch.

Fionn started the car, rolled down the windows. A pale hand appeared on his chest. Slid down.

A whimper escaped Lyse's tight throat.

He turned off the car. His seat eased backward, giving her a better view of his face. It was the perfect face. Not as pale as most gingers. Wide green eyes that could narrow into intimidating lasers when he was angry. A strong nose, high cheekbones. A full mouth that made women fantasize, especially when he gave you that grin. Panties melted away when the man grinned.

Just like he did now, as the woman crawled over the center console and shimmied her way onto the floorboard between his knees.

A fist clamped down on Lyse's heart.

Fionn seemed to prefer risky locations, in his job and with his women. Tonight appeared to be no different. The woman bent forward. Lyse didn't know if the door blocking her view was a blessing or a curse. Somewhere in the back of her mind, she knew this wasn't only punishment; this was all she'd ever have of Fionn. As close as she'd ever get to her fantasies of him, the ones filled with the gravelly grunts and groans that escaped him now, she was sure. She'd imagined them over and over through the years. Hopeful years. Stupid years, filled with stupid fantasies for a stupid girl.

And yet her body heated at the thought of being between his legs, touching him, taking him in her mouth.

Stupid. What kind of woman watched a man with someone else and got aroused?

A desperate one. A damned one.

She clicked the mouse again, and the camera zoomed in just in time. Fionn's face tightened. A soundless cry escaped him, his body jerking, emptying himself in the ultimate pleasure. Lyse watched, unblinking, until her eyes burned and her throat closed completely. Until the hard knot in her stomach grew so big, so full of bile and self-hatred that it rose up her throat and forced her away from the screen.

Thank God the trash can was close by. *No puking on the keyboard, Sheppard.*

When the heaving finally stopped—and when she could walk without her knees giving out—she carried herself and the trash can into the bathroom down the hall. The chilled water felt good on her flushed face, rinsing the bitter taste from her mouth. Hot tears mingled with the cold, but she pretended they weren't there. Pretended she was okay. It was the only way to get through each day. Giving in to the pain didn't help when it would only come back tomorrow. And the next day. And the next.

Avoiding her reflection in the mirror kept the illusion of control intact for a few more, precious seconds.

She couldn't even hate Fionn for what she'd seen. He was the resident lady's man at Global First; everyone knew it. And it wasn't like he wasn't made for it. The man was an Irish god—one she wished she'd never met, most days. But then she wouldn't be able to tear her heart out night after night, would she?

She walked back into the bedroom, grateful that whatever he'd done with the woman, she'd at least missed that part. Though watching him cradle her on his lap, his big hands running over her hair and down her spine, might be worse. Lyse could practically feel those long, rugged fingers on her skin. She shivered beneath the dream touch, then shuddered at her sick imagination.

The clang of water running through the pipes jerked her back to reality. Sean in the bathroom. Her next-door neighbor must have an early shift at the restaurant. Though their shared wall was insulated enough that they both had privacy, nothing could quiet the noisy pipes that ran through them.

She glanced at the clock display in the bottom corner of her computer screen to confirm the time, and relief flooded her. Time for coffee. It might be the middle of the night in Georgia, but here in Ireland the sun was just over the horizon. Though she didn't deserve the reprieve, she clicked off her view of Fionn and began to cycle through her regular checks—Deacon's property, Trapper's apartment, the Global First compound—grateful when emotion began to ebb in favor of her critical thinking. Ones and zeros, observations didn't require feeling. With anyone else she could shut it off, do the job. Retreat when the fuckup that was her life became too much to handle, which was exactly what she did now. Retreat. There was no shame in regrouping, right?

Right. Keep telling yourself that.

She rubbed at the ache in her chest, eyes on the screen.

The last house on her list wasn't a team member; it was a house here in North Quigley Village. A quiet neighborhood off one of the main streets that bisected the town. The houses were small, cottages really, with bigger yards that allowed for plenty of the gardening that flourished in Irish country summers. The owner would be getting up soon, following her normal routine. Lyse paused her surveillance and rewound twenty-four hours, quickly scanning the video. Nothing unusual. Her finger tensed, about to close the program.

And that's when she saw it—a shadow. Not near the house, but up on the street. The neighbors were all in bed, everything still, quiet in that way that only occurred in the dead of night. The dark, amorphous shape near the top-right corner of the screen didn't cross in front of the house, simply lingered there near the hedgerow. Someone else might've thought it was a shadow cast by the full moon or a neighbor's still-lit lamp, but Lyse had watched hours of surveillance on this particular house. She knew every branch of the trees, every nuance of the night hours as they passed. This shadow shouldn't be there, but it was.

The emotional girl inside her retreated, allowing the intelligence-trained woman to take over.

An hour later her analytical mind and quick fingers had supplied a face, a name, and a trail that led her back to a part of Fionn's life he'd kept a closely guarded secret from everyone but Mark Alvarez and Deacon Walsh. A secret she shouldn't know and had prayed would never rear its ugly head—but it had.

She knew it and the shadow knew it, but Fionn didn't. And now she had a decision to make: keep herself safe, or protect the one woman Fionn had always loved?

Pick up your copy of *DESTROY ME* at your favorite retailer now!

∞

"I have a handful of authors that write books that I consider comfort reads. I can typically rely on these books to bring me joy when I'm in a reading slump. Ella Sheridan is one of those authors."

—*Blogging by Liza*

About the Author

Ella Sheridan never fails to take her readers to the dark edges of love and back again. Strong heroines are her signature, and her heroes span the gamut from hot rock stars to alpha bodyguards and everywhere in between. Ella never pulls her punches, and her unique combination of raw emotion, hot sex, and action leave her readers panting for the next release.

Born and raised in the Deep South, Ella writes romantic suspense, erotic romance, and hot BDSM contemporaries. Start anywhere—every book may be read as a standalone, or begin with book one in any series and watch the ties between the characters grow.

Connect with Ella at:

Ella's Website – ellasheridanauthor.com
Facebook – Ella Sheridan: Books and News
Twitter – @AuthorESheridan
Instagram – @AuthorESheridan
Pinterest – @AuthorESheridan
Bookbub – Ella Sheridan
E-mail – ella@ellasheridanauthor.com

∞

For all the latest news, sneak peeks, quarterly contests and man candy, sign up for Ella's newsletter at her website.

41989689R00189

Made in the USA
Middletown, DE
13 April 2019